'Barbara Boswell bursts the blister that covered the scorching testimony at the Zondo Commission of Inquiry into State Capture and Corruption. Some politicians are as immoral at home as they are in the halls of government. *The Comrade's Wife* is a wonderful account of the political made personal.'
Rehana Rossouw, author of *What Will People Say?* & *New Times*

'*The Comrade's Wife* is a brilliant commentary on the politics of gender reflected in the most personal of domains – the romantic relationship. Dr Boswell writes with care, allowing us into the innermost thoughts of Anita whose experience with abuse reflects the experiences of so many. What a thrilling read! I could not put it down.'
Terry-Ann Adams, author of *Those Who Live in Cages* & *White Chalk*

'Tender, delightful, frightening. *The Comrade's Wife* is testimony to Boswell's inexhaustible vision.'
Pumla Dineo Gqola, author of *Female Fear Factory*

'Wonderfully plotted, emotionally rich, clever and full of intrigue; in *The Comrade's Wife*, Anita narrates her unbreakable commitment to her husband Neil, to her country, South Africa, and the immense personal toll of both these loyalties.

'Find a quiet comfortable corner and settle in because you won't want to leave Anita's superb company until she's finished her story.'
Nadia Davids, author and playwright

The Comrade's Wife

This is a work of fiction. Any names or characters, businesses or places, events or incidents portrayed in this work are fictitious. Any resemblance to actual persons, living or dead, or actual events is purely coincidental.

First published by Jacana Media (Pty) Ltd in 2024
10 Orange Street
Sunnyside
Auckland Park 2092
South Africa
+2711 628 3200

www.jacana.co.za

© Barbara Boswell, 2024
All rights reserved.

ISBN 978-1-4314-3444-2

Cover design by Studio Warburton
Editing by Helen Moffett
Proofreading by Lara Jacob
Set in Sabon LT Std 10.5/14.5pt
Printed and bound by CTP Printers
Job no. 004152

See a complete list of Jacana titles at www.jacana.co.za

The Comrade's Wife

Barbara Boswell

In loving memory of Nadia Goetham

Chapter One

No matter how I try to change it, the story always starts like this – with his devotion. When I think about him now, after all this time, the word that still best describes him is devoted. It's what comes out first on every page I draw close to write his story. Our story. Stories so intertwined that they became one.

The work of untangling them, of taking my story back, so that it once again belongs to me, is the impulse that drives me to that blank page in an attempt to write, rewrite, recast. And because that word won't leave, let me accept it and start with this simple statement: my husband is the most devoted person I know.

He is fastidiously committed to duty, his family, his comrades, his country; is equally devoted to caring for me, to making me happy. My mind goes back to the bedroom, the stage for so many of the scenes that make up our life together; the place where we spent most of our time at home together: loving, fighting, questioning; the site of our many conversations, him probing, wanting to know how to please me.

"What do you need from me, right now?" he asks as I watch him get ready for bed. I look at him, really look at him, as I consider his request.

Dark brown skin, burnished and even. Slanted black eyes, hinting at Indonesian origins. Full lips. End-of-the-day silver stubble dotting his jaw. He keeps his head shaven; the result is a clean look.

He wears a crisp cotton robe, which he will remove when he gets into bed; he sleeps naked, no matter the season.

What do I need from him? This is a language he has learned from me. It does not come naturally to ask, or even to want to know. But in close to one year of marriage I have started to train him to consider what I might want and need.

My eyes trace the contours of his body, now disrobed. Muscular and lean, he takes meticulous care of himself. As he opens the drawer of his bureau, the chiselled muscles of his back ripple under his dark skin. His body glows, accustomed as it is to being scrubbed, exfoliated, pummelled and polished to a high sheen at the most exclusive spas across the city. He smooths cologne around his chin and neck – he always professes he wants to come to bed smelling good for me. With one practised movement, he dives onto the bed and leans towards me.

"No reply, my precious? Speak to me. What do you need?"

I want to tell him about the grey spot in my stomach, the hand that compresses my chest when he is away. Thandiswa, in one of our energy healing sessions, has tried to get me to describe the grey spot. "How does it feel, how does it sound?" she asks.

The nearest thing I can compare it to is the grey static of a TV when you can't get a signal – a jarring energy underneath my navel, jumbling my insides.

How do I put this into words to Neill without sounding completely mad? He who deals only in facts, certainties, verifiable information. I can't even articulate it to myself. How do I tell him, and not sound like the worst thing a woman can be: clingy, needy?

He has been away this weekend, returned late on Sunday. The trips are becoming more frequent. I hate them, but this is how I knew it would be, what we talked about endlessly in the early days when we were deciding if this thing between us had legs, and where to take it.

That we wanted each other was a given; that we wanted to spend the rest of our lives together, the agreement, spoken clearly – the reassurance often given when things became difficult between us. We had both been married before, had witnessed those unions implode; we knew love was not enough.

Both independent and self-sufficient to the point of not needing anyone, we were wary of merging our lives, but, at the same time, inexorably drawn to each other. I fell almost instantly in love with him; yet I felt so much ambivalence as our relationship progressed. I wanted this, wanted him, but had doubts about whether we could commit fully and make a way together. Would we be able to let go of our separate, hard-won lives and blend our histories, families, professions to create something lasting?

"Don't worry," Neill would placate me when I'd reach the cusp of having enough. "We have the rest of our lives. I'll make this up to you."

Those words, at first, would melt me. Later, once the phrase had become threadbare, I'd simply shake my head.

Tonight is not a night for such a fight, though – I just want peace; reassurance that he is happy to be back with me, that he won't leave me again too soon.

He moves closer, reaches his hand around my body, settling it in the small of my back. He leaves just enough space so that I must complete the task of closing the gap between us. Quintessential Neill – never forcing, never coercive. I must always do the work of meeting him where he is, even when it is he who wants me. It is an excellent strategy, successful at always making me want him more.

The scent of his cologne pulls me in. I answer the question still hanging in the air by inching towards him and planting a kiss on his jaw. Warmth radiates from his body, and I bury my face in his neck, inhaling the distinct, sweet, Neill-fragrance, a blend of sandalwood and citrus and something else I can never quite make out.

The knot in my stomach unfurls; my body releases the tension, held all weekend, of not knowing his whereabouts or when he'd be back. I am happy for this reunion, in no mood to resuscitate our recurring argument.

He is gone a lot. His job requires it, and yes, I knew this from the start, that his work would take him away from me, that I would spend more time without him than with him. Sometimes I am okay with it – mine was a full and busy life before we met, after all – but at other times, like this weekend, I'm not. I can state this over and over again, answering the question, "What do you need?" with the simplest of answers: "You, more of you. Your presence."

But it won't change a thing. He reminds me often that I knew the deal from the beginning: his demanding role in public life; the frequent need to travel; that he belongs to others – the party, his constituents, the country – more fully than he belongs to himself. And since we were no longer young and starry-eyed, we both knew this would take work, effort, compromise. I knew fully what I was getting into and raising the old gripe now, with his warm body pressing against mine, seems pointless.

He kisses me back and I let it go – the anxiety, the resentment clotting my stomach. It is easy when he is here, full of smiles and endearments, touching me, feathering his fingertips along the length of my spine, to let myself go in his expert hands.

My husband is an excellent lover – thank God for this – not one I have merely had to endure. He is creative, innovative, uncannily in sync with my body. He knows when to take his time and when to be quick – knows exactly where and how to touch me. I try not to dwell too much on how he's honed this particular skill. This has been one of the delights of our marriage, the thing that softens the jagged edges between our togetherness and his absences. Our differences can always be worked out in bed. We might snipe, but there is a strong instinct in both of us, having come to each other later in life, for harmony. When harsh words flare, we are quick to compromise; one of us will reach for the other, who will be only too grateful to accept the peace offering of skin.

We have been married for just under a year. I met him online – how else does a woman of a certain age meet a man these days? I don't tell people how we met, except for Claire and Thandiswa, my closest friends. They have lived this relationship vicariously from the outset. It's one of their favourite stories to tell and retell, when we are two or three cocktails in, on our nights out – how I met the love of my life on the internet. Just like that!

"There is still hope for me!" Thandiswa loves to shout when the drinks kick in, knowing full well that my kind of domestic setup would have her running for her life in a matter of weeks.

Thandiswa and Claire were there from the start, as they are for most other significant moments, big and small, in my life. I met them both on our first day at university. All three of us outsiders, in an institution not built for the likes of us. Young women who came from different townships of the Cape Flats, we banded together and became inseparable. We were put into a "bridging" course to learn the skills needed to succeed at university; skills the administrators assumed we would not have because of the colour of our skin, and the high schools we had come from, even though we had all been the top matriculant at our respective schools.

The experience had bonded us, seemingly for life, given that we were now in our forties. We took different professional paths: Claire went into law and runs a successful practice; myself, an academic now teaching at the same institution where we met; and Thandiswa came close to obtaining her MA in psychology, but left the programme after her husband-to-be died in an accident. When she felt ready to return, she realised she no longer wanted the degree. She has flourished as a social worker who also specialises in a range of alternative healing modalities. She got her calling in her late twenties, resisted it for years, but eventually stopped running from it and went to thwasa. Her credentials include initiated traditional healer, making her one of the most sought-after health consultants in Cape Town, if not the country.

From humble beginnings, we've all made good, living the lives we dreamed of in those early days when, awkward and unsophisticated, we had to brave a university that might as well have been a foreign country. We're successful, making it on our own terms, each in her own way; but it takes only the whiff of a margarita for us to revert to the raucous, wayward ways of our early twenties.

Claire and Thandiswa were the first to see Neill, before I had even met him in real life, at one of our regular get-togethers at a restaurant on Kloof Street, as I whipped out my phone and showed off his dating profile on the app.

Neill, 55. Cape Town. Three well-chosen photos: one close-up in a suit, another mid-range shot of him sitting at a restaurant table, smiling; the last one of him out hiking, showing a man in good shape. None of the red flags I had come to avoid on dating apps: couple pictures with a woman, kids-as-accessories to drive home the point that they are loving dads; flashy cars; or muscle-bulging gym bods.

"Ooh, good-looking!" cried Claire.

"He looks familiar," said Thandiswa.

"Not one of your old flames, I hope, Thandiswa!"

Thandiswa had never gotten over the death of her first love. It seemed, from where I was sitting, that the risk of loving and losing yet another man had led her to avoid trying to replace him. Once she had recovered from Bulelani's death, she started dating again, racking up a string of lovers – but none good enough to replace him permanently. She zipped from one man to the next like a bee pollinating flowers, lingering just long enough to leave them smitten and pining after her inevitable brisk departure. Her cheery, life-and-soul-of-the-party persona became a defence against letting anyone get close. Men, young and old, black, white and every hue in between, courted her, proposed to her – tried to privatise her, as she called it. She wasn't having any of that. Life was to be enjoyed because it could end at any moment, and for Thandiswa, enjoying life meant sampling as many men as possible. It was not entirely implausible that she'd be familiar with my prospective beau. Thankfully, she wasn't.

"So, tell us everything – when are you meeting?"

I had been talking to him for a while after we matched on the app, and our nightly conversations were becoming a ritual. He was unfailingly polite, almost old-fashioned in his courtesy. He asked intelligent questions and really listened to the answers – remembering insignificant details and raising them in later conversations – signs that he knew how to pay attention. He was curious about my work, and had even started sending me articles or news snippets relating to it. We had been speaking for two weeks, some nights into the early hours. What struck me most was his kindness and empathy, all wrapped up in gentle humour, as he spoke about his extended family and adolescent twins, a son and daughter. He was a lawyer by training but had changed careers a few years ago – he kept this part of his life vague during our chats, and I didn't probe too much.

He had eventually asked me out on a date, just for coffee. We both knew the rules of the game – don't invest too much in the first date so that you can walk away quickly should something weird come up. Coffee is low-stakes, not too time-consuming, and good to get a feel for whether you'd like to see them again. I was looking forward to meeting him in person, as I had come to look forward to our daily chats as I settled into bed.

I relayed all this to my friends, who were "oohing" and "aahing" at every turn.

"What will you be wearing?" asked Thandiswa, the fashionista among us.

"Well it's just a coffee, so probably my usual jeans and T-shirt."

"Nooo!" she cried. "At least a nice top, something low-cut and sexy. And please go get your nails done. And your hair. This guy is a catch!"

"Stop it, Thandiswa! It's a coffee date."

"But please make an effort, Miss Serious Intellectual. You know, it is possible to be clever and hot – the two are not mutually exclusive!"

We burst into laughter. This is Thandiswa's constant complaint when assessing me from the point of view of a prospective date.

"You're too serious, too straitlaced, too nerdy. Men can't relate to you. You think too much. Yes, those are admirable qualities at work, but men want a woman they can have fun with, laugh with!"

Claire concurred, as always. "You live too much in your brain. Get in touch with your body, your sensuality, woman! You need to learn to live in your body."

"Well, this is news! Please tell me, Claire, where the hell have I been living all of these years?"

We screech with laughter, causing the mostly pale heads in the refined establishment to turn in our direction.

As we lower our voices, Claire and Thandiswa plan the exact outfit I should wear to my coffee date with my prospective boyfriend, Neill. I take it all in, nodding and smiling. I have zero expectations going into this date. I've done this dating thing for far too long, with very little positive net result. But this man is different, I feel it in my bones. Warmth and kindness are constant currents running through his voice, unlike so many others, who seem to have some invisible stopwatch timing how quickly they can get a woman into bed.

"I'm thinking of this as anthropological. Just going to observe an outlier from that species."

"Oh dear God, no! Trust you drain all of the fun out of this by making it some kind of case study!" chides Thandiswa.

"Yes!" Claire chimes in. "Even though it's just coffee, you should probably have a little drink or two before you arrive to loosen up."

Thandiswa's rule for dating is when you meet someone, you should immediately assess whether you are attracted enough to kiss them. If you can't imagine an intimate kiss with the person sitting in front of you, you might as well leave.

This is the yardstick I take along to the date. We meet at a coffee shop at the Waterfront and for a few moments after "Hello", we just stare at each other. Somewhere in my body, a sun rises. I am aware that my heart is racing a little. To calm down, I visualise the hormones that have just been released into my bloodstream. It's just chemical, I tell myself, although I know that chemicals do not account for the smile I feel spreading across my face.

Over the preceding few weeks we had shared intimate thoughts with each other about our childhoods, our disappointments, our dreams. And here we are, wordless, with nothing to say.

He breaches the awkward pause, speaking with a deep voice: "So lovely to meet you at last, Anita. And if you don't mind me saying so, you are even more beautiful in person than your photos have led me to believe."

"Good to meet you too, Neill. And no, I don't mind you saying that at all."

The forty-five minutes we had scheduled turns into one, and then two hours. It feels like talking to a friend I've known all my life. He remembers everything we've talked about, references even the names of my students I've dropped in passing. When it's time to say goodbye, he walks me to my car. He opens the door; we say our goodbyes rather formally before I slide into the driver's seat and he shuts the door behind me.

I've been home for about fifteen minutes when he calls.

"I really like you, Anita. Our date went beyond my expectations. When can I see you again?"

I abandon my caution, and all I have come to know about spacing and pacing. "Whenever you want."

I see him the next day, and the next, and the one after that. Lunches, dinners at the kind of fine restaurant I could never afford on my salary. Walks on the beach. He picks me up in a black Mercedes SUV, the leather passenger seat already heated by the time I deposit my bum on it. He bears flowers, often, and not those ready-made bunches you pick up at the local Engen garage.

Yes, I met the love of my life at age forty-five on a generic dating site. Yes, we married less than a year later, despite our respective fears of commitment and much-vaunted love of independence. Yes, the past nearly two years together have been mostly bliss. We have merged our lives, his mother and siblings love me, and his children have started to accept me, once the frost that greeted my arrival thawed.

My own mother loves him – I never thought I would hear her utter the words "the son I never had", and my friends adore him, adore our sweet love story. When we are together, driving, hiking, talking, or making love, I look at my life and wonder if it truly is real. How could I get so lucky?

And yet the moment he leaves, the static in my stomach starts. There are times like tonight when he has delayed his return home for no good reason. When plans I have made are cast aside without a thought or apology. When I have spent a perfect spring day waiting and waiting for him to arrive, while he's barely acknowledged the texts I've been sending to get an idea of when to expect him. These are the times when, alone and feeling abandoned, I seethe.

But then he walks in, all smiles, smelling delicious, scoops me up in his arms, and I melt. I breathe a sigh of relief: he is back – we can resume our golden life together. His presence, his gaze, the sound of his voice, his skin against mine – that's what I need. That's what settles me.

In bed, he lifts my chin and whispers, "I missed you. Won't you kiss me?"

Despite my earlier resolve not to pick at it, I find myself asking about the delay. "What happened today, though?"

"Don't start. Not this again. You know how it is. I can't always predict things. I can't just brush people off. I work for them. I work for the people."

He rests one palm on the nape of my neck while tracing the contours of my lips with the thumb of his other hand. "Don't start a fight now, my precious. I'm here now. Don't spoil it."

Let it go, I will myself and shut my eyes. He kisses me – a long, slow kiss that wipes away the words still lingering on my tongue. I pull him towards me, into me, unleashing all the emotions I have swallowed with my body as I offer it to him. Sex with him, as always, induces somnolence – a blessed relief.

We wake the next morning, balance restored. He's up early, cheerful as always, while I linger half-asleep in bed, where he brings me his usual morning gift, a cup of coffee. I am still sleepy as he bends down, suited and tied, impeccably dressed in a black suit, white shirt and black tie. He kisses me goodbye. It's 6.30am and he is off into the world to change it.

I languish for another half an hour, can afford to go slow this morning; I have no classes to teach, just one committee meeting at the university at noon. My thoughts turn to a proposal I need to submit for a huge grant, the type that can be career-changing, and I berate myself for not yet having set up a suitable office space in Neill's home. Our home.

I've been living here for almost a year, but sometimes I still feel alien. Writing, the lifeblood of an academic – the most necessary thing I need to do if I want to go any further on my chosen path – has fled my life. It is so difficult to write, and there is something about this house, and our merged lives, that conspires against it.

It is not for lack of time – God knows, Neill is gone for a lot of it. Nor is it for lack of trying: I scribble down words at the kitchen counter, the huge oak dining room table, the patio table next to the swimming pool, or at a dresser in the spare bedroom. I manage in this way, but I am aware that to take myself seriously as a writer, I need a dedicated space where I can focus, uninterrupted by chores, visitors, or Neill's comings and goings. It is not that there isn't enough space – most days, the two of us rattle around in this house at the foot of the mountain. I just haven't made it a priority – the carving out of a designated space to think and write. The thing I swore to myself I would not allow when we started to get serious, has crept in – my tendency to put my work last, to focus on his needs, to make sure he is taken care of before all else.

Love has made a bit of a mess of me. It bothers me, this neglect of my intellectual life. But it is still early days, I placate myself, still the adjustment phase of the marriage – I'll find my stride again, eventually.

I arrive at my university office at the Department of Social Studies around nine, winding my way around a throng of students in the quad to enter the building that has become my second home.

I feel lucky still to be working in a beautiful, older building; all wood-panelled corridors and Oregon pine floors – not one of the more modern monstrosities that have sprung up as the university has grown. My footsteps reverberate, announcing my presence to everyone in the corridor. I unlock the door to my office, settle at my desk, and turn on my PC. My usual open-door policy, adopted so that students and colleagues can drop in for a chat when they see me, will not do for today. The door will remain firmly shut as I try to finish this albatross of a proposal.

I have lived in this office every weekday and often weekends too, for the past eight years. Over time, I have decorated the shell presented to me on my first day with pleasurable comforts – a small couch draped with bright fabric, an earth-toned kelim, a beautiful ceramic teapot, and mismatched hand-painted mugs. On the wall facing my desk hangs a poster for a Mary Sibande exhibition, the first thing I stuck up with Prestik after tossing out the Irma Stern print left by my predecessor. I have since framed the poster and had it properly hung, along with various other prints and photographs.

The Sibande poster, featuring the artist in a billowing worker's overall overlaid with a white apron, reminds me daily where I come from as the child of a domestic worker; and what I too could have become, were it not for the sacrifices made by that domestic worker, who pushed me to escape the prison in which apartheid had trapped her. Yes, there are quite a few of us here; PhDs and professors, respected, and esteemed, who come from such beginnings. But we won't tell you that, not unless we've known you for years; and even then, it will be cautiously, once we have proven to you, over and over, that we belong here.

It took a while for me to feel at home in this office, but gradually I've made it my own. I burn incense, aromatherapy oils, and when necessary, imphepho – which got me a lot of funny looks at first, and into a bit of trouble with "Buildings and Safety", the department charged with upkeep. I argued that this was my cultural practice and that not allowing me to burn my smudges and incense discriminated against me. Now they just steer clear when they smell the pungent aroma of smouldering herbs wafting through the hallways. Thandiswa makes a special smudge stick of imphepho for me, adding lavender, geranium and her secret fynbos blend – meant to bring my ancestors into the office with me, while protecting me from people with bad intentions.

I often tell her to set up an online store selling her medicines and potions – even the fancy wine farms are now selling imphepho at extortionate rates as part of their "lifestyle" products, but Thandiswa insists that she must know the person in order to make them a unique stick that will heal and protect them. She's not going to commercialise her work to make quick money. Her khoigoed bundles work – they have certainly cleared the air of some pompous stuck-ups around here. And as the only black woman in the Department of Social Studies, I relish that. I've paid my dues and deserve to be left alone to get on with my work.

My PC takes forever to start. I need an upgrade, but we're entitled to one only every eight years, and I am due for mine in December. While I wait for the computer to reach full wakefulness, I dream a little bit about my hopes for this proposal – my version of putting my intention out into the universe, something Thandiswa is always telling me to do. I am that nebulous creature known as the mid-career academic, having languished at the Senior Lecturer level for seven of my eight years here. I've carved out a small niche for myself at the intersection of sociology and psychology, an interdisciplinary field of my own making. I tried for *ad hominem* promotion to Associate Professor in my fourth year, and was turned down. When I appealed the decision, I was told that my research agenda was not considered rigorous, my output paltry, and my methods not suitably scientific.

The proposal I'm working on now envisions a national study on high school learners' perceptions of race and racial identity. I have gone to great lengths in the methodology section to describe a grounded research approach, which views participants as just that – participants, not subjects from whom data will be extracted. A grounded approach will see me presenting my findings to the students, inviting their input, and amending my findings to consider and include the ways participants respond to my analysis. It is their perception I am studying, after all.

The way my project is structured builds in time to deliver feedback to the participants. This is why my research takes longer than that done by many others in my department – it centres participants' voices, not my own as the "expert". I could abandon this topic and do something easier and less time-intensive; work with a less vulnerable population, and not give participants the opportunity to give input into the process of analysis. I could churn out work at a rate that pleases the university, bringing in the all-important government subsidy for every article published. But this population – adolescents – is important, understudied, and in need of advocacy research that will translate into policy that could change their lives, or the lives of those who will come after them in a few years.

If I receive this grant, it will allow me to travel around the country for a year, visiting schools in both rural and urban areas. I have good contacts in high schools, but need money to make this study a reality. My proposal budget has a line item for doctoral students who will be trained in participatory methods, which hold the potential for transformation in the next generation of scholars.

Transformation. How I detest that word! Yet I pepper it throughout the proposal, knowing the assessors who evaluate grant proposals score each proposal using a points system. I will literally lose points if I do not show how my proposed study contributes to transforming South African higher education. I am part of that transformation, was hired eight years ago with a special Vice-Chancellor's fund established to fast-track transformation at our university, which had remained stubbornly un-melanated in the teaching demographic.

Brian, then the Head of Department, welcomed me stoically on my first day, leading me through the department to introduce me to my colleagues. "Meet Dr Anita Fredericks. Our new transformation appointee," he said.

My new colleagues smiled and told me to "just ask" if I needed anything.

I was hired on the strength of the designated boxes I ticked in the "race" and "gender" categories of the HR form submitted as part of my application. No one really cared what my research specialisation was, or how it might "transform" things, and one year after my appointment, at the mid-probation mark, it was noted that I had not yet published anything. I've been lagging ever since. My colleagues frown upon this, I know – I found the minutes of one Research Committee meeting on our shared departmental hard drive, in which they had commiserated about the inevitable attrition of publication that goes with the lowering of standards. That was when I stopped caring what they thought of me.

I might not care about my colleagues' opinion of me anymore, but I do care deeply about my research. I need to do it properly, include the subjects in an ethical way – or it would feel like stealing from people. Because knowledge can be stolen, too. They've built entire disciplines and universities on stolen knowledge. I refuse to be part of that.

My proposal will be done tomorrow, and I will send it off to the current head of department for his feedback, and his all-important signature, the stamp of approval that will launch it on to the Research Office for a final decision. Getting the head of my department onboard is the first hurdle I need to clear if this project is ever to get off the ground.

The writing sweeps me up, and it is hours later when my phone pings. There is still that frisson of excitement when his name pops up.

"Quick chat?"

I reply with a thumbs up.

Neill calls and we discuss dinner plans. This has been one of the adjustments of marriage – I have never had a fixed time for supper, sometimes even forgetting to eat when absorbed in work. We decided early on that we'd try, as much as we were able, to eat one meal a day together, setting aside space to connect and share our days. Never again wanting to see the inside of a divorce court, we sat down and talked about how we would make time, despite our busy lives.

We settle on a time for tonight's dinner. The duty of choosing a venue and making a booking falls to me. I don't like it, but he's busy, busier than me, and he flatters me when I complain that this is gendered labour: "But you're so good at it!" His job is incredibly stressful, and I remind myself to be the good helpmeet I promised I would be. After speaking to him, I make a reservation at a new restaurant we've both been wanting to try, and forward the details to him.

I'm fully absorbed in the proposal for the rest of the day. When I arrive at the appointed restaurant, he is already there, absorbed with reading something on his phone. His face lights up as I walk towards him. I feel that warm sun inside of me, the same as that first day we met. It is that rarest and most beautiful of feelings: pure joy.

Chapter Two

On our third date, I learned what he did for a living. He had been an attorney who built up a thriving practice over many years in Bloemfontein. But having been part of the movement since his teenage years in the late 1970s and early 1980s, and later, the political party that came out of that movement, the time had come for him to take up formal leadership.

The movement was his life. He had always been involved in its structures: a disciplined branch member, he had worked as a legal advisor, sometimes formally, at other times, behind the scenes, more of a strategist. In the late 2000s, he decided to step fully into the leadership role he was already covertly taking. Reluctantly, of course, after being deployed by the leadership. Because of his acumen as a lawyer and businessman, he was placed on the party's provincial list and became a member of the provincial legislature of the Free State. Later he was deployed to the national legislature, which accounted for his last few years in Cape Town. He is a backbencher who shuns the limelight; not at all a political grandstander or populist. He has grown to love it – the work, the city – what was not to love? – and it has become, more or less, home. I wonder, out loud, how he has remained below the radar. He is hardly in the news, hardly makes headlines, nor is he photographed at political events.

"Well, I've applied my work philosophy from practising law to my work as a politician."

"Oh? What is that?" I ask.

"I prefer to work behind the scenes. Exercise power softly, quietly, if you will. I don't want to be known as a political player. Sometimes that stands in the way of doing the real work."

I nod.

"There are benefits to remaining in the background. In politics, I've learned, you can be a street-fighter, or a strategist – a chess player."

"And you are … which one of those two?"

I am teasing, flirting with him. The tone of our conversation is light, convivial.

"Oh, I don't know," he smiles. "Let's just say, I hope, for your sake, you never have to find out."

The smile is meant to signal lighthearted banter, but his answer chills me.

I look at him, so calm and relaxed, a study in ease and confidence. What lies beneath that polished exterior?

"Oh, don't look so serious. It was a joke – or a poor attempt at one, it seems."

I plaster a smile across my face, take another sip of my gin and tonic. Getting to know people in the age of the fourth industrial revolution is a strange pursuit. Were I to Google him, there'd be a multitude of snippets and news items all over the internet. There might be social media profiles, showing how affable and friendly he has been; I might be led through a string of ex-wives or ex-girlfriends. I could know, within a few keystrokes, how much he earns, the properties he owns, the number of children he has, the names of his relatives. You can get so many insights, slivers of light, into a person's life, freely and publicly available, but so often these are the shells of their lives; carefully crafted personas declaring: *Look at me! I'm so rich, so clever, so productive, so kind, so compassionate. I love my family, love God, the church* – whatever currency they need to trade in.

Transparency and hypervisibility have, paradoxically, made it even more difficult to know people. Lives are curated, managed, manicured like lawns. You think you are getting to know someone; yet it's possible to know everything and nothing about them at the same time.

I Google him as soon as I get home, and am impressed with

what I find. A solid cadre, committed to the cause of freedom from a young age. Being a backbencher does not mean that he snores away his days in the plush leather seats of the House of Assembly. He is active in a number of portfolio committees. Most strikingly, he chairs the Portfolio Committee on Women and Children, where he has put in a great deal of work. Within no time, I've pulled up Hansards in which he is named or cited, and find he has been a tireless advocate for the introduction of a Basic Income Grant. His argument supporting the grant rests on the idea that poverty in this country is gendered; that providing such a grant is a step towards lifting women, who are increasingly heading households, out of poverty. I read his addresses in Parliament, where he maps out the potential the grant has to diminish the abject poverty and food insecurity many children live with, stunting their opportunities almost from the cradle. His speeches are passionate denunciations of the feminisation of poverty, but his attempts to codify the Basic Income Grant into law have been thwarted numerous times. I trawl through the parliamentary record until the early hours of the morning, and when I am done, go to bed satisfied that my new suitor is one of the good ones – if "good" is ever a word that can be applied to a politician.

A few days later, Neill's profession is the main item on the agenda of our monthly sister meeting – or the coven gathering, as we like to call it. Thandiswa and Claire are hungry for more details of this budding affair – and my aversion to his job.

"I really like this man. There is something very special about him. But a politician? One from that party, no less? We know what a mess they are. Should I get further into this?"

I myself was once a card-carrying member of the party, years ago, when things were new and bright and full of optimism, hope and gratitude. A better life for all, we were promised. And had the party not delivered that? Hadn't it liberated us, ushered us into a new era where we could at last stand proudly as full citizens, cast off the yoke and indignity of poverty and oppression? How else could a girl like me, having grown up in a wendyhouse in someone's backyard in Athlone, have made this leap into the life of the mind, this life I love?

Yes, I am clinging to that coveted black middle-class status by the very tips of my unmanicured fingernails. But I have a job, and more than that, a career; I own my own modest home, have food to eat, access to medical care when I need it. Yes, I pay black tax to several relatives in my extended family and friend circles – school fees, petrol money, chipping in for the rent – but I have it better than 90 per cent of this country. And there are legions of us – not the disaffected "born frees", but the ones who came of age at just the right time, when universities and technikons were affordable and you could pay your own fees by working one part-time job; when we were actively headhunted and absorbed into the professional force, before the youth unemployment rate skyrocketed to 47 per cent.

We are the generation that has done well out of this transition. Yes, we criticise the party for selling out, for the negotiated settlement that didn't return the land, for the naked corruption that has festered over the last decade or so. But where would a woman like me be without the party? Still scrubbing some white woman's floors. Still living in a ghetto for people who look like me. Still forced to go through the back door of the post office. Isn't that why we continue to vote for it, years after the rainbow-magic has faded, to be replaced by rot, graft, and a hollowed-out public purse?

I take pride in my academic work, which I often describe as critiquing power. And there is a great deal to critique about the ways in which the liberation movement has moved into power – the corruption, the cronyism, the leap to embrace neoliberal market forces after coming to power on a socialist manifesto. But, let's face it, I am a beneficiary of that power system, over and over again. That fact rankles, but remains true. I have eschewed traditional forms of power while lurking at the margins, happy to benefit from the large systemic changes brought about by the movement. Am I a hypocrite to turn my nose up at someone who has not been uncomfortable with power; who has actively sought it and fully inhabits it; who is not afraid to wield it?

Thandiswa and Claire unpack the issues with me over mojitos.

"Does being a politician have to be a dealbreaker? What's his overall vibe? I mean, his aura, his light. Do you get good vibes, is what I would ask myself."

"Oh my god, Thandiswa!" I enthuse. "He's attractive, intelligent, witty, charming – a little bit on the suave side, but all in all, a great package. Of course, I'm getting good vibes! They're called pheromones! You of all people should know this. Take a look at his picture again, my friend. Who wouldn't be getting good vibes being around this man? I am positively vibrating!"

Thandiswa spits a bit of her drink as she erupts in laughter.

Claire pretends to disapprove: "You two are gonna get us kicked out of yet another fine establishment! Seriously though, Anita…" she shifts into analysis mode. "I know a politician is not your dream man. But it doesn't have to be a dealbreaker. Not all politicians are corrupt. Given his credentials and the portfolio committee work, he probably isn't. Maybe he's one of those idealistic souls who believes he can change things from the inside."

Claire leans forward: "Him being a politician actually works in your favour – there are probably lots more ways for you to check his bona fides than just your regular Joe. There's a lot of information in the public domain. Never mind Hansard – check his annual parliamentary declaration of interests. He's got to list all business interests and gifts there. You could learn a lot about him through those channels, at least professionally."

"Oh, you have got to be kidding!" I scream, imagining myself turning into a detective, sniffing out his business on the internet. Quite a romantic start to a relationship.

Claire reads my mind: "And it's not snooping. You need to do due diligence if you are seriously thinking about letting this man into your life. If you want to have a short fling with him, by all means, go ahead and enjoy! But I haven't seen that look in your eyes for years – you're smitten!

I laugh, but it's true.

"And this is where I see so many of my clients go wrong. They're in love and they don't stop to ask themselves, who am I really getting into bed with? Metaphorically and literally, of course!"

More laughter erupts around our table.

"I am serious, Anita! Women fall in love and ignore all kinds of red flags. Jump into marriage without securing their assets, buy properties together without getting their names on the title deeds, move in with men without cohabitation agreements. Legally, I can't do much for them after they've taken these huge leaps, and the man turns out to be a less than upstanding citizen."

Claire is in full protective mode by now: "And then there are men who target successful women – appeal to them to take out loans, bankroll their business ideas, or just blatantly sponge off them. You need to take care!"

I protest. "It's not like I'm rolling in it. I make ends meet, have a comfortable life, but my lifestyle is very modest. I'm not exactly sugar-mommy material!"

Thandiswa guffaws and starts a more drunk-than-sober rendition of "Pour some sugar on me".

But Claire remains serious in her quest to educate me on seductive scammers. "From your point of view, yes, you live modestly. But even if you don't have that many assets, you could still be very attractive to a con artist. You own a home? Fully paid up? Have a bond? A pension fund? Your credit standing is good? There are men out there who target modest-living women like you, who aren't necessarily wealthy, but have their financial lives together. They siphon off small amounts, but over years, it can add up. Or they can force you into debt by bankrolling lifestyles they think they deserve – a nice new car paid for by, guess who? You! Men love to pull out the gold-digger stereotype when it comes to women, but in my practice, I'm starting to see the genders reversed far more than before."

"Oh yes! Preach, sista!" Thandiswa picks up the baton as Claire pauses for breath. "And don't forget the hobo-sapiens!"

"The what-now, Thandiswa?"

Thandiswa straightens up, swigs from her glass, and takes a deep breath. "You haven't heard about hobo-sapiens? Girl! Let me tell you! Lazy men without jobs or a place to live. They find you, woo you, and next thing you know, they're moving in with you. You know what they say: no one falls in love more quickly than a man without a place to stay! Jy moet pasop, meisie!"

We scream with laughter. Once I recover and catch my breath, I thank them for their warnings. "I hardly think Neill is wanting for money. I'm not in danger here. In fact, he has been quite generous."

Claire is not convinced, "You can't be too sure. The lovely Mercedes will be a government-issued car. And his housing will also be subsidised. Yes, he's probably well-off financially, having practised law for many years, but there are other ways in which men can drain us. Time. Care. Women do so much emotional labour in relationships. I have clients who've stayed home to look after kids to allow a man's career to flourish, only to have said man leave her once the children are grown and his career is soaring. That's when he takes off with a young hottie from the office where he's spent all those late nights. And if you haven't made provisos to take care of yourself, you can be financially devastated when such a man leaves. Obviously, that's not the case with you – I can't see you giving up anything for a man. But there are ways we invest and over-give to men that we are never compensated for. So, make sure before you decide to invest in this man, before you fall in love with his mind, or his body or his ... whatever: make sure that he's worth it."

Claire is the only one among us who has been and stayed married – for almost twenty years. She has the odd complaint about Frederick, but from the outside they look like the perfect couple. I've always put her gripes down to her wanting to make us feel better about the often tumultuous state of our love lives.

Her comment gives me pause: the sadness in her eyes as she cautions me about over-investing emotionally betrays something. I make a mental note to ask her about it another time, when we're alone.

"Claire has a point," says Thandiswa, deep into her third mojito. "You can't be too careful. You know how they say it takes a village to raise a child? Well, if you ask me, it also takes a village to have a successful long-term relationship."

She is suddenly serious. "Back in our youth, when we first started going out with men, the pool was pretty small. You dated someone from your street or your neighbourhood, or someone you went to school or varsity with, or a guy you met at work. And there were networks around you – people who could tell you what was what with a man. Your brother used to play cricket with him; his dad used to work with your uncle; your friend attended class with him. We had people who could vouch for love potentials – you could ask them straight: is so-and-so a good guy? Will he treat me right?"

Claire and I nod.

"These days most singles looking for love meet people on the internet. And even those who are hitched are there, on the dating apps. It's tricky. On the net, you're a blank slate. You can completely reinvent yourself. And the innocent, trusting fools that some of us are don't have any way of checking that people are who they say they are. Not until it's too late, and you're more than halfway sucked in and entangled with them."

Claire takes yet another turn. "Listen to Thandiswa. You can't be too careful, Anita. Especially at our age."

"Our age? We're hardly geriatrics!"

"Of course not, but your eye should be on retirement. Do you have enough to live comfortably? Will you have somewhere decent to live once the salary stops coming in? And will a new man have his eye on that prize – the house you may have paid for, the pension fund? I'm telling you, I'm seeing more and more women in this predicament. Once the panties drop, it's like they become mesmerised, happy to kiss their money goodbye until they wake up one day, and money and Babes are both gone. 'I wanted to build a life with him,' they cry in my office while I pass the tissues. There are no ways to recoup those losses if you gave the money freely. This is why I advise clients to think twice – hell, four, five times – before jumping into a relationship that involves sharing money or merging assets."

"You two are enough to put any woman off men forever!"

Thandiswa laughs. "Oh no, no, no, my love! Men are wonderful if you keep them in the right place in your life. Do what I do. Have fun with them, have great sex with them, but watch out once your emotions come into play. This is why I avoid falling in love!"

Claire is less cynical. "Fall in love, if you must. But do your research. And meet his people early on. They'll give you a sense of who he is."

Solid advice. And ultimately, this is how I found myself on a flight to Bloemfontein one Friday afternoon.

I had asked Neill when I would meet some of his friends, and he'd suggested a visit to Bloemfontein, his home town, where those closest to him lived. I could also meet his family, a suggestion that sent me into a panic. Was it not too soon for that? I asked. We barely knew each other, had been seeing each other for less than two months. We didn't yet know where this would go.

It wasn't too soon for him, he replied. And he knew where he wanted it to go, but if that overwhelmed me, he would back off. That was the last thing I wanted. I found his forthrightness endearing, his self-assurance in knowing what he wanted – me – disarming. Wasn't I always complaining to the coven about men who didn't know what they wanted, who were too afraid to commit? And here was this beautiful man saying everything I'd ever wanted to hear from a love interest. No games, no testing me, no disappearing and reappearing on a whim. Why, now, was I finding it all too much, too soon? And so I agreed to spend a weekend with him in Bloemfontein.

My business-class return ticket arrived in my inbox minutes after I texted him my ID number. This is how it would always be with him – I would express a desire or agree to a request, and minutes later all arrangements would be made – for travel, for buying anything I wanted, for acquiring the finer things in life. This is how he shows his devotion. Everything will be taken care of, from this point on. I am loving the vibe of this brand-new relationship. If I had to sum up the feeling of being with him in one sentence, it would be: "Your wish is my command." Like I said: devotion.

He is already waiting for me when my plane touches down in Bloemfontein. I text as soon as I'm allowed to switch the phone back on – "landed!"

The green notification lights up the screen seconds later: "Been here for half an hour! Can't wait to see you!"

We are not the type of people to recreate movie scenes in an airport arrival area. But the air around us crackles as we stare at each other and giggle with excitement at being reunited. I lean into a hug, and the familiar scent of sandalwood greets me as he kisses me, sending a delicious current through my body.

He relieves me of my luggage, and soon we are gliding down the highway from Bram Fischer Airport in a glittering black Porsche – his own, not a government-issued vehicle. Once safely ensconced behind its tinted windows, he relaxes and reaches for my hand. He strokes it playfully, then lifts it to his face and plants a flurry of kisses into my upturned palm.

"Welcome to my home town. Thank you so much for coming all this way to visit me." He has been away from Cape Town for a week – first to Pretoria, and then to visit his constituency – the longest period we've been apart since meeting. I've missed him – seeing him makes my heart lurch recklessly about in my chest. I study his profile while he drives, pointing out landmarks, his eyes full of light. I am touched by his excitement at seeing me again – he is usually so calm, betraying very little. I run the back of my hand along his jaw – feel the stubble already threatening to push through what I know to be a freshly shaven face. His skin against mine feels like home.

This feeling catches me off-guard. I've been cool until now; watching him, watching myself step forward and then retreat from him, observing my feelings expand and retract with a detached eye. Even here, on the cusp of love, feeling that falling, yet pulling myself back, I find it impossible to switch off my analytical mind – to just feel, for once.

Since I've met him, I've been both object and subject of study in a private ethnography. He is different to all the previous men in my life. My daily journal entries attest to an almost compulsive need to record the experience – create my own data, so to speak. My mother has so often berated me for this tendency: the need to analyse life so much that I forget to live it. But it is a habit, difficult to switch off, and what is more, comforting. My need to analyse is a way of distancing myself from my emotions, which are often so messy.

I've tried to counter this tendency, *feel* my emotions – God knows, I've sat through countless mindfulness sessions, tried meditation, prostrated myself on the couches of too many therapists to count. But I am at the age where I've accepted the basic structure of my personality. There will always be this need to record, remember, observe the patterns that shape my life, and try to make meaning of them.

Neill takes me on a lightning trip through the downtown area, pointing out the Supreme Court of Appeal, the lake, the zoo. It's a quick twenty minutes from the city centre to his home, where we will tidy ourselves before supper with his family.

We're waved, with a smile, through the entrance to the Golden Hills nature estate where he lives. Until this moment, I didn't know it was possible to live in a gated estate that doubled as a nature reserve where kudu, eland and zebra roam. Neill lives alone in a luxurious five-bedroomed house, which we enter through an intricately carved wooden front door, made locally by copying photos taken on a holiday in Tanzania. A small, cosy reception room opens into a much larger, light-filled atrium, all glass and steel, allowing the tawny late afternoon light to spill across the entire living area. Persian carpets anchor abundantly stuffed leather chairs and couches. Abstract wooden sculptures populate the room like old friends.

"Your home is stunning!" I try not to sound too awestruck as I take it all in.

He beams at my wide-eyed surveillance of his home. "I'll take you on a tour of the rest of the house in a second. But first…"

He scoops me into his arms and pulls me into a long, passionate kiss. Here he is a different Neill to the one I have come to know in Cape Town, where his demeanour is measured and calm. When he draws away from me, his eyes shine, giving him the look of a boy who has just unwrapped a new toy on Christmas morning.

"Please make yourself at home. Whatever you need, just ask, okay? Come, let me show you everything."

He takes my hand and pulls me along. It's as if I've stepped into the pages of *Architectural Digest*. He whisks me through the marble-clad kitchen, a wood-panelled study – more library than study – with a fire already crackling in the fireplace, a formal living room with bespoke cream couches, the sunroom, the swimming pool, the gazebo.

He explains how he chose the house for its good bones, then stripped it right down to those bones to have an architect redesign it and throw down most of the constricting inner walls, letting in the light and harmonising the interior with the stunning exterior. Living in a game reserve, he wanted to make the most of the natural setting, to bring the outdoors – the lush colours, the changing seasons – inside. His vision was for the house to be a backdrop to the outdoors – not too showy, not in competition with nature. He had the best interior designer in the country fly in to work with the architect to fulfil this vision.

Next he leads me up a granite staircase. Five bedrooms, each with their own bathroom. A wrap-around balcony that affords each bedroom its own uninterrupted view of the game park. Neighbours are a mere insinuation – you know they must be out there, somewhere, but they cannot be seen.

I can't help but think of my own humble semi-detached home on the hill in Woodstock, sandwiched between rows of similar semis.

Houses in the same mould, each with the same long passage, two bedrooms, a living room and kitchen, and the only bathroom at the back of a tapering house. On a quiet day, I can hear my neighbours flush their toilet. It must be wonderful to live like this, unencumbered by the daily invasions of privacy that close communal living entails.

The twins' bedrooms are pristine. He loves being an MP, but the heartbreaking flipside means that he doesn't see his children as often as he'd like. They're twelve, on the brink of the turbulent teenage years, a boy and a girl – some people just get lucky like that. Neill's ex-wife has primary custody of them, amicably agreed to, he assures me. It's best for the children to have a solid home base, and he's allowed to see them whenever he wants. This he does as much as his work schedule allows, even if it means a short hour here, a quick car ride there, a chance to drop them off at their extramural activities when he is in town with a bit of free time.

Their beautifully decorated bedrooms have an unlived-in air about them – they're far too neat for children's rooms. No tacky teenage heartthrob posters torn from *You Magazine* taped to the walls, no empty cups, no hastily discarded shoes, no scuffed teddy bears. These rooms have not been disturbed by anyone other than a cleaner in weeks.

We've agreed that I will not meet the twins this time. The adults in the family are fair game, but with children, you have to be careful. There'll be dynamics to negotiate, attachments to be formed – and, no doubt, resentments to get over. It is better to tread carefully, wait until we're both one hundred per cent certain of our stakes in each others' lives before going that route.

Neill leads me into the guest bedroom. A domestic worker has discreetly unloaded my luggage from the car, and I find it neatly stacked by the foot of my bed. A fresh bouquet of pink and white roses adorns the dresser.

"I thought you'd be more comfortable in here," he says.

I'm disappointed. We have not yet slept together – Neill has been a perfect gentleman about this. He asks to hold my hand, asks, "May I kiss you?" the first few times we kiss.

I complain to the coven that it all feels a bit stilted.

"A man who understands consent? God, it's a miracle!" exclaims Claire.

To which Thandiswa adds, "You're so used to dating trashy men, you don't realise when a gentle-man is genuinely courting you!"

Courting. It sounds so old-fashioned. But the chivalry I routinely baulked at in my younger, militant feminist days now evokes a feeling of safety.

"Seriously, babes, he sounds like a keeper."

And here my keeper was, protecting my well-worn honour by releasing me from any obligation to have sex with him. And on his home turf, no less. His gallant behaviour twists my heart a little bit. I want him to respect me, yes, and obviously I want this relationship to be about more than just sex, but I also want him to desire me. Is he really happy to have me here for the entire weekend with zero prospect of some between-the-sheets action? Am I just not that irresistible?

He reads my mind. "My bedroom's just across the hallway. If you want to indulge in a midnight visit, by all means, do. I will leave it up to you."

This, I will come to know, is his way: never pushy, never insistent. He comes halfway towards me and leaves a space between us which I must work to fill. A glow spreads through my body. I muster every ounce of restraint to stop myself from dragging him into the bedroom right that minute.

He leaves me to settle in, and we each freshen up in our respective bathrooms. I check mine for evidence of a feminine presence anything left behind by my predecessors – but there is nothing; only generic, unopened shower gel, shampoo, conditioner, luxury hand soaps and body lotion. The cupboards in which I hang my clothes are empty.

The drive from Golden Hills estate to Heidedal, where Neill grew up, takes less than thirty minutes, but is several lifetimes away. After we leave the estate with its discreet electric fences, booms and obsequious security guards, we head back south on the N8. As we exit the highway to make our way to his family home, the landscape changes. More potholes, open fields with litter and rubble, and tightly packed houses competing for space. It's early Friday evening, and the streets teem with people on their way to the corner shops, off-sales and taverns. On the side of the road, a group of boys kick a deflated soccer ball around. The township feels instantly familiar to anyone who's grown up in the standard two-bedroom-kitchen-living room-outside toilet house you will find in any coloured housing scheme in South Africa. You could plop a block from Heidedal down in Bokmakierie, Athlone, next to my mother's street, and it would blend right in, along with the young men loitering on the corner, eyeing the Porsche.

Except, in my day growing up in the township, they were doing Mandrax, injected into our communities by the apartheid state to quell the riotous urges of the 1980s. Now it is tik, dragged into the lungs through a different kind of pipe – the lollies, not the broken-necked Black Label bottle pipes. The effects are equally devastating, but infinitely more gruesome than the "buttons", the pills that when crushed and smoked made the user kap om and sleep it off. Tik leads to rapes that end in bloody murders, stabbings, mass shootings. Homes being trashed, beloved parents and grandparents beaten and slashed. The fungibility of the coloured South African township is a depressing fact. Neill's jaw tightens as we pass another group of young men. He looks at them, is recognised and waved at; he waves back and smiles, hooting cheerily. This, then, is the ever-demanding constituency that will take him away from me so often.

We flow with the traffic through the township towards a subdivision where the homes stand further apart from each other, have larger gardens, well-maintained fences and freshly painted exteriors. Neill parks the car outside a modest white house, with a garden demarcated by a painted vibracrete fence.

His mother waits in the doorway, smiling: tall, proud, clad in a dress that would normally be reserved for church on Sunday. We're introduced, and she folds me into a long hug, declaring how wonderful it is to meet me, how she's heard so much about me, and to call her Aunty Sophie.

She is an energetic woman in her seventies, slim, with proudly squared shoulders and perfectly coifed, pitch-black hair. Her only problem, she soon shares with me, is arthritis in her hands, the result of years of domestic work in white people's homes, scrubbing floors and washing laundry, sometimes by hand. It was worth it, though, she confides, because look at how her children turned out. All four of them have a university education, have made something of themselves, are contributing. She would do it all again in a heartbeat, knowing how proud they would make her. And how proud she is of her boy, her oldest. He, who had to become the man of the house at far too young an age, who started working at the age of ten, doing odd jobs around the neighbourhood, selling fruit and vegetables in order to supplement her meagre income after their father just up and left them. This when she, still in her twenties, had no family of her own to count on besides Neill. But look at how it all paid off. Breathless praise for him spills from her lips as she leads me into the living room, before I have even taken a seat.

"We didn't always live like this, you know," she waves her hand around the modest living room, spotless, with the kind of suite I know only too well, having helped my own mother lay-buy one at OK Bazaars.

"My kids had a hard childhood. We didn't always live in a house like this, with bricks and a good roof over our heads. I only got this house when Neill was almost finished with high school. But look at the goodness of God. Through the help of my children, I can live here now. In my own house. And they take care of me. I thank God for that every day."

Neill's sisters and their husbands start arriving for supper. They greet me politely, with the requisite phrases, we've heard so much about you, so pleased to meet you. Each of his three sisters arrives with a side to complement his mother's main dish of roast lamb. They hug their brother, ask after his health. They joke and tease. I note their body language when they talk to him, deferential, eyes wide with respect. There is no hint of sibling rivalry in their interactions. I catch and chide myself – for once, stop analysing. Just be with them, be a human being. It's a kind of an armour I've built up, I suppose, to distract from any awkwardness when I meet new people. I watch them closely, which often makes things even more discomfiting for those who feel my gaze. But they do not notice, wrapped up as they are in welcoming their oldest brother.

After the introductions, we sit down at the dining room table while Neill says grace. He is short and perfunctory: his mother takes over after his "Amen", thanking God for bringing all her children together again safely, with Neill travelling so much they never know when they will see him again. She goes on to thank God for providing for her and her family, and for bringing me to her home.

His sisters are reserved, but somehow still warm. They ask me questions – nothing too probing – do I have children? Thankfully, there are no follow-up questions when I answer no. When Neill excuses himself to go to the bathroom, the eldest sister, Nicolette, asks my age.

I answer truthfully, forty-five.

Relief brightens her face. "Oh good! You look great for your age – much younger. But that is a good age for someone like Neill, not too young. He needs a mature woman, someone who understands the demands of his career, and who isn't insecure about it. He knows a lot of people – is admired and respected. Any woman in Neill's life needs to understand that she cannot be the only one to lay claim to him. He belongs to the people. You must have patience with that."

"I will certainly try my best. We're still getting to know each other, so there's lots still to find out about him, and him about me."

"I see," says his mother with a smile. "But you know, you are both grown-ups. Mature people, professionals. You've both lived lives by now. You've both achieved a lot. And when you get to a certain age … let me just say, you are not getting younger. And when you're older and mature, and you meet someone of good character and good values, you know, there is no need to wait and see for too long. If you find a good person, at your age, at Neill's age … commit to it. Life is short. You've lived more than half of it already, and good people don't come into our lives every day."

Neill returns from the bathroom, and his mother cuts the conversation short before I can answer.

"Now what are you gossiping to Anita about me, Mum?"

"Ah my son! I am just telling her how lovely it is to see you happy. That is always what I have wanted for you. To be happy. Settled."

"And have I not been? I am just about the happiest man you'll find, Mum."

"You know what I mean, Neill. I have been telling you all these years, you could be happier. With the right person by your side. There is a deeper contentment to be had when you find your helpmeet, the one that God has intended to help you carry life's burdens. And you do carry a lot, my son. You do. To have someone next to you as you carry what has been set out for you to carry … there is simply nothing that compares when you have that knowledge of a true friend next to you."

"Thank you, Mum. Now you go on like that, and you will scare Anita off. She will start wondering just what is wrong with me to make you so desperate to palm me off."

The sisters laugh in unison. Aunty Sophie takes her cue, turning back to me: "There is nothing wrong with my son. He is wonderful. He is clever. He is strong, respected by everyone. Always helping others, even when they don't deserve it. Always doing the right thing. Always caring for me and his sisters. You will not find a better man than my son."

We are quiet in the car as we drive back to the estate after supper. Neill is in a world of his own; I can finally relax after the stress of meeting the family and trying to make a good impression. I lean back, sleepily, watching the street lights whizz by in a blur.

"Why are mothers like that?" Neill laughs. "Here I am perfectly happy, living my life. I would say I haven't done too badly, and yet she won't be happy, won't consider me a success, until I have a wife."

"Mine's the same," I answer. "It's not that they don't consider us successful – more that they don't want us to be alone."

"But surely alone is not so bad?" he asks.

"Well, no. But from a parent's point of view, I suppose, it makes sense to want to see your child with a partner. Clearly you don't need help materially. But emotionally? She must wonder who is there for you when you are lonely or sad or stressed."

Silence hangs between us. I break it with a question that's been on my mind almost since I've met him. "Who is there for you, Neill? I have Thandiswa and Claire. We're closer than sisters. But you never speak of friends."

"Well, I don't really have the time. And I just don't have a high need to analyse everything. If things bother me, I speak to my mother. Or my sisters. If I'm upset, I go to the gym. I watch a series, have a few whiskies, and go to sleep. I don't know. I haven't ever really needed this thing you call emotional support. Sounds a lot like navel-gazing to me."

"Okay, the strong and silent type, I get it, I get it!" I say. "But you know that's why your gender has higher stats for strokes and heart attacks, right? From keeping it all in, not needing support, not showing emotion. Men have been socialised to be strong, stoic. Emotion isn't a sign of weakness."

"Analysis, analysis!" he barks. But then his voice goes soft again. "What a heavy discussion for a Friday night. I'd rather be cuddling on a couch with you." He reaches for my hand. I lean over and kiss him on the cheek.

"Well, you were a great success. The whole family liked you, especially my mother. I could see that. Doesn't happen too often. Not that I've brought many women home."

I've wondered about that, and the quiet, polite focus with which his sisters observed me. It stands to reason. He's a successful, wealthy man. Any close family would be suspicious of a potential partner and their motives, given his status. I remind myself that although I am here to be subjected to a series of tests to gauge my suitability – for what, I have yet to fathom – I am also here to do my own discerning. Due diligence, as Claire calls it. It is not only about me being liked, being chosen; but also making my own informed choices based on what I see of his home, his family and their dynamic.

He takes my hand, flattening it, palm down, on his thigh, and covers it with his. It warms my whole body, and as the car cuts through the night, I imagine us continuing to drive like this for hours. His family has confirmed what I have intuitively felt – that he is a good man. In his presence, I feel safe, protected, held. I could stay like this next to him forever, journeying through time, uncertainty and the unknown, the knowledge of him holding me like this being enough.

I wake as we pull into his garage. Exhausted, we bid our goodnights on the landing between the bedrooms, and I turn in immediately. I toss around the expanse of king-sized bed, hoping that he'll appear and jump in next to me, but if my suitor is feeling amorous, he is committed to being a complete gentleman. I consider making my way to his bedroom, but decide against such a bold first move. Disappointed by his lack of advances, I fall into a restless sleep.

I'm a late sleeper, but set my alarm for 6.30am – I know he rises early, and don't want to delay him in what will be a busy day. He must work in the morning, an imbizo with members of the party; then we're due for lunch at his mother's. We'll go for a drive in the afternoon.

The smell of fresh coffee awakens me on Saturday morning. Neill is opening my door, in hand a feast of bacon, scrambled egg, toast and coffee. He places the tray by my bedside, greets me with a kiss, and sits down next to me on the side of the bed.

"Wow, what a treat! Can't remember the last time I've had breakfast in bed," I say.

"Think about it – this could be the start of every day."

I giggle. This kind of joke makes me uncomfortable, but I say nothing – who wants to be a curmudgeon when you've just been brought breakfast in bed?

Neill wears a white T-shirt and jeans. Unlike me, he looks like he's been awake for hours. His gaze on me is steady as we eat. I am self-conscious: this the first time he is seeing me without the armour of make-up. Not even a smidgeon of mascara. It feels as if a layer of skin has been peeled from my entire body.

"You look so beautiful. And your morning voice, so soft and sleepy, it's very sexy."

I groan to myself without letting the smile slip from my face. It's too early for this. I haven't even brushed my teeth, and I need two cups of strong coffee before I am anywhere near fit for human company.

Neill is chipper and chatty, rattling off a list of potential sights for us to visit in the afternoon after work is out of the way. Still half in dreamland, I catch only the tail-end of the locations he's considering.

"What do you think, Anita?"

"You decide. Since I haven't really done any sight-seeing in this part of the world, any place you take me will be new to me."

After breakfast he leaves me to get showered, and soon we are on our way.

I am spending the morning with his mother, who wants to get to know me better. He'll rejoin us for lunch. I am petrified of the thought of four hours alone with the woman who raised him, and what her astute eye might see, or find lacking in me. He senses my nerves.

"Don't get too anxious. She already likes you. Just continue to be yourself, and she will love you. Because there's so much to love. Before the end of the day, she'll have fallen in love with you – just like I did!"

His words surprise me. This is the first mention of love between us. It makes me uncomfortable, as it always does in relationships. The timing of saying the words out loud to the other, the politics of who says it first...

Thandiswa's rule is that the man always must declare love first. It is one of the intractable arguments we have over cocktails. What, are we in the 1950s? I always declare in disbelief. Such a retrograde notion that the man should say it first – who cares who says what first – if you feel, say it. Thandiswa argues that a woman who says "I love you" to a man before he does, gives away all the power in a relationship. The man now has the upper hand, and since they already have all the power thanks to patriarchy, why give them even more, creating an even more unbalanced playing field?

Soon I'm back at his mother's dining room table, a pot of tea and an array of sandwiches and little cakes spread out before me. Neill makes a hasty exit, leaving just me and his mother in the house, this time with no buffers between us. My stomach lurches as I sit down, facing Aunty Sophie's direct gaze. She pours tea, starts asking polite questions about my life – work, family, where I grew up.

"So you're divorced, how long ago?"

"Ooh, it was so long ago, I even forget – more than fifteen years. We were so young when we met at university, and we married soon after. We were far too young."

"People give up on marriage so quickly these days," she says. "Any children?"

"No, we never got around to that, thankfully," I lie.

"Thankfully? That is a funny thing to say. Children are a blessing."

"Well, I didn't mean it like that. I always wanted children. The time was not right then, and I didn't meet anyone after my ex-husband who I thought would make a good enough father. I really wanted children, but it just didn't happen for me."

"And now? You're still young."

"It's a bit late now. I am forty-five. It might still be possible, but I feel that my life is more or less set on its course now, so why would I want to have a child at this point?"

Another lie.

I hardly know this woman, and I am not getting into this with her. Yes, my first husband and I divorced, but not because we were too young when we married. The memory of it still singes: the months of waiting for a pregnancy that never appeared, a wait that turned into years. Hope spiralling into dizzying cycles of disappointment, month after month; watching my husband Keith's face coming to mirror the despair in my heart. Three years of trying, two more of cycles of in vitro fertilisation, a second mortgage to pay for it – and nothing, nothing at all to show for it. My attempts to get him to agree to adopt a baby were futile. Thandiswa's offer to be a surrogate, which he would not countenance. Keith's decision to leave the marriage, my begging him to stay, knowing that I was doomed to fail at that, too. Trying to rebuild my life while watching him go on to remarry and have the two children – the pigeon pair we'd always dreamed about, had even chosen names for. Seeing his new wife, Marguerite, slip effortlessly into the life that should have been mine.

No, some stories are best left untold, especially to the mother of your new boyfriend.

"Well, good," Aunty Sophie says. "I'm glad you have no plans to try and make my son a father again. He is too busy for that, and it is not a good age for him to start a new family. I see a lot of men doing that, taking second wives who are so much younger, who want babies. It's madness!"

I smile, not knowing how else to respond. I made a tentative peace with not having children a long time ago.

"I'm glad Neill has chosen a mature woman as a companion. That is what he needs now: stability, security. And not only the things that money can buy. Someone to care for him, emotionally, spiritually. His work is extremely demanding. He needs that softness that only a good woman can provide for a man."

I nod. And what about me? I wonder silently. What about the needs of a woman in the life of a man like Neill? My cheeks start to hurt from holding the smile on my face.

Not that Aunty Sophie notices. She carries on: "That is what my son needs. A helpmeet. Someone who will stand behind him, care for him. Someone who will make a home for him. The way he lives is not living. He needs the love of a good woman, soft, but strong. I see that in you. I saw it the minute you walked through my door. I hope you can be the one who provides that for him. It would comfort this mother's heart to see him settled. More tea?"

I thank her for thinking so highly of me and say nothing more. Her words unsettle me – Neill is hardly a child who needs looking after, and I most certainly am not the type of woman who will coddle a man in the way Aunty Sophie thinks her son deserves. I don't want to complete the task of raising a man-child. It is as if she wants to hand over the baton of caretaking, to find her son another mother. Neill is fifty-five and has made the type of life for himself that he desires. I am sure he could have been married and happily settled by now, had he wanted that. A man like him gets what he wants.

I allow her to pour me another cup of tea, take a deep breath, and reply. "Neill and I have not known each other very long. But from what I have learned of him so far, you have raised a wonderful son. He is a good man. And he cares for himself very well. His life is evidence of that."

"You are very gracious, my child. But a mother knows. He needs a woman by his side, not one who will forsake him like Nicole did. Think about it. I have a good instinct about people. You'd make a good wife for Neill."

"Time will tell," is all I say in reply.

We turn to other topics. She shows me her garden, lovingly tended over years. When Neill arrives, he finds us poring over photo albums of grandchildren.

As we depart her house, she stands at the gate, waving. I unclench my jaw; at last I can relax. The day stretches out before us, a luxurious promise. I am happy to be beside Neill again and recount the conversation with his mother.

He grimaces. "I don't know what it is, this pressure to settle down. I am sorry that she laid such heavy stuff on you – I thought she'd wait a bit to get to know you better before diving into that kind of talk with you."

"It's alright. I understand it, in a way. As I told you last night, I get the same from my mother. I suppose the maternal urge to see your child happy in one of the only ways that makes sense to you is quite strong."

He disagrees: "But it's not as if she had this blissful experience of married life. My father deserted her when we were all very young. Life was brutal. We often went to bed hungry in those early days after he left. I got a little job at the corner shop to help out. My mother had to become a domestic worker – the lowest of the low. I suppose security to her can be measured in a strong partnership between a man and a woman."

His musings hang in silence in the car, as I take in the endless sky, dotted with clouds that skim the rust-coloured koppies. Neill, too, is lost in his thoughts for a few minutes, then quietly declares, more to himself than me: "Perhaps she's right."

Over late-afternoon coffee at a farmstall, Neill reminisces about his childhood. How they lost their modest home after their father left them, and were forced to live in a shack, mother and four children, the youngest merely four months old. How he became the man of the house, such as it was, at ten – the title filled with the weight of responsibility he feels to this day. Aunty Sophie would tie the baby, Christine, to her back while working, cleaning different madams' houses – a different boss every day of the week, with different predilections, eccentricities and rules. How the task of starting supper would fall to him after coming home from school, while also tending to his two younger sisters, who were too old to accompany their mother to work. No electricity, no running water, just a communal tap in the backyard in which they lived; an open fire on which to cook, paraffin lamps and candles by which to do homework and read.

As they grew older, his second-eldest sister became the surrogate mother to the other two, freeing him up to work harder at school. He was the clever one, something drummed into him every day by his teachers, his mother, the extended family. He could become something – if he wanted. This is what he strove for, what kept him going through the icy winters without any shoes, with hardly anything to line his stomach. And thank goodness for libraries. The library became his second home, a place where he could complete his homework uninterrupted by the chores of a home life characterised by unease, lack and want. After finishing his homework, he would go on to devour almost all the books in the modest municipal library, and was bereft when he realised there was nothing more to read, no more worlds to escape into.

Not that this kind of escapism was the norm in the 1970s for a coloured boy in South Africa. When he entered high school, the struggle beckoned. Fuelled by the lack and indignity that was the substance of his daily life, Neill was a willing recruit into the struggle – led by that outlawed nascent movement, its parameters, membership, and structures by necessity ill-defined. But he grew into it, grew up in it. He had been part of this movement since the age of fourteen, and as much as he made that movement by being one of its soldiers, it made him. He had risen through its ranks as a student activist, and by the time he was in matric, he was a regional leader, often on the run, hiding at safe houses around Bloemfontein, or in Natal province, so as to stay one jump ahead of the security police and their sinister detentions.

Despite this turbulence, he excelled in matric, winning a bursary that took him to Cape Town, to the only university providing unfettered access to our kind. He studied law, did his articles for a firm in Cape Town, and returned to Bloemfontein to work at a law firm where his mother had cleaned windows a few years earlier. Later he started his own firm. It was the right time – there was a new democracy, a new regime that had just introduced the policy of Black Economic Empowerment; being fully BEE compliant, Neill's firm soon raked in contracts from both the private and public sectors.

His telling of his story gives me the opening to ask the question that's been on my mind since I met him. Why did he become a politician, especially when he was already established in a successful career?

"I've worked so hard for everything I have, and the odds stacked against me were monumental. But it was really my mother who provided the bedrock for all I've been able to achieve. And it is really because of my mother – women like her – that I got into politics. After a certain stage in my career as a lawyer, there was nothing more to achieve."

He pauses: "Yes, it's good to have money. I love my house and it's wonderful to live in, especially coming where I come from. But it was for women like my mother that I decided to change my career and enter formal politics. I could have made a lot more money through my law firm than what I could earn as a politician. But to have the opportunity to make change at the policy and legislative level – that's been a new challenge for me."

His eyes come alive as he speaks. "I know how degrading poverty is, how it feels when other people look down at you as if you're nothing – because you have nothing. I know what it did to my mother. To me, being in the legislature is a way to make a change that's about dignity. Pride. Helping people to restore the dignity that apartheid and poverty took away from them."

He leans across the table: "I know politicians have terrible reputations. But if enough people like me entered the right power structures, people who are there for the correct reasons, I truly believe things can change. We've got the tools for it: our brilliant Constitution, the legal framework, the Chapter Nine Institutions. We have the right infrastructure, we just need ethical people to make it succeed. And who was I to sit by the sidelines and criticise, if I wasn't prepared to do the work myself?"

I have never before experienced such intensity from him – it's as if a private bubble separates us from the other people in the coffee shop.

"Spoken like a true politician!" My trite joke breaks the spell.

"I know you're a sceptic. I don't blame you, and I suppose it's pointless to try to persuade someone into believing one has integrity. But you'll get to know me, you'll get to see it in my actions, in my life."

Something in the way he says this, as a simple statement of fact, moves me. His words hang between us; nothing in the tone of his voice makes me feel like he is trying to convince me. He is utterly without defensiveness, with nothing to prove – *this is who I am, take it or leave it.*

It's already dark when we arrive at his home, after the long drive that followed our coffee break. We both retreat into our bedrooms. I run a bath and sink into the comforting warmth of the water, replaying the day in my head. A day of discovery, of getting to know him and his mother, and what makes them both tick. It has been revealing, in a good way, of the kind of man Neill is, and how he might fit into my life.

I take in my body stretched out and fully relaxed in the warm water, detached, as if looking from the ceiling above. I run my hands around my navel, allowing them to travel up to cup my breasts. I think about Neill's hands exploring my naked body in this way, close my eyes, and imagine the weight of his body pressing down onto mine.

After my bath, I get into bed with a book. From across the hallway, I hear the faint sound of the TV in Neill's bedroom. I wonder if he's still awake, but try to take my thoughts off him by dipping into the thriller I picked up from the airport bookstore. Relationship guru Thandiswa's voice spools through my head – never make the first move, not to ask for his number, not to touch, not to initiate sex – at least not in the beginning. Men are hunters. They love the chase, want to pursue. Don't make it easy for them.

Yet another thing we clash about: I am a feminist, after all, and enjoy my sexual agency. If we are to be equals in a heterosexual relationship, I counter, then each should have the freedom to initiate and do what they want. Her views are retrogressive, essentialist, sexist. Thandiswa always comes back with "Yes, feminist all you want, but I'm telling you, that's the nature of most straight men. Go against it at your own peril."

This usually launches the perennial debate about nature versus nurture, which brings Thandiswa's final riposte: "Well, South African men haven't been nurtured to see us as equals. So if you want to make a job of nurturing, training and teaching them how to be, good for you! I will stick to working with their elemental nature. I don't have time to raise grown men."

I chuckle at the thought of Thandiswa. I know what she would advise: "Stay in your bed. Let him come to you. That is the problem with you – you've taken your feminism too far. You act like a man, and are surprised when men don't like it."

I decide to ignore my inner Thandiswa, slide out of bed, do a quick ruffle of my hair in the mirror, and slick on some nude lipstick. I change out of the t-shirt I normally wear to bed into a silky nightdress I brought, just in case. My neck is dotted with perfume – not too much – and my breastbone too, all the way down between my breasts.

Outside his bedroom door I knock, holding my breath. No reply. Perhaps this is a good moment to turn around, head back to the guest room and be the ordentlike meisie I was raised to be. But my body takes over, silencing the tortuous debate in my head about feminism, agency, sex rules, and women acting like men. I knock again, louder, and hear shuffling from within.

"Come in!"

I take a deep breath and enter. He is lying on the bed wearing his robe, a crumpled newspaper next to him.

"Well, hello," he says, his voice warm as red wine. "Fancy seeing you here!"

Trying to appear sultry, I stifle a giggle.

"Well, are you just gonna stand in the doorway all night? Come on in."

I walk over to the bed, my bare feet sinking into the plush carpet.

"Is there anything I can do for you?" He tries to suppress a smile.

"I was feeling a bit lonely, not to mention cold," I tease.

He shifts from the side of the bed to the middle, clearing a narrow space for me, which he pats. "Come and sit here for a while. Perhaps I can help you."

I sink down next to him as he wraps his arm around me, and bury my head in his chest. His scent is heady, that familiar combination of sandalwood and citrus.

He kisses the top of my head, then strokes my chin, tilting my face upward so our eyes meet. His kiss starts out tender, his lips parting mine gently; then becomes insistent, probing. He runs his fingers lightly across my shoulder, snagging the straps of my negligee. Hands travelling, he slips first one thin strap down, then the other, tugging the flimsy nightdress down over my chest, belly and hips. I slither out of it, a snake happy to be rid of dead skin.

He moves over me to dim the light on the nightstand, then plants his lips on my throat, mapping a trail of kisses down the front of my body. From my chest, he continues down to my stomach, grazing my skin with the lightest of kisses. I'm exultant as his tongue flits around my navel, his breath an invisible string tugging my body up towards him. My sighs bloom into soft moans. He continues to trail kisses down my lower abdomen, pausing to rub his lips against the mound of my pubic bone, each kiss sparking further delight.

"I've been waiting so patiently to devour you," he murmurs, looking up at me through hooded lids.

My response is to run my hands around the back of his neck, willing him to go deeper. He obliges, sinking his lips and tongue into me. In just a few seconds I dissolve, screaming, then float weightless on the waves of pleasure pulsing through my body. He comes up for air with a sardonic: "Are you okay?"

I moan in reply.

"Some water?" he asks, reaching for a carafe on his nightstand and pouring its contents into a crystal glass. "Here. Drink. You sound parched." Indeed, I am.

As the ripples of pleasure in my body subside, the thought starts circling in my head: he is so practised at this! I gulp down the water and chide myself for this ungenerous thought, reframe it. He is an experienced man, good at what he does, and I should be praising the patron saint of good sex and mind-blowing orgasms, whoever she may be.

He strokes my hair, planting gentle kisses once more on my forehead. He returns my empty glass to the nightstand. Then he is back on top of me, kissing my mouth with renewed vigour.

"You are so exquisitely beautiful. I can't get enough of you," he whispers.

He starts again, eating my lips, moving on to my neck while caressing my breast with his hand. This time he is slower, more deliberate, taking in the way my skin reacts to varied touches of his fingertips, lips and tongue, differing pressures. I run my hands down the length of his back, revelling in the tautness of his muscles. My hands glide down into the v-shape of his waist, where his back narrows and flares back out again into muscular hips.

I slip my hands under the waistband of his shorts and tug them down before wrapping my legs around his back, pulling him into me. He sighs as he enters me, burying his head in my neck as he thrusts – each stroke summoning greater peaks of pleasure. My body transmutes into pulsing light. We breathe each other in as tongues and lips intermingle, gasping, each greedy for the other. He makes sure that I climax again before he does, then collapses next to me. Our breathing evens and he kisses my forehead. I open my eyes and look into his, become aware of his hand possessively resting in the wetness between my legs.

"How are you feeling?" he asks.

And that's when I break the cardinal rule. "Like I love you."

The words slip out before I'm aware that they were forming on my tongue. They startle me. He, on the other hand, looks unsurprised. Just smiles tenderly while planting a kiss on my nose, before murmuring, "I know."

Chapter Three

His mother bids me goodbye with a long hug and a kiss on each cheek.

"Travel safely, my child. Thank you for coming all this way to meet an old lady. Look after my son back in Cape Town."

I thank her for making me feel so welcome.

Neill drops me at the airport just before noon, and is also full of thanks for my visit. He'll remain in Bloemfontein for a few more days and will see me back in Cape Town soon. He doesn't know the exact day he'll be back. I've become used to the unpredictability of his schedule in the weeks we've been seeing each other, but this goodbye feels different.

I've met his family, by all indications a measure of the seriousness of the relationship to both of us. And then – our lovemaking the night before. With the relationship consummated, I feel a new possessiveness creeping over me. He feels like territory I've staked a claim on, and I want to guard this new possession – want to know that he'll come back to me, and when.

Thandiswa's voice pops into my head again. "Well, the female orgasm will do that to you. Flood your body with oxytocin. It's the same hormone a mother releases when she's just given birth to a child. It makes the milk come in. When you've had a great, delicious orgasm – same chemical. No wonder men begin to behave like children once they've made the conquest."

Hormonal, emotional, psychological – who knows? All I know

is that this attachment is real. Whereas before I have skirted around the edges of my feelings, detached, watching from afar as I made a game of moving close and then away again – after this weekend, a boundary has collapsed. I may have said it too soon, and (woe is me) first, but the truth is that I'm in love with Neill. And although he hasn't reciprocated in words, there must be something serious there. Why else bring me to meet his mother and his sisters? Why take such care showing me around his home town? He wants me to know him, know his life. I know that this has not been done lightly.

We kiss passionately at the drop-and-go zone.

"Don't miss me too much," he calls as I jump out of the car.

I turn around before I enter the sliding doors and take a last look at him in the car, watching me depart. He blows me a kiss, and I smile.

Once I touch down in Cape Town, I text to let him know I've arrived safely. No reply. Probably working. I head home, where the Sunday blues descend on me with a vengeance as I prepare for the week ahead. I spend two hours evaluating capstone assignments, then call my mother to let her know how the weekend went. She dispenses with any pleasantries and cannot wait to shame me as soon as it's her turn to talk.

"I hope he still respects you after you went all that way, running after him. I hope you slept in separate rooms."

"Of course we did, Mum."

"And I hope you *stayed* in your own separate rooms, both nights."

"Of course we did, Mum."

"Good, I didn't raise you to go and jump into beds of men who aren't willing to put a ring on your finger."

"No, you certainly didn't, Mum."

The conversation makes me want to scream. This has been her refrain since I started puberty. Take care of yourself. Don't be the sort of girl that opens your legs for any man. Save yourself for marriage. Even if you are engaged, don't give it up, give your virginity away for nothing. Make sure you have that coveted wedding ring on your finger first. Because once it's gone, you're damaged goods. Her own story, projected onto me.

What is implied, but never spoken is: how she gave it to her first love, resulting in the pregnancy that birthed me. My father deserted her right after learning she was pregnant, leaving her, at nineteen, to struggle on her own. Her parents put her out onto the streets. She worked in a shop in Athlone all her life, and also took on domestic work in her free time. Despite working almost constantly, she could only afford that little room in the backyard of an uncle's friend. Her family never looked at her again; it was only when I was in high school that they thawed towards us, and I met them. I have never met my father, nor do I know his name. I asked once, and after the smack in my face that knocked me across the room, I never dared ask again.

It has always just been the two of us, Mum and me. And I've worked damn hard not to be the woman she became: studied hard at school, got a bursary that allowed me to enter university, kept my legs closed until I married Keith, whom I met during my final year at university. I had been the good girl who reached the goal of marriage without an out-of-wedlock pregnancy, who earned a degree in sociology from one of the top institutions in the country instead. I know how proud that made my mother: how my success in landing a solid, middle-class guy, a beautiful home in Rondebosch East, a job doing HR for one of the top four banks, vindicated her. All her sacrifice, the rejection, people whispering behind their hands when she passed them in the street, had been worth it for this crowning achievement – a successful daughter who had it all in life, at the age of only twenty-four.

Except I didn't have it all. Life didn't work like that, did it? My fairytale lasted exactly one year into marriage, at which point I went off the pill and waited. The much-hoped-for baby didn't arrive. Not that year, nor the next, nor the next.

"God is punishing you for something," my mother offered, helpfully. "Cleanse your heart, pray, fast. Get your life right with God."

But wasn't I doing all of that already? Going to church faithfully every Sunday? Honouring my mother? Obeying my husband? I did everything right: was the perfect daughter, the perfect wife; and still, no baby.

My mother and I both fell into depression. When I cried and argued with her that I had done everything, there was nothing to set right between my Creator and me, she started blaming herself. This must be God's way of continuing to punish her for her looseness, for me being born. The sins of the father, and all that ... I refused to accept this outlook; decided that a God who could be so cruel was a God I wanted no business with, and, in the words of my mother, I abandoned the faith.

As the childless months snaked on and the love in Keith's eyes turned to pity, then waned altogether, I went back to university to do a postgraduate degree – a blessed relief that helped me structure my days and long nights. My professors urged me to enroll for an Master's degree, and I veered off-path to Gender Studies, where I found a kind of home. Theories of race, gender, class, intersectionality: these gave me a language with which to describe and analyse what I was living, and to see the trap into which my mother, and her mother, and her mother before her, had fallen. The trap I had sleepwalked into, practically shackling it to myself – the sexism and racism internalised from one generation to the next. Women like my mother created our cages; men no longer even needed to do that. And once I saw it, I couldn't unsee it. Academia, feminism, the thirst for knowledge, for ways to use these newly acquired skills to break out of the cages in which I and others found myself: these became my new religion.

Keith's leaving devastated me. But reading, research, progressing with my writing a few hundred words at a time: these anchored me to myself, prevented the despair from destroying me. Little by little, one sentence, one paragraph at a time, I built something new for myself, a world of knowledge; and so, I also rebuilt the me I might have been with the husband, children and happy family I imagined would be my fate. I found strength, went on to do a PhD in Sociology, and got a job almost immediately at the same university in Cape Town at which I'd done my undergraduate degree. The effortlessness that I had been denied in my quest to become a mother seemed to overflow in my career.

Yet, I harboured a secret no one knew: not my mother, not Claire, not even Thandiswa. It was difficult to admit to even myself. I still loved Keith, still pined for him more than a decade later. When he left, we had severed all contact. Claire tried to soothe me by pointing out that we were lucky in a way that nothing bound us together – there would be no custody battles, no co-parenting disputes, no ongoing wars about parenting rules and ideologies. I bitterly pointed out that my so-called luck was what had led to the dissolution of the marriage in the first place, leading to her offering a grovelling apology for her insensitivity. It was unlike her to say something without meticulous consideration.

Keith married Marguerite just over a year after our divorce became final. She was beautiful, accomplished, younger than me – and fertile. I shamefully tracked the progression of their relationship through Facebook, watching as she posted every relationship milestone with glee. The engagement ring, more expensive than mine; the wedding, a tasteful affair in the winelands, where guests lodged overnight, turning the ceremony into a weekend-long celebration. The pregnancy announcement six months later; the pictures of her first sonogram, showing a healthy baby; the gender reveal, which I silently condemned as retrogressive and over-the-top even as I trawled through her account in the early hours of the morning. I hated her, then wept from jealousy and guilt for despising another woman. For what? Being chosen by the man I loved with all my heart.

Their firstborn was perfect too, naturally, and was followed almost exactly a year later by the birth of a little girl. The perfect pair. The perfect life, which Marguerite loved to show off on Facebook and Instagram, her perfect wardrobe with her perfect skin and hair. I blocked and unblocked them in cycles, determined to move on with my life, but maudlinly curious about how they were doing. I checked in periodically for news of a crash, or at least cracks in the glossy façade of their perfect lives. But none came.

And I knew Keith. He was loyal, committed. Had I been able to give him the children he wanted, it would have been me in the yearly professional photoshoots with the whole family dressed in jeans and matching tops. I would have been the one glowing with maternal wholesomeness, barefoot and smiling. Gorgeous enough to be an influencer, Marguerite shilled beauty products by filming elaborate tutorials, most of which featured her in various states of undress, with nary a stretchmark in sight. I made a point of boycotting everything she endorsed.

After almost a decade, I started dating again, but my heart was never in it. Even on the first date, there would be comparisons to Keith. After I turned forty, with a string of short-lived affairs behind me, I took the advice of the coven and signed up for a serious dating site, not the kind you go to for hook-ups, but the kind of app where one paid a hefty fee to meet men of a certain calibre. Professionals, accomplished in life, with high net worths. Seeking similar. No gold-diggers allowed; they vetted for that – you had to state your annual income in the questionnaire. This selling point rankled so much, I almost didn't join.

"Get off your high horse, or you'll never find a man!" Thandiswa scolded.

Annoying, but she had a point. And as half-hearted as I was about men, I didn't want to spend the rest of my life alone. If I could turn this corner, leave Keith in the past where he belonged, and meet someone who wasn't interested in having children, perhaps I would have a chance at finding a happy partnership.

I cycled through men, virtually at first, then, if mutual interests dictated, in person. At first, I dreaded the modern mating game, but soon it became a part of my life I could focus on or put on the backburner as needed. When busy with work, with friends, with life, I didn't bother to meet many men. But when I was at a loose end, the app became my go-to – a quick fix for loneliness and the thrill of chasing or being chased.

The men were mostly pleasant enough, searching for varying levels of engagement: some only sex; others, a companion – emotionally and physically. Then there were the ones who made me feel like I was auditioning for the role of wife. These dates were the worst. Usually there would be an enquiry about my cooking skills, which evoked a bristling response, spoiling the date.

There were times when I quit it all and deleted the app. But that was usually when the lectures from Thandiswa and Claire would start again: the "How-will-you-ever-find-someone-if-you-don't-try; surely-you-don't-want-to-be-alone-for-the-rest-of-your-life?" monologues. They induced enough guilt to convince me that I should at least be trying.

Trying what? To find the elusive "one" who would complete my life? But my life already felt complete. I loved my work, had good relationships with friends, worlds that I moved in and out of at my own pace and volition. The cycle of meeting and dating men became one of those worlds, but nothing or no one I met ever stuck. Until Neill.

And here I am, for the first time since Keith, in love. Genuinely, head-over-heels in love. As I lie in bed, waiting for sleep to claim me, I turn the weekend over in my mind. I can't put my finger on the moment my heart capitulated. But I find myself missing him, with this quiet knowing, a bruising tenderness blossoming in my chest. I don't know how, or why; I just know that I love him.

I wake before my alarm goes off at six on Monday morning, and immediately grab my phone from the nightstand. There are no missed calls, no replies to the two texts I sent after I landed, not the usual goodnight kiss emoji sent promptly at ten every evening since our first meeting. I check his "last seen" time stamp – 8.30pm the night before. This silence is unusual. An unsettling feeling creeps into my chest. I hope nothing has happened to him. Then, as I stare at the unanswered blue-ticked messages, he comes online. Relief washes over me.

"Hi!" I type, watching this one word balloon out in a green bubble across my screen. But before the two ticks can turn blue, he is offline again. Last seen: 6.03am.

I am even more uneasy now. Why is he not answering me? I give myself a short lecture about staying cool, then dial his number anyway. My call remains unanswered. I think about our last few hours together as I ready myself for work. No argument, nothing off; we had been warm, affectionate with each other.

Over breakfast, Neill had been the perfect post-coital companion, lavishing attention on me – his eyes never straying from me, his mouth confirming that I was beautiful, wanted, adored. And now the spotlight of his attention has inexplicably gone away, and I am puzzled, lost. What have I done wrong?

I am about to walk into an 11am seminar when my phone grudgingly burps out a curt "Hi."

"Hello Neill," I type in reply as I sit down in front of the class. "Everything okay?"

"Fine, yes."

"I was worried about you when you didn't return my texts or calls."

The words "typing... typing..." flash across my screen. I cannot let my students, who are shifting impatiently, wait a minute longer, and switch off the phone to start my class.

Two hours later, I switch it back on.

"Told you I'd be busy with constituency work. Fell asleep early."

None of the usual terms of endearment.

In my head, the faint voice of my mother, which has been on loop all morning, breaks into a roar: *See? This is what happens when you give it to men. They lose interest. Done with you once they've got what they've wanted. If you are stupid enough to just give it away.*

I place a call, which is declined with a curt "In a meeting" text.

I can't help but feel hurt.

"Okay, call me when you have a moment," I text back.

We eventually speak around seven that night.

"Hi stranger, what happened to you?" I try to keep my tone light, the anxiety out of my voice.

"I told you I was busy. And fell asleep early." His voice is flat, brittle.

"Okay, I hope I didn't tire you out too much."

My attempt at a joke is met with silence. I try a different route back to the Neill I know. "Are you well? How did work go after I left?"

"Fine."

An uneasy silence stretches between us. I had expected one of our delicious long conversations, reliving the visit, discussing how it had gone with his family, him reporting back on whether they liked me, asking what I thought of his home town. Perhaps that was the problem? His mother and sisters didn't like me? But my time with the most important woman in his life had been warm, after the initial formality had worn off. Our parting had been especially sweet.

"Well, my day was fine too," I say, breaking the silence, as if he had asked about my day. "I was just worried about you – it's been the longest we've gone without talking."

"I told you I was busy! What else do you need to know?" he snaps.

"I know, I know. I'm sorry. It's just been weird."

"Don't tell me you're going to be like that now! One of those women who needs constant updates. I'm telling you now, I'm not clocking in with anybody. I told you I'd be busy. Let it go. I'm really not in the mood to answer the same question over and over again."

I am shocked by this abrupt shift in tone. This is a side of him I've not yet encountered; his voice, usually dripping with honey, is now ice-cold.

I try to counter. "I am sorry, but you didn't actually tell me you were going to be so busy. And I haven't been asking the same question. I'm expressing myself – clumsily perhaps – to try and start a conversation," I stutter. "I've just really missed you."

"Christ, this is tedious! I don't have time for this."

And just like that, the call is over.

Who is this man? Not my warm, kind, considerate lover of the past two months.

Something's up. I know I should let it go, but can't. Did his family not like me? Did I commit some faux pas I'm not even aware of? Was it my saying "I love you" in the heat of passion? Have I scared him off?

This is ridiculous, I tell myself. We are adults, not teenagers. I have expressed my feelings to a man I love, or think I love, at least; expressed concern when our regular pattern of communication dried up without warning. Why do I feel like I'm being punished?

I know I shouldn't text, but I do.

"Seriously?"

No reply, except for two blue ticks.

I scroll through our WhatsApp messages of the past few days, as if reading them again will reveal some new, hidden meaning, something I've missed in our communication. But all I can conjure is our wonderful weekend together, our leisurely but deep conversations, his body against mine, the warmth of his eyes.

Perhaps he needed space after the intensity of our time together. If that was the case, surely he could have just asked. He is intelligent, connected to his emotions, articulate about them in all other spheres.

I sigh and pull out yet another pile of essays to mark. Working till late at night, I keep checking my phone for the usual cheerful, "Hello my precious". Nothing. Not the regular good night, no interesting snippet of news he occasionally sends with a "thought of you". Just a heavy silence.

I lose track of time and crawl into bed at 2am, having just entered all my students' marks on a grade sheet. The essays have all melded into one giant, poorly written script, swimming in my head as I lay it down on the pillow to fall into uneasy sleep. Maybe my mother is right. It's just that I have not before cared how or when men contact me after we've had sex for the first time. Some of them I did not particularly wish to hear from again. But with Neill, I do care – deeply.

His silence stretches into the next day, and the next. By Wednesday evening, I have convened an emergency meeting of the coven to discuss this latest development.

Thandiswa, as usual, is ready to take it all apart and stitch it back together again. "Not unusual behaviour at all," she declares. "Neill may be one of those men who gets off on the chase, the thrill of not knowing whether he can get a woman. The challenge of hooking her. And then, when he has her, the excitement is gone. Could very well be!"

Claire nods sagely.

"I mean," continues Thandiswa, "he must have lots of women throwing themselves at him all the time. A man like him: rich, good-looking, well-spoken, powerful. Hell, I wouldn't mind throwing myself at him, given half a chance!"

Claire laughs, but I fail to see the joke. "You two are not making me feel any better. You're supposed to reassure me!"

"Sorry, love. Is he very religious?" asks Thandiswa. "It's just that the religious types will have a fine time with you in bed, but then write you off as having no virtue, as if they didn't enthusiastically partake. Your sin, in that case, is being a woman who enjoys sex. The Madonna-Whore complex!"

"Sis man, surely that complex has a more politically correct name by now? And no, Neill is not particularly religious," I bristle.

Thandiswa replies: "But even the non-religious types have been steeped in these prehistoric ideas about women's sexuality and morality. They will say it doesn't matter, but still think less of you if you give it up too quickly."

"Oh my God, you sound like my mother!"

Thandiswa cackles. "Some men think their penis is so special that putting it inside a woman changes her for good. Damaged goods, et cetera, et cetera!"

She swishes her drink above her head with an extravagant wave to punctuate each et cetera.

"How utterly depressing. God, I can't believe we are still in the 1950s."

"You can argue as much as you like, dear Anita, about the politics of it all. That won't take away the realities of how most men in this country see us. You don't come through fifty years of apartheid and Calvinism unscathed, as much as you might profess to be liberal. They're liberal until they've chised you into bed. And then all that nonsense comes out. Remember, not everybody has two years of postgraduate gender theory under their belt."

There it is again, that dig about my education. Thandiswa and I have fought good-naturedly in the past about how I think my degrees are better than her training in traditional medicine, and her studies to become a sangoma.

"You need to decolonise your mind, sister," she teases, not altogether joking. Normally I let such ribbing about me being an educated snob slide, but coupled with my unhappiness about Neill's silence, tonight's dig stings more than usual.

Claire catches the look on my face. She chides Thandiswa: "Come on now, Thandiswa. You can see that our friend is upset. Go easy."

I feel my face sagging. I don't need this, not Thandiswa projecting her insecurities about her unfinished degree all over me, nor Claire's condescension.

I drain the last drops of wine from my glass and rise from the table. "See you next time, sisters," I announce and leave.

By Thursday I have given up on Neill. After taking me home to meet his family, a beautiful weekend, and then not hearing from him, save for that one detached and sullen call, it is clear that our budding relationship is over. It puzzles me: to be ghosted, as my students would call it, like this after ushering me into his most intimate spaces. Initiated by him, not me. But before allowing myself to wallow in self-pity, I remind myself that I've been seeing him for less than three months; this is not the end of the world. But after years of not letting anyone in, not finding someone even remotely interesting enough to consider for the long haul, Neill felt like that person – and his abandonment hurts.

I spend Thursday night dusting off my Billie Holiday playlist, her mournful voice striking just the right chord over my glass of whisky.

I go into the office for a few hours on Friday morning, attend to some admin, and gather books I need from the library so I can spend the weekend reading. I don't make any plans – I prefer to be alone to process this non-breakup, this most undignified ending of the first relationship in years I've allowed myself to believe in.

I am deep in the *Journal of Southern African Studies* that afternoon at home, when the doorbell rings. Outside my front door I find Neill, wearing the look of a boy who has been chided by his mother, a huge bouquet of red roses in his hand. I stare at him in disbelief.

"Well, aren't you going to invite me in?" he says, throwing in a wink.

"I'm really surprised to see you."

"Well, come on now, don't be rude, Anita. Don't keep me waiting on your doorstep looking like a fool with a bunch of flowers."

I gesture for him to come through the door. In the living room, he makes an ostentatious gesture of presenting me with the flowers. "For you, my precious!"

I take the roses into the kitchen and drop them in the sink. "Thank you. And what the hell just happened?"

"What do you mean?" He is all innocence, as if he hasn't just blanked me for five days.

"What I mean is, what happened between us? You take me home to meet your mother, lavish attention on me, have sex with me, and then: not a word from you! Besides telling me not to bother you? What the hell is up with that?"

"My God, you're really angry." His voice is soft, the look on his face perplexed.

"Yes, Neill, I'm angry. Angry and confused. Nearly three months of constant contact, calls, good mornings, goodnights, and then you take me home – and then: nothing."

"Wow, Anita, I told you I'd be busy."

"Too busy for even a quick hello once a day?"

"What can I say? That's the nature of my work, my dear."

"Well, you've had the same job the whole time we've been together. What changed in the past week?"

I am desperate for a fight to get rid of all the pent-up anger of the week, but he's not biting.

He sits on the couch, pulls me down next to him, gives me an avuncular pat on the shoulder. It works. The touch of his hand on my skin settles me a bit. And he smells damned good, too.

"I've tried to tell you, but perhaps I haven't been clear enough, and for that I apologise. My job is more than a job. It is my life. It never ends. When I am here, there are the long hours in committee meetings, in the House itself. And reading, research. Hours and hours of reading."

He stares, unblinking, straight into my eyes: "When I am home, in my constituency, I do everything I can for others. There is visiting and listening to them, and trying to find solutions. Connecting them to the people who can help when I can't. The poor single mother who comes to me and cries because she cannot pay her brilliant son's school fees, and fears for his future. A future we should all care about. The mother whose electricity has been cut and whose water is about to shut off. The parents with four kids living in a backyard shack, who have been on a housing wait-list for years."

His gaze is still direct, his fingertips now caressing my bare arm. "This is why a relationship never sticks. I want one, and not just with anyone – I want this with you. It's just that work can be so all-consuming. And sometimes it's not fair on a partner."

He looks away, and stares into the distance. "This is why my marriage failed. Why I hardly see my children. I regret that. If I could take back the way I treated my ex-wife, my God, I would. The neglect. But this is the life I have chosen. I can try to be better. Want to be better for you."

He leans back towards me to deliver the clincher. "I am sorry that the way I've been has made you feel neglected, and uncared for. Please, please stay on this journey with me. I will try – no, not try, I *will* do better."

The arm around me rests firmly on my shoulder; his other hand grips my hand as it rests on my lap.

"Please give me the chance to learn how to do this with you.

There is no one else I want to do this with, this relationship thing."

I look into his dark brown eyes, earnest and bright. My thaw quickens to a full-on melt. I kiss his cheek. I feel his body relax into relief. He cups my face between two warm hands, planting a tender kiss on my lips. I rest my cheek against his, the stubble on his chin against my neck sending a current through my body.

"Come now, my precious. Forgive me. I'll make it up to you."

It doesn't take much for him to reel me back in. I release the last bit of resentment and sink into his arms, and he is ready to take full advantage of my capitulation. He kisses me passionately, and I am swept right back into his slipstream. He lifts me from the couch as he straightens up, embraces me from behind, dotting the lightest of kisses around my neck as he walks me into the bedroom.

"Let me show you how much I've missed you."

Sweet words seal his capture. I am hungry now for him, tugging his blue tie, close to ripping the buttons off his shirt as he covers my neck and shoulders with kisses.

Our bedroom reunion is joyful, spirited. Neill is energetic, inexhaustible. There is a new, different energy about him as he teases my body into sexual submission, until I am almost begging him to enter me. He does so with a surprising gentleness, a restraint that makes it clear my pleasure is the aim. He drives himself deep into me and just as I feel that familiar wave of pleasure about to wash over me, he stares straight into my eyes, and murmurs: "And yes, I love you too."

I move completely back into the palm of his hand, back into the fold of Neill.

We make love for hours, pausing only to fuel up on what meagre scraps of food remain fresh in my fridge. We doze, wake up, and do it some more. We leave once to get mutton salomies at Golden Plate, in my home suburb, Athlone, then race back to bed.

He stays with me until Sunday, and we talk, setting down ground rules for what to do when he gets too busy. I am busy too, but this is never discussed. His work is important, having a wider-ranging impact on a lot more lives. My essay marking and classroom preparation are not quite in the same category. When he leaves just before midday on Sunday, our relationship is back on track. He will try to communicate more when things are pressured; I will try to understand when his absences grow too long. We seal it with a kiss as he heads out my front door.

So begins a new phase of dizzying relationship heights. He is not around much during the week, but keeps faithful to his promise to stay in touch. We speak often, he pinches time off here and there during his day to come and swoop me away to the most expensive restaurants in the city. Weekends, when he is not in Bloemfontein, are a feast! I am wined, dined and sexed in the most exclusive five-star hotels across the country – on the Wild Coast, the Whale Coast, the Garden Route, the Dolphin Coast, the Berg. Game farms, where all the drives and other amenities are wasted on account of us frolicking in bed for hours; exclusive country retreats tucked away in the winelands a few hours out of the city. We spend another weekend in Bloemfontein – this time, I spend almost the entire time with his mother. He rents me a sporty BMW and the two of us drive around together: she shows me the places where he grew up, went to school, played soccer, the safe houses where he hid when the police came looking for him; spaces she calls "formative" in making Neill the man he would become. His time in hiding almost broke her, and when he came back home to live with her after his excruciating absence, there was a secrecy about him she hated. He had learned, on the run, to operate on a "need to know" basis – a habit she knows her son still struggles with. He had nightmares about police coming for him for years afterwards. Yes, the struggle shaped him and his sense of justice, but it also warped him. There were little things about him that were lost forever, could never be retrieved. The woman who partners with Neill would have to understand this background, be patient with him.

Her stories make me fall even more deeply in love with him. That might well have been the aim of appointing Aunty Sophie as my tour guide. Who better to persuade you to love a man than the mother who loves him more than her own life? Not that I needed persuading. I am gone, finished for him!

My mother and the coven complain that they hardly see me. I bring him to meet my mother. I have avoided introducing them, knowing her disapproval of the first man I've loved since Keith would crush me. Like me, she has never quite gotten over my first husband. She didn't know what he saw in a girl like me, and felt no qualms about sharing her bemusement at his choice to be with me. When our marriage fell apart, it came almost as a relief to her, since she couldn't see me holding on to a man of Keith's calibre. In her mind, it was a fluke that I got him in the first place; she believed that once he realised his mistake, he'd be compelled to leave.

I should not have worried about my mother and Neill. He dialled the charm up to megawatt levels, and by the end of their first meeting, he held her in his palm. A bit more lightly than me, but it is safe to say that my jaded, long-suffering mother adores him. She, too, is whisked away on a five-star weekend with us, sealing yet another deal for Neill. She will adore him with obeisance, taking his side against me in any future disagreements.

Things are solidified. I am his girlfriend – I train him to call me his partner when introduced. I blossom under the gaze of the sun that is Neill, as his warmth, wealth and power help me to unfurl from the grey, nondescript woman I was before he entered my life. Now I am a beauty, glowing with contentment. It is his love, yes; but also his money. A few thousand rands here and there to get my hair done, the gift of an exquisite dress or pair of shoes at the mere hint of my admiring them, the weekly massages and beauty treatments. I have fortnightly hair appointments now in the City bowl to maintain my caramel highlights.

The coven crows about my refined new look.

"Love looks good on you," toasts Thandiswa.

Yes, I am in love and glowing, but what they don't know is that my new gloss is as much down to microneedling at the most exclusive spa at the Waterfront as the hormones coursing through my body at the thought of my beloved. I don't want to shatter the myth that a well-loved woman can be identified by the glow of her skin, the way she carries herself.

I am loved. Finally loved. Well-loved, at that. And I love him back. I'm softer, smile more, am happier at work. My research quietly takes a back seat; why would I spend weekends and long nights slogging away at it when a mini-holiday beckons almost every second weekend? And besides, spending time in my lover's bed is far more pleasurable than burning the midnight oil over the latest, indecipherable, poorly written rubbish that passes for research in the churning-out factory. We're in the honeymoon phase of our love story. This will settle down, I tell myself, and I will get back to work soon. For now, I want to enjoy this magnificent man and all he offers.

And then it stops. Again. Without warning, without reason. My beautiful man turns cold and taciturn, leaving me with no clue as to why.

He goes home to Bloemfontein. Disappears. No phone calls, messages, no replies to my attempts to communicate. I call his mother to find out if he's okay. She says she hasn't really seen much of him since his arrival, and I regret worrying her. This prompts a terse, two-minute phone call from Neill – I am busy; leave my mother out of our relationship! I try to protest, but am cut off before I can finish my sentence. I text a long apology and realise, to my horror, that I am blocked. I start shaking in disbelief. I try calling on and off over the next few days, but am sent straight to voicemail. I avoid my mother and the coven, fearful that they will know just by looking at me that something is terribly wrong. I don't want to share this with them, partly because they will think less of him, and by association, me; and partly because speaking this out loud to others will cement it in truth.

There is no excuse for this kind of treatment, I know. If one of my students came to me and confided that she was being treated like this, I would warn her about the dangers of such inconsistent behaviour from an intimate partner, tell her that something is seriously amiss if a man blows this hot and cold.

I wait, puzzling over this situation not only in terms of what I might have done to cause it, but also turning inward. Is this what I want? Neill being gone like this feels like a hole in my chest. I feel his absence in a myriad ways: in the morning when we'd usually have a wake-up call; having something funny happen and wanting to share it with him; wanting to describe the latest microagression I experience at work, and having him affirm that it really did happen and was wrong; wanting to see him, touch him, kiss him.

This is not a healthy relationship. Though my experience is limited, I do have the measuring stick of life with Keith, which taught me what genuine love feels like. I read and reread bell hooks on love: the six elements that signal its authenticity and durability. Communication, respect, trust, care, knowledge, commitment, responsibility – none of these are on display right now. How can they be when my partner has simply vanished? Not a goodbye, no indication that there would be some pressing matter keeping him away. Love is not only a feeling, but a set of actions, she reminds me. As wonderful as the past few months with Neill have been, there is nothing now that enables me to hold on to any illusion that he loves me.

By the time Neill returns, nine days later, to my doorstep, it is over. I am done. He senses this as I let him in. I might be done, but I'm not so heartless as to break up with a man on the pavement of the busiest street in Woodstock. This time, there's no playful banter, no naughty, lovable rogue performance. There is not touching, no fingertips trailing my skin to soften the story he's about to spin.

"I can explain…"

I don't allow him to finish. "No need. It's over."

I hope he doesn't notice my quivering upper lip.

"Anita, please don't overreact like this."

"Overreact? You must be joking! You disappear for more than a week. Not a single word. I thought you might be ill, dead. But even in death, I would have known more about your whereabouts than I did about your life this past week."

"Look, you're angry. I understand. And you have every right to be. I'm sorry."

"No, you're not. Why do this in the first place? We spoke about your behaviour the last time you disappeared. You gave me assurances, you gave your word you would not do this again. Does that mean nothing to you? Anyway, it doesn't matter anymore, Neill. I'm done."

For a moment he looks as if he might burst into tears. Then something in his demeanour changes. The warmth takes flight from his voice. "My God woman, get a grip. If you calmed down for a moment, you would realise that these are your abandonment issues speaking. All that stuff about your father leaving your mother, leaving her on her own to raise you. And then Keith leaving you. You are dragging all of that baggage into this relationship. You won't even listen to me. Come on now, you are not a child anymore!"

I am stunned into silence. My deepest wounds, those I have shared with no other soul but Neill, are now being hauled out of an artillery chest and used against me.

I find my voice. "How dare you! How dare you use the worst moments of my life against me like this? I entrusted this information with you as my partner, my lover, my friend. And now is the time you choose to haul it out for point-scoring?"

The tears I despise roll freely from my cheeks. Neill takes a deep breath, ready to fire the next round. But then I see it on his face – the shadow of something shimmying across his features. Something pulls him back. He checks himself; stops the argument.

I start to sob like the child he's wounded with his words. He leans in, takes me in his arms. I allow him to hold me, soothe me – the child who needed this years ago, being comforted against the strong chest of a man.

I am not sure how long we stand like this. He allows me to cry and cry some more, letting out all of my pent-up pain from the past few days. He is right. This pain stretches down years of my life, way back to a time before I was even born. I was conceived in pain, bathed in my mother's pain inside her womb.

Neill strokes my hair, kisses the top of my head. When the last wracking sob has left my body, he speaks, slowly, deliberately. "My precious Anita. I am so sorry. I was wrong. I did abandon you, yes. Things were going so well. Too well. I started feeling nervous, caged-in. I panicked. I do that sometimes. I told myself I needed space."

I listen without saying anything.

"I am sorry that I disappeared without a word to you. Now you know my reason. I've been a stupid, idiotic man. Overwhelmed. And you've done nothing wrong, nothing to deserve this. I am here with a mea culpa and a plea that you forgive me. I'll work on this, work on my tendency to run away. I need to stop it."

His words soften me.

I know I need to end this. But here is this man I have grown to love with an intensity I've haven't experienced in years, articulating his wrongs, laying them at my feet, and asking me to help him do better. He is asking for help, willing to learn. And I want him – his presence, his body, the way he looks at me, the ideas he shares with me. There is nothing I would love more than to fall back into his arms and his world, because I've missed him, missed life with him. I am on dangerous ground, I know, but how can I not forgive him, my sweet Neill, and have our life return to the beautiful way it used to be? Perhaps his behaviour this past week is an aberration. And isn't this what love is? To see the other in their full nakedness – the ugly, the beautiful, the dysfunctional – and still choose them?

He kisses my cheek. "I swear to you, this will never happen again."

Another kiss follows, on my lips.

I sense his confidence growing. I have not yet spoken a word, said that I would forgive him, but he knows it already from the language my body speaks against his.

"I don't know, Neill. I am old enough to know this about me – I can't be in a relationship with a man who just disappears like this."

"Oh my God, Anita. Please forgive me. I have been insufferably stupid."

He pauses, searching my face for signs of absolution. I say nothing.

"In a way, my stupidity has been a good thing."

I draw away from him, my eyes questioning.

"I have realised just how much you mean to me. How I don't want to go another day without you. I can't imagine my life without you. I want to wake up every morning and know you'll be by my side, always."

His eyes are moist, awash with love. He fumbles inside the inner pocket of his blazer and pulls out a ring.

"Will you marry me, Anita?"

There is no question in my mind about saying yes. Fresh tears spring from a well of joy. I accept his ring, let him slide it onto my finger.

"Thank you, my wonderful woman. You've made me so happy!"

We kiss. He holds me in the tightest hug. It feels as if he will never let go.

"I promise you, I'll do my very best to make you happy, Anita. You deserve nothing but the best."

We kiss and hug some more.

"Champagne! This calls for a toast," he laughs.

Since there's none in the house, given that I don't have a champagne budget anyway, we drive to his favourite hotel at the Waterfront. I cannot believe the dazzling rock on my finger belongs to me, a symbol of our future together. Tucked in a leather booth in a tastefully muted room, we sip his favourite, Moët. He cannot keep his hands off me – and I cannot stop kissing his cheeks, his hands, his neck. Our eyes are locked, and soon our lips are too.

"Let's go back to my place before we're told to get a room," he jokes.

On the way, his calls his mother to share the news. "She said yes!" he says. "Anita. Yes, of course I mean Anita."

I look at him quizzically. Why would that even be a question for Aunty Sophie, when we spent so much time together during my last visit in Bloem? Perhaps she had sensed trouble when I called her to ask the whereabouts of her son last week. I shift the thought out of my mind, concentrate on the joy of the occasion. We go to his home and tumble into bed, drunk on love, Moët and each other.

With the decision made, Neill goes into action mode. There is no time to waste, he declares. We're not young, we know what we want, and now that we're engaged, a wedding should follow as soon as possible. He hires a wedding planner, and we set the date for a month ahead. And this is how I come to marry Neill, a mere nine months after clicking "yes" on his picture on a dating site.

Chapter Four

The wedding is a small, tasteful affair at his house on the estate in Bloemfontein. His family attends; my mom, Claire and Thandiswa are flown up and accommodated at a beautiful hotel close by. The twins, whom I meet for the first time a week before the wedding, are in attendance – well-behaved, polite and eager to please their father. My wedding dress is a simple sheath from Gavin Rajah, who is brought on board after I complain that I can't find anything suitable in the local shopping malls. Neill, as always, looks impeccable in a bespoke suit. We both brim with adoration during the simple civil ceremony, conducted by one of his friends.

A reporter from the local newspaper calls me a week before the wedding to ask if they can attend, or at least get a picture to mark the momentous occasion. Neill has long been one of the most eligible bachelors in the city, she chuckles; many hearts are about to be broken. She congratulates me for pulling off a feat many women have attempted but failed.

Neill bristles when I relay the request. "I hope you didn't give him any information. Why did you even take the call?"

"We spoke. She's a person. I wasn't going to be rude. I answered her politely."

"Well, that is something you'll have to learn not to do. Your life is about to change. You cannot speak to journalists, please. You might give away sensitive information without realising it."

"I'm hardly a fool," I say, going into defensive mode. "Of course I know not to say anything of a sensitive or confidential nature to a journalist."

His mood darkens even more. "You just don't get it, do you? I am telling you now that you will not speak to journalists again once you become my wife. This is not negotiable."

Since my interaction with journalists has been a fat zero until now, I hardly see the point of fighting a battle about this. I don't like him telling me who I may or may not speak to, but it makes some kind of sense: he has a high profile, is set to rise through the party ranks, and needs to remain discreet in his movements. I remember his mother's caution about his habit of dispensing information on a need-to-know basis. He doesn't want the media to know where he lives, where the twins go to school, or his travel schedule. And I have already breached that boundary by telling the journalist that we are to be married at his home.

I apologise and leave it at that. It isn't difficult to accept this rule – it seems reasonable. I remind myself that communication and the art of compromise are essential for a solid relationship, and promise that I will never speak to journalists about anything to do with him again. And, no, we'll not supply the media with wedding pictures, nor share any of them on social media.

Several high-ranking members of the party attend: the Secretary-General, the Premier of the province, the Deputy Chief Whip of Parliament. Then there are comrades from the next tier of government: the mayor, council members, Directors-Generals. I don't know them, but take my cue from Neill and smile quietly upon meeting them. No spouses are present. He doesn't really know their wives, Neill tells me in the days leading up to the ceremony, and it's best to keep this type of gathering small. Neill disappears with a few comrades for a while during the sunny afternoon. I find them in the study smoking Cuban cigars, and drag him back outside to mingle with our guests.

We have a lavish dinner at dusk in the garden, fairy lights draped around the garden twinkling on as the sun dips below the horizon. We dance our first dance as husband and wife on a portable dancefloor to Eta James's "At Last". I lean into him, marvelling at the perfection of the moment, how the heartache I'd endured after Keith left has been transmuted into a joy so pure it leaves me breathless, by this man I love so completely.

In my speech during the reception, I read from a poem by Elizabeth Barret Browning: "I love you not only for what you are, but for what I am when *I am with you*. I love you not only for what you have made of yourself, but for what you are making of me. I love you for the part of me that you bring out."

His love in my life has been transformative, a force that's shaken me out of a decade-long stupor, a numbness that became my state of being after Keith left. In Neill's arms, under his gaze, I come alive again – not only to him, but to myself and life itself.

We are about to leave for our honeymoon at Victoria Falls the next day when Neill breaks it to me that a crisis is brewing within local party ranks, and that he has been asked by the highest leaders of the party, the national executive, to mediate. To this call to duty, he cannot say no. He suggests that I go ahead to the game reserve on my own, with him to follow as soon as the crisis is brought under control. I baulk at the idea – who leaves for and arrives at the destination of their honeymoon alone? I cannot think of anything sadder.

Neill's annoyance flares at my dissatisfaction.

"Look, Anita, we're married now. If there's one thing you have to come to terms with, and quickly, it's my place in the party. And the party's place in our lives. The party has been and always will be my life. I make no apology for that, and I was clear about it. Now if you know me at all, you should know that I will do my very best for you. But please don't get in the way of my work. Don't make me feel like every time I have to go to work, I'm not choosing you. Please, for the love of God, don't make this a competition."

"But this is not just any old thing – it's our honeymoon! How does this set the tone for the rest of our lives together?"

He becomes more rigid: "This is who I am. This is who you married. Please don't make it harder than it needs to be."

He turns and leaves the bedroom, ending the conversation. I hear the ice clink inside his glass of Macallan – an 18-year-old, nothing less – in the living room bar, and the buzz of his always-vibrating phone.

I go on honeymoon on my own. He promises to join me when

he can. I spend my days swimming and reading by the pool, eat sumptuous gourmet dinners by myself, wearing the cocktail dresses I shopped for while imagining our evenings together, away from the pull of work and the demands of the party. At night I read novels in bed before drifting into restless sleep. I lie to Thandiswa and Claire when they text to ask how it's going, and request pics. I send selfies by the pool, Instagram-worthy snaps of my dinners and the beautiful vistas, but no photos of the honeymooners.

Neill never arrives. I get the odd text and phone call telling me how much he misses me. After four days, I cut my solo honeymoon short, and head back to Cape Town. Neill has promised to pick me up at the airport, but I am met by a driver in an anonymous black SUV, who calls me just after the plane lands to let me know where he is waiting for me. His instructions are to take me to Neill's house in Higgovale, where we have agreed to live, but none of my things are there yet, and I am tired, hurt and angry. I just want to sleep in my own bed, so I redirect him to my home in Woodstock.

Newly wed but alone, I struggle with my suitcase down the passage of my house. After a shower and tea, I head to bed. I refuse to text him. As I turn to switch the bed-lamp off, there's a knock at my front door – and once again, when I open it, I am confronted with a sheepish Neill on my doorstep. He crushes me into his embrace as soon as he enters.

"My precious! My wife!"

He covers my face with an abundance of kisses. He smells of whisky and that familiar sandalwood.

I wrestle out of his arms.

"Fuck you, Neill!"

"You're cross. Disappointed. I get it. I am so sorry I couldn't be there. It's unforgiveable, really."

The words are contrite, but his expression is playful. "But you are my wife now, you're coming to live with me. So I'm here to help you pack a few things and bring you home. Take off those pajamas and put on some clothes. And don't bother to unpack that suitcase – it's coming with us."

"Your audacity astounds me. Imagine not showing up to your own honeymoon, and expecting me to be swept off my feet and come home with you!"

"That's exactly what I've come to do. Sweep you off your feet," he laughs as he picks me up again and swings me around. "Come, come now, my precious Anita, we've wasted so much time already. Let's not waste another minute in starting our life together."

I feign anger, but am happy he is here. I don't want to make that too obvious, though.

I pack an extra suitcase. He doesn't ask how the hotel was, or what I did. It's just as well – I want my memory of the last five days to be erased, and set back to the day of our wedding. My bags are packed with a few necessities, as I will be back for the rest of my things over the next few days. We've discussed this – I will move in gradually, as there is no rush to vacate my house. I will keep it as an investment property and rent it out once I've settled fully at his place.

Neill is sitting on the bed, watching me fold and pat down clothes into a second suitcase. He looks around the room. "I think you should sell this place." His tone is light; casual.

"Really? Why?"

"Rental properties like these can become a nightmare to manage. It's not that great a space – surely this cannot be your dream house? You don't need the extra income. You've got a stable job with a good income. And you're my wife now. I'll take care of you."

I am taken aback. We might have married in haste, but Neill did not neglect to draft a prenup that clearly protects each of our assets. I glossed over it and lifted my pen to sign straight away when he presented it to me. He scolded me for being reckless, said that I should have my own lawyer look it over. I argued that I loved him, and trusted whatever arrangement he thought best. He told me that I was too trusting, that I should not let matters of the heart cloud my good judgement, especially where money was concerned; that I had a duty to look after and out for myself. I found myself thinking that I had done that all my life so far, and had managed pretty well; that I trusted myself and my sense of him.

Nevertheless, I sent the prenup to Claire. Pretty standard, she said. We were entering and would leave the marriage with the assets we brought into it, with neither having a claim to the other's existing assets. It gets tricky though, she added, when one tries to quantify types of support that are not monetary. A spouse staying home to raise kids so that the other's career might flourish, enabling a high income. Sacrifices made by one spouse so that the other can advance. She advised me to add some type of provision for spousal support in the event of the marriage ending, with amounts incremental to the number of years of marriage. This struck me as cynical, extractive. We were not having children. I earned my own income and was financially independent, and would presumably continue to be so were the marriage to end. I was moving into a house with him where I'd be relieved of any financial obligation. I'd be living very well for nothing!

"Even so, I would add a provision for spousal alimony should the marriage dissolve. It might actually deter him from straying, if he's inclined to that."

"That's ridiculous, Claire. He's not the type to cheat. He's not that type of man. Also, if having to give me a hefty payout is the only thing deterring him – well, what kind of loyalty is that?"

"Please Anita, join me in the real world. Fifty per cent of marriages end in divorce. The main causes of these divorces are money and infidelity. I'm sure Neill is a standup guy, but statistically there is a fifty per cent chance things may go wrong. You don't want to be left out in the cold when that happens. Neill seems solid. But he's a politician. And a man. They lie. I hate to sound jaded, but I see it all the time in my practice – how men hide things: money, assets, mistresses, second families. Could you readjust your rose-tinted glasses for a few minutes? You are thinking with your heart when this decision needs a clear mind."

I thanked Claire for her advice and promised to sleep on it. The next day, I handed Neill the signed prenup, unchanged. We did not speak about it again. Having separated our financial lives, I am now surprised by his unsolicited advice to sell the house.

"Neill, it means a lot to me that you want to take care of me. But I have been taking care of myself for a long time now. Surely you know I am not the type of woman who will leave everything to a husband? This house may not be much, but it's mine. I worked hard for it, and I love it."

"Alright," he says. "Was just thinking out loud." He drops the subject and carries my bags out to the car.

As I step out, I look back at the house I have lived in for much of my adult life – my refuge, a shelter against the buffeting storms of life. Here I had grown up, made something of myself. It was my favourite place: a little harbour of peace – sometimes an island of frustration on which I was shipwrecked – but always a space into which I could retreat to replenish myself, remake myself. I swallow the lump in my throat as I close the front door for the last time. A new, different life awaited me, with one of the most precious gifts life has to offer: the steadfast love of a partner who adores me; who has promised to love me for the rest of our lives.

We are quiet as we drive through the muted city streets. At his home – our home – he stops the car some way from the front door, so that we have to walk up the long, winding driveway. At the end of it waits my wedding gift – a gleaming red BMW Z4. I squeal with delight as Neill whisks me into his arms and kisses me. We jump into my new car, me stroking and caressing it like the newborn baby I've never had; Neill watching me with delight, eyes shining. Tomorrow, we'll take it for a spin, but tonight will be our first night together as a married couple. He picks me up and carries me across the threshold, into our new life.

"Welcome home!" Neill laughs as he plops me down in the reception room, filled with dozens of red roses. He leads me into the kitchen, where he pops open a bottle of Moët, and pours it into two waiting flutes.

He raises his glass: "To my lovely wife! To us! To our forever!"

I sip my champagne and I am back under his spell. Forgotten – the missed honeymoon, the lonely days by the hotel pool, the lies to my friends, the tearful flight home. I am with him, in his arms, beside myself with love.

Chapter Five

We've known each other for only nine months, I tell myself over and over again when the going gets rough. Which it does, with frightening regularity. The fights are mostly about his absence, his lack of communication, my taciturn reception upon his return, what he calls my capricious moods.

He leaves often and with barely a moment's notice. There are patterns in the occurrences that pull him away: constituency work, time in Pretoria, crisis in the constituency; crisis in the party at provincial level that National needs him to sort – he is the only one from the province trustworthy enough to operate at both levels. The twins having problems at school, needing their father, one of them playing truant; family therapy with his ex-wife Nicole and the children, to support them through this particular rough patch of adolescence.

I meet Nicole briefly. She and Neill are civil to each other, and she is civil towards me, for which I am grateful. I don't ever envision a day when we will call each other "sister" over drinks, but she is respectful, and I reciprocate. I want this to work, I want to love his children, and for them to love me; I want to have a cordial relationship with their mother.

Neill's absences vary in length. Sometimes he is only gone for a day, at other times a weekend, on rare occasions, up to a week. He does his best to remain in touch, and forewarn me so that our joint plans are not too badly scuppered. Yet there are times when I find myself alone at a dinner with friends, the theatre, or a beautiful picnic in Kirstenbosch that I have packed for us, simmering with resentment. If his absences were regular, like a certain day of the week, or a predictable length of time, I could work around them. It is the unpredictability of it all, never being able to make firm plans with him, the non-sacrosanct nature of almost any commitment, that throws me. Even when he is home, there are long days at the office, stretching into the evenings and nights. It is rare for us to have dinner together, despite our pledge to try and share at least one meal per day.

The coven commiserates: it takes a while to settle into marriage. You'll adjust and find your rhythm, they say. But it feels like I'm the one doing all the adjusting here, I complain. I am a placeholder, a bedwarmer. They nod and smile, but offer no further comforting words.

My mum's advice is to turn the time without him towards homemaking – whatever that is. I ask her to be specific.

"Make the house nice, you know. Warm. He's been a bachelor. Add a woman's touch."

I stifle a laugh as I picture my mother's idea of adding warmth to Neill's house. A set of large, crocheted doilies on the marble coffee table. Doilies draped across the back of his Eames armchair. That print of Jesus and the twelve disciples at the Last Supper above the mantelpiece, competing with the abstract gouache painting on the opposite side of the room. Knitted toilet-seat covers and matching knitted rug taking the chill off the Caesarstone minimalism of the bathroom. Gatti's ice-cream containers, repurposed as skaftins, rubbing shoulders with Le Creuset coffee mugs. Athlone, meet Higgovale!

I have learned not to tamper with the décor without consultation. When I tell Neill I am hiring a mover to bring my worn but comfy reading chair, his eyes widen. Don't I want a new one? I reply that I like the one I've been using for years: it's cosy, a chair in which I can sit for hours without my back hurting. He arranges a meeting with an interior decorator, Gwyn, who hands me a wad of catalogues. We'll find the perfect chair, a new one, she chirps, to go with the décor she has so lovingly curated – with Neill's guidance, of course. We settle on an off-white wing-backed chair for the study. It sits in the corner beneath a floor lamp, guarded over by a Sophie Peters painting – a gift from my husband to appease my longing for the scuffed-up chair.

The rest of my belongings suffer the same fate. They remain in my house in Woodstock, to which I retreat occasionally in the early days of marriage, when my new home becomes too large, too gloomy as the sun sets on yet another solitary day. These guilty trips to my old home bring little joy. It is no longer home; it feels unlived in, too pristine. Yet I cannot settle into the new house, make it my own. I am stuck in this no-man's land, living in luxury, but without a space that feels comfortable, like the pair of slippers you change into after a long day at work. That is how I want home to feel. In the Higgovale house, I walk in and see nothing reflecting me. Yes, there is the Sophie Peters painting in the corner of our joint study, but that, too, was chosen by Neill. None of the bright wall colours, the fabrics I love to drape to soften a room, or the large framed posters of my favourite films and exhibitions have followed me here.

I miss the sounds, the textures of my own place: the mellifluent tones of the Adhan punctuating the days as the faithful are called to prayer; the laughter of children playing on the pavements. I could walk out of Neill's house forever and neither my absence nor my presence would register. The house would remain as it is. I have entered into some sort of hermetically sealed cosmos, wrought by Neill's hand, with no prospect of the joy of building a home together with furniture, art or objects that have meaning: ensconced in memories of a journey we've taken, an antique piece spontaneously bought on a roadtrip, or a precious inherited piece of china. Everything is new and shiny, chosen from a catalogue. I berate myself for these thoughts. I have everything, and yet here arises a nostalgia for used, old things – scuffed and worn – the kinds of things we should not be dragging from our drab pasts into shiny new futures.

After one too many depressing returns to my old house – filled with guilt for missing this ordinary space when I now live in a designer, magazine-worthy house; for not being more grateful for what I've received; for the house sitting empty in the middle of a city struggling with a housing crisis – I take Neill's ever-more insistent advice and sell it. I hope that the finality of letting it go will sever my relationship with the past, and anchor me more firmly in the new.

With my house gone, I spend most of my time, when not at work, in Neill's house. He chastises me when I say this, reminding me that it is now "our" home.

"I don't understand your uptightness. Make it your own, it's your home now. What will it take for you to settle?"

"You," I blurt out before I can catch myself, knowing full well the potential for one loaded word to spark an argument in the powder keg of our emotions.

"Not this again," he sighs. "This is becoming tedious! I thought I was marrying a grown-up."

The words sting, marking a new progression in our relationship: the personal insult. Until now, he has verbalised his exasperation only about our situation. This is the first time he has attacked me personally. It soon becomes a pattern. Still, I don't know which is worse: the insults, or his silences when away.

Four months into our marriage, he is away on an ever-extending stay in Johannesburg (work for the party) when I manage to track him down by phone.

I hear in his terse tone that an argument is looming. I try. I keep my voice soft, pliant, pleasant. Ask how his day has been, who he's been with, how work is going. Monosyllabic replies ricochet back at me: "Fine", "good", "the usual", "Tim", "tired," "yes", "no".

He is not even making an effort, nor any attempt to find out how I am, how my day has been.

Anger rises in my throat. I swallow it back down. "Do you know when you might be back?"

He explodes with rage: "For God's sake! No! I don't know when I will be back again. And I'm tired of fielding the same question, to which you *know* I don't have the answer."

The phone connection dies in my ear. I don't bother to call back. I allow my tears to flow freely, wondering how things have become so bad so quickly, fearful for the future.

When I return from work the next day, the living room is filled with roses. Neill comes out of the bedroom, dressed in a linen shirt and jeans, not his usual suit. He walks over to me and cradles my hands in his. He kisses them gently. It is such a relief to feel this warmth from him that I start to cry.

"My precious. I'm sorry."

We embrace and I am grateful, grateful that he is here, contrite, kind to me, that he still wants me. Here is the Neill I got to know, the Neill I fell in love with: not the stranger bellowing at me down the phone last night.

He leads me to the sofa. I nestle against his chest; my body feels like it is dissolving with the sheer relief of having him back within arm's reach. We sit like this for a few minutes, me listening to the steady beat of his heart and his even, relaxed breathing. Being like this with him calms me down, makes me feel that an integral part of me that has been missing, is restored again.

"My darling, I need to make a proper apology. I am sorry I was so short with you. It happens when I'm tired, and last night I was exhausted. But this is no excuse for how I spoke to you. I'm sorry, my love."

His apology soothes my raw nerves. I can deal with conflict and harsh words if, at the very least, he knows there is a problem and is not too big a man to apologise. He goes on talking in that calming, steady way of his: he knows that saying sorry is not enough, that he has to work on changing his unhealthy workaholism. It's just that he has been alone for so long, has allowed work to consume him, has very little need for the day-to-day intimacies that constitute a loving relationship. He has forgotten how to do that, but is now he is committed to me, he knows he needs to do better. To feed this relationship, nourish it, avoid repeating the mistakes of the past. He wants to make me happy. He wants to be happy. We're both reasonable, mature, empathetic people; we have the ability to create the beautiful life we envisioned when we fell in love. He is willing to go to couples therapy with me, if that's what it takes.

His apology makes me whole once more. Life is beautiful again. I'm back in love, delighted to be Neill's precious wife.

Although I am dizzy with love most days, there is no doubt that marriage has been an upheaval. One moment I'm blissfully happy, enamoured with my soul mate, excited about the future that stretches before us and the life we're building together. The next I am wracked with insecurity and doubt. Am I built for this? An intimate relationship where the other is an absent presence? I have left my home for this, forsaken my freedom. And almost everything in my new life is wonderful. Except when I am alone in the gilded cage, wondering where he is, when I will see him again.

There are always plausible reasons for his absences, well-considered explanations why he could not pick up the phone to say goodnight or answer a frantic series of texts from me. Not that I am often frantic anymore. He has trained me very well not to question too much, not to allow my voice to betray any anxiety when I speak to him from a distance. I soon take over that role from him, training myself into obsequious obedience. My tone is supple, even in the most difficult conversations, in case I elicit a "Don't you trust me? I don't know where we go from here if by now, you still don't believe that I have your best interests at heart."

"Trust that I have your best interests at heart", becomes the shorthand reassurance he peppers into every conversation in which I even begin to express doubt. It's culled from the sit-down discussion we have about my "trust issues" two months after the wedding.

He is calm. My eyes are red from crying from fear of what he is doing when he is away, and the frustration I feel with myself for not being more secure, not being able to accept his explanations, not being a better wife.

"We need to put this to rest, Anita. Once and for all. So that we can enjoy the rest of our lives together."

As always, I am comforted by his tone – calm, authoritive. He knows what he is saying, knows what he is doing. Rational, reasoned. I am the overemotional one, overwrought by my feelings, not being able to shake my need to know his every move.

My emotional state verges on controlling, he tells me, with a concerned look on his face. "Without trust, there is nothing. Trust is the bedrock of any relationship. This relationship. If we can't trust each other, what do we have? Nothing. We might as well pack it in, give it up."

My eyes widen with fear. Not giving up – not so soon – not ever!

"I am a grown-up. I've lived a whole life. Heaven knows, I haven't been a saint. But I'm a good man, or at least I'm trying to be. I want to be a better man for you, Anita. Don't you see me trying? Maybe you don't see my efforts, or appreciate my efforts, but I am trying, my dear Anita. Especially since I met you."

My tears gush. I know he tries. I know he listens to me, wants me – us – to be happy.

He continues his monologue, his voice warm and without a hint of resentment or impatience. It is as if he is soothing a beloved child. "And every time you doubt me, I ask myself, why does she not believe in me? My own wife. And a bit of what I'm trying to build with you breaks a little. It breaks a little more each time."

He pauses for the full effect of his words to sink in. It is like a political speech, directed at an audience of one. Were this in a town hall or a stadium, this rhetoric would be answered by a roar of love from his adoring crowd. Here, in our beautiful home, on the plush white couch, his hands on my knees, my muffled sobs fill the silence.

"I don't want us to break, Anita. I need you to trust me. To trust that I hold what's best for you at heart."

I believe him. How can I not, looking into his gaze, the eyes holding me steadily, sincerely. I say nothing, but nod. I want this to work. I want to show him how much I love him – how there is not a shred of doubt when I am sitting like this with him, the smooth brown contours of his face within touching distance, anchored by his smile.

I believe my husband. And I believe in him. I say it over and over again, to make it so.

He has my best interests at heart. He has said so. This is my mantra when I wake up at 2am, alone in our hand-carved sleigh bed, ensconced in 800-thread count Egyptian cotton sheets that grate in his absence. *He has my best interests at heart* is the supplication I offer to the gods at 3am when I haven't heard from him for twelve hours, or have received only one cursory "sleep tight xx" text message in two days. *He has my best interests at heart* is the protective prayer I mumble to myself as I nod off at 4am. I bolster this belief with the small white pills, benzos, that my doctor prescribes for my anxiety and sleeplessness, imbibing wholehearted trust as I swallow them. I will believe in my husband even when he is not next to me in bed at 5am on any given morning; I will believe that he has my best interests at heart, even when I don't know what exactly I am being asked to believe about his absences.

Chapter Six

I focus on work, pouring all hours not devoted to teaching or administration into my new research project. The proposal for "The Making of Race in South African Secondary Education: Learners' Perception in a Transforming Democracy" is almost done. As I edge closer to the finish line, a familiar lethargy creeps in. I know this about myself: I have trouble completing things. Wrapping them up with a nice bow on top. This is feedback I've received increasingly as my years at the university have lengthened into a decade. My ideas are lofty, but do not transmute into the gilded currency of academia – publications.

I defend myself vigorously: the type of participatory research I do takes time – often double the time taken by more conventional topics unattentive to power and systems of oppression. But there is more than a grain of truth in the Head of Department's feedback every time the yearly performance review comes around. I do struggle to complete things. I've read dozens of articles about imposter syndrome, while hating myself for fitting the stereotype of a black woman, first-generation academic, so exactly – as if I were a textbook case study. After all these years, the feeling that I don't belong, that I got into the university by accident, that I will be discovered to be a fraud, still skulks around the dark corners of my mind.

"Internalised oppression," scoffs Thandiswa, who suffers no such lapses in confidence.

Yes, I know that – intellectually. But that knowledge does not help me when I struggle to wrap up an argument on the page, and procrastinate for days about submitting an article to the top academic journal in my field, before ultimately "forgetting" to press the send button. This damned thing stalks me, no matter what I do. Knowing the psychological roots of imposter syndrome doesn't shield me from the gutting despair of yet another "Rejected" email in my inbox, carefully automated, so that my resentment cannot be pinned on any particular colleague in the field. The impersonal nature of the rejection stings almost as much as the rejection itself. Because who then can I ask what to do next, how to improve?

The anonymous reviewers' reports became a circle of hell I avoided for some time, to the detriment of my career. In my first few years as an academic I'd pore over them, astounded by the cruelty that anonymity spawns. "Reads like a hastily slapped-together graduate paper"/ "A disembowelling and dismembering of Lacanian theory of subjectivity"/ "Trite" / "Unsophisticated thought"/ "Mere descriptiveness, seemingly incapable of theorising" – these and other anonymous reviewer gems have remained with me, word for word, popping up as if projected onto a huge screen in front of me when I sit down to write, reminding me exactly what my "peers" think of me. These words immobilised me for years, until I slowly clawed my way out of the pit into which they'd sunk me. My publication count has grown modestly since then, but not enough to guarantee the coveted promotion to Associate Professor.

My hope against hope is that the grant proposal will drive a final nail into the coffin of my fears of failure. I've written into the grant space, time and money for the writing itself: regular writing retreats, and a developmental editor to coach me and the graduate students I'll recruit to this project, so that our work will be burnished into print.

Gary, the Head of Department, chooses a Friday afternoon for me to present the proposal to him. Obtaining his signature is the first of many hoops I must jump through to get this grant approved. First, I need the department's buy-in, then the faculty's, and finally the central research office of the university. The higher up it goes in the bureaucracy, the larger the committee that will need to stamp their seal of approval on my project. Gary's support does not guarantee that I will get the grant, but without his signature, it cannot move any further up the chain.

When I emailed him a soft copy of my proposal, I sent off a silent prayer that he'd sign the electronic copy without needing any further discussion, and return it to me that same day. But it is not like Gary to pass up an opportunity to give me a detailed exposition, in person, of the shortcomings of my research plans – a teachable moment, he likes to call such oversight of my research, as if I am a perpetual student. He replied almost immediately: "Thanks for this – happy to discuss it further over coffee next Friday. Free at 3?"

The death hour on this campus – Friday at 3pm, when faculty have already left for the weekend and students are getting a head start on their partying. I've dressed for the occasion: long black shapeless pants and a black buttoned-up shirt, finished off with a tan blazer. My neck is adorned with a royal-blue and purple paisley satin scarf – a gift from my mother when I graduated from my Master's programme – a kind of talisman. A few years ago, after I kept arriving for happy hour with Thandiswa and Claire, seething from a wounding staff meeting where tempers and voices had flared, Thandiswa advised me to wear a scarf to meetings, draped around my neck. That way, I'd be covering both my throat and heart chakras, warding off energetic attacks on my centres of speech and emotion. I laughed at her, but started wearing my scarves anyway. Today, as I knock on Gary's door at 3pm sharp, I adjust the paisley print to cover every bit of flesh between my blazer and face: a covering of the jugular, really.

He opens, smiles, and with a practised sweep of his hand directs me towards the couch. I would have preferred the more traditional arrangement: us seated on either side of his imposing desk, creating a safe distance between us. Sitting on the couch is a nod towards flattening hierarchy, but also blurs the boundaries – which is the danger with Gary. He sits down next to me, and like the arm of a jukebox picking out a vinyl, chooses and clicks his persona into place.

"Tea or coffee?"

"No thanks," I say. I want to keep this meeting short and professional.

My heart pelts my ribcage like a drum. I am dizzy with the sound of blood pulsing through my veins. It is well known among university women that alone and behind a closed door with Gary is not a good place in which to find oneself.

Part of the informal induction of every woman here is to whisper to the others, the new ones coming in: which man is safe, which man can be trusted. But as the first black woman recruited to the department, this courtesy was not extended to me by my white women colleagues. They were civil enough when I arrived, smiling at me in passing, but they omitted sharing this crucial, unspoken survival guide for a woman in a place like this.

Gary, then an up-and-coming Associate Professor and not yet the department head, had been the only colleague to show me some warmth. We hit it off. He was the one who would pop his head around my door to ask how I was settling in, and whether I needed anything. He shared his tricks for negotiating a bloated bureaucracy – which secretary to finesse to get this or that application through in record time. Who to call when a student was having difficulty. Never too busy to offer a quick pep talk when panic rushed through me at the thought of facing a lecture hall with three hundred pairs of expectant eyes trained on me. We lunched, we laughed. We bonded over our shared love of country music, graphic fiction and gin. He was in his late forties, divorced, charming; adored by faculty and students alike. I liked him, this affable friend I could rely on in otherwise hostile terrain. I didn't notice the raised eyebrows, the pointed looks across the table when I took a seat he'd invariably saved for me next to him at staff meetings. Or perhaps I didn't want to notice those looks.

It happened the night of my first end-of-year staff party. We'd both arrived at the restaurant early, and found ourselves together in the lift. We'd bantered, laughed. I was close enough to smell his cologne and the alcohol on his breath. He said I looked sexy. I joked back that he didn't look too bad himself, and thought nothing more of it as we exited the lift.

I sat next to him, as usual, at the end of the long table set for twenty people. We ate, drank, unravelled a bit, got raucous. At a moment of particularly high-volume frivolity around the table, Gary stretched one arm across the back of my chair, drawing me towards him as if to whisper something private. I moved into his embrace with a giggle, then froze in horror as I felt his hand move between my thighs. I stiffened as his hand moved on, fingers firmly pressing against my crotch. Our eyes locked: him, smiling; me, stultified into a silence for which I still despise myself. Around us, our colleagues, oblivious to what was happening, roared louder.

I knew I should have said something, swatted away his errant hand, slapped his face. But I didn't. Couldn't. All will to move left my body; I left my body. Like Lot's wife, I turned into a pillar of salt, a grimace fixed on my face. Fingers now tugged at the sides of my panties. Rough. Hard. I felt his nails scrape my flesh, but my body sitting at that table remained immobile, rigid as a rod. Mouth dry, words caught in throat. Scream, damnit! Those words flashed on in my mind like a neon sign. But I couldn't. Our eyes remained locked, his grin growing bigger, his leer saying, "Got you!" If anyone else noticed, they didn't say anything. They were complicit in this act, but so was I: by saying nothing, doing nothing.

I snapped out of his grotesque spell and toppled a drink in the space between us, spilling red wine on his white shirt and on myself. His hand jerked up, and he laughed that familiar, affable laugh: "Oh how clumsy!"

To the rest of the table, he announced: "No more wine for Anita!"

He handed me a napkin to mop up the wine spill.

The rest of the table erupted in laughter at a joke made at the other end. I cleaned myself up, tears prickling my eyes.

Gary turned his back to me and rejoined a conversation with our colleagues. I sat frozen next to him, waves of nausea crashing against the walls of my stomach.

Did that really just happen? With my friend, my only real friend in this place? The only one I could ask to check my lecture notes, the one who looked over my work before I submitted for publication? The one who said "Chin up" after I got verbally battered in a staff meeting? I retreated into the bathroom, and left the party straight from there, without taking leave of anyone.

The university closed for the break, leaving me with a month to think about what, if anything, I could do. Ruminating is more like it; I obsessed, replaying the scene endlessly in my head. Why hadn't I stopped him? Moved away? How could I have avoided the incident?

"The incident" – that is how I came to think of what happened in the weeks that passed. Not an assault, certainly not that, because where would that leave me? Gary, so friendly and charming, well-liked by colleagues, adored by legions of students. Harvard-educated. White. Who would believe me? And how would I set foot on campus again, sit in staff meetings with him again? I told no one – not my mother, not Thandiswa nor Claire.

In the new year, I reported to the university's Office for Diversity and Inclusion – ODI for short – where I spoke to an intake officer, who sympathetically guided me through a retelling of "the incident".

The next time I went in, I met with a much more senior member of staff. She would be handling the complaint from that point, given the standing of the man I'd accused of sexual assault. Grace was a Professor of Gender Studies who also played an oversight role at ODI. She listened attentively to my retelling, nodding at the appropriate moments, and making low, cooing sounds of commiseration.

Then she asked: "You were drinking? I'm sorry to ask this, but were you intoxicated? I ask only because that may have an impact on your recollection."

For a moment I was swallowed by silence. After all the work of women's movements and feminist writers dispelling rape myths, here I was, coming up against the most pernicious one less than half an hour into my intake interview reporting a sexual assault at a progressive university. The previous semester, I'd taught a class on Pumla Dineo Gqola's *Rape: A South African Nightmare,* in which we carefully considered a catalogue of myths around rape and sexual violence. I would never have dreamed that, just a few months later, I would be made answerable to these myths, projected on my body at a university office I thought was designed to protect me.

"Well, if you aren't going to believe me, who else will? How will I get some kind of remedy for this?"

Her empathetic demeanour shifted to something more officious, business-like. "I didn't say that I don't believe you. I'm asking questions to clarify my understanding of what happened."

I stared at her, unable to believe that I would be subjected to this at ODI of all places. I refused to answer the question. "Well, I know what happened to me!" I seethed.

She moved back in her chair and straightened her spine. "Look, you have two options here. There's the formal route. You lay a charge of sexual harassment or sexual assault, or both, against your colleague. Formally put it in writing to your Head of Department. The HoD then takes it up to the Dean, Human Resources gets involved, and a formal hearing is held. He is entitled to legal representation at that hearing. You too, if you'd like, but it's not necessary. If he's found to have perpetrated the act you accuse him of, there'll be some sanction. A suspension, a written warning, maybe even dismissal. Let me be honest, the latter is highly unlikely."

After a pause to let her words sink in, Grace continued. "The other option is to take the informal route. We appoint a mediator. The mediator meets with each of you separately and then together. It's an attempt to constructively resolve the problem. Restorative justice instead of retributive justice, if you will. We ask the defendant to apologise to the complainant, if they are able and willing to admit wrongdoing. They don't always. They might be ordered to go on a remedial course to educate them about why the offense is wrong, and its impact."

The matronly, speaking-to-a-victim tone returned as her eyes brimmed with concern. "In your case, the second option might be your best bet if you want to feel that the issue has been addressed."

I tried to check my anger, but failed: "Well, I find the second option ludicrous! Imagine having to attend mediation with your aggressor. Who thought setting things up this way was a good idea? This man assaulted me! It was sexual assault! The power differential between the two of us was already enormous before this even happened. Him groping me was an act of asserting power, violently. And you propose we sit and talk it out, like two friends having a beer at a pub? No! Surely not! This is no remedy! It's a further assault on my dignity."

She snapped back: "Well, we haven't yet determined that a sexual assault actually took place."

"What do you mean! I've just told you that it did. Is my experience and retelling of it not evidence enough for you?"

Droplets of saliva hurtled out of my mouth, landing on my neatly folded hands on the desk. I knew I needed to calm down. I was tilting dangerously into angry-black-woman territory, a precursor to getting my complaint dismissed. I breathed deeply, willing my pounding heart to slow down.

Grace kept her reply professional: "Again, I did not say that I don't believe you. But it's university policy to at least make sure the account makes sense. That the story remains consistent. We are bound by that policy. Any investigation and remedy needs to be fair to all involved in an accusation like this. Your accusation is serious. And Prof Simmons is quite prominent. This could severely damage his reputation, the impact of his scholarship, his legacy. One has to tread very carefully here."

The room started spinning. I felt my face flushing, and willed myself to continue taking deep breaths.

"But what about me? What about my career, my scholarship? This assault has already damaged me, my ability to sleep, my ability to concentrate and work. What about my dignity?"

She stared at me for a few moments without blinking, before the carefully constructed mask of concern dropped.

"Let me be frank, Miss Fredericks."

"It's Dr Fredericks," I corrected her.

"Dr Fredericks. Professor Simmons is a world-renowned expert in his field. He's on advisory boards of international journals, widely published, highly cited. He is a public intellectual who appears regularly in the media. Sought out as keynote speaker at annual conferences here and abroad. And then there's you. You're at the beginning of your career, new to this university. No major publications if your CV is accurate, no large grants to help us navigate these times of austerity. No PhD students graduated. You have yet to prove yourself at this university and, dare I say it, as an academic. You will need scholars like Gary throughout your career, to vouch for you, write letters for you, recommend you for opportunities. Gary's credentials are well-established. And he is well loved by students and staff alike. It's not so much that they won't believe you; it's that they will not want to believe it of him."

A deathly, emboldening calm settled over me. "The unspoken part of your little lecture is that he's a white man and I a black woman. You know this."

"I don't like your insinuation, Dr Fredericks. Race has nothing to do with it. Full of accusations, aren't we?"

I felt myself floating outside of my body, detached, watching this conversation from the corner of the room's ceiling. I heard a voice belonging to me. Its even tone surprised me. "All you've done is defended his position, without even looking at what he has done. How this has affected me. All you've done since I've walked into this office is advocate on his behalf. His career, his reputation, his standing. Who advocates for the victims here?"

"The victim? You are hardly a victim, Dr Fredericks! A grown woman. Drinking with a man, your colleague at a work function; flirting with him by your own admission, and then crying foul when he touched you as you leaned into him. Is that not how you described the events of that evening?"

A gate opened inside of her and her rage came rushing out. "Don't talk to me about victims, Dr Fredericks. Between the two of us, you are not the one scraping young women off the floor every Friday night, rushing them off to Victoria Hospital for a rape kit. They are the ones whose lives are actually destroyed."

Now she was the one flushed. "You, on the other hand, are a grown-up who went to a party and didn't have the good sense to know how to comport herself there. Think about your career. Think about his! Go ahead with this claim, and I guarantee you, one of you will lose your career, and it sure as hell won't be him!"

A putrid silence hung between us. I staunched the tears that started to well. She was correct, of course. I allowed that knowledge to sink into me as she rose from her chair and pulled two sets of forms from her filing cabinet.

She sat back down, shoving both forms towards me across the desk.

"Now, which will it be? Are you lodging a formal complaint, or do you want to go the informal route?"

"Thank you, I won't be choosing either of those options."

She sighed, looking down at her hands, then pulled the forms back.

"I think you've made the right decision. I believe you. I believe what you say happened to you. But taking this further will not end well for you. Go home and do some self-care. Get a manicure and a massage. Talk to your friends or a therapist – I can refer you to someone if you need a good psychologist. Get it out of your system that way."

I nodded wordlessly.

"Now, is there anything else I can do for you?"

"No, no thank you. And thank you for your time."

I slunk out of her office, the shame of what I'd allowed to happen clinging to me like a foul odour.

A week later, I stepped into Gary's office. He was thankfully not yet the HoD, just a colleague – a much more senior colleague.

"Hello Anita!" he said. "Oh you look cheerful," he proclaimed with his usual sardonic humour.

I sat down on the seat he offered, watching his demeanour change as I asked if we could talk.

"Yes of course, what's on your mind?"

"I want to talk to you about what happened the other night, at the staff dinner."

"What happened the other night?" He seemed genuinely bemused by the question.

"Between you and me, at the table…"

"What do you mean? Nothing happened, Anita. We ate, we talked shit, we drank too much. Everyone had a good time, everyone made it home."

My dour expression transferred over to his face. "What on earth do you mean, Anita? What are you talking about?"

"You touched me. Under the table. Inappropriately."

He jumped out of his seat. "What on earth? No, I didn't. Most emphatically not. I brushed against you once or twice, maybe, but touched you inappropriately? That's preposterous!"

"I know what you did. I didn't imagine it, Gary. And there is no way it could have been an accident. You shouldn't have done that. It was violating. Not only of my body, but of my trust. You were my friend Gary, my only friend in this department! And you've broken my trust!"

"I have no idea what you are talking about. You drank a lot, Anita. We both did. You spilled a drink all over yourself, remember? Was it when I tried to clean you up? Now maybe I was sloppy. I apologise if I was. But definitely I did not do anything to hurt you. Not planned, not deliberately."

"You grabbed me between my legs, Gary. Pulled my underwear out of the way to touch me. How could that have been an accident?"

Despite my resolve, I started crying. I'd wanted to keep this curt, professional. I wanted him to know that I knew what he'd done, that even if there was nothing I could do within the university system, I wasn't going to let him get away with it.

I wanted him to know the sting of betrayal; what it meant for a woman to think she was completely safe with a man, only to have that sense of safety cruelly ripped from her. What it felt like to be preyed upon in a moment of complete ease and openness with a man you trusted.

As women we do this all the time – make snap judgements about the men around us. Is he safe? Is this a man with whom I can let down my guard? Is he safe to walk past, or do I cross the street to avoid him? Is he safe enough to get into a lift with, work closely for hours in an office with a shut door?

Because whether we like it or not, whether or not we acknowledge it, in this country we are prey. And those preyed upon have to think for not only for themselves, but also live in the minds of their hunters, imagining what the aggressors' next move might be. We do these calculations almost unconsciously every time we meet a man, decide to get into a car alone with him, or make a decision about inviting him into our homes after a date. We've been socialised to think like the men that might harm us. Is what I'm wearing provocative? Is leaning my body in a certain way seen as an invitation to touch or more? Is my dress too short, too revealing? Am I at fault for driving in this neighbourhood alone at night?

Except that our whole country is that wrong neighbourhood, where we could be attacked and hurt at any moment. We are well aware, through messages from the media, the church, our communities, that if we do get hurt, we will be made the ones to blame. What was she doing there at that time of the night? Why was she wearing that, what did she expect going into his house for a nightcap? And hadn't I learned that the week before, at ODI?

What had I been thinking, drinking with Gary? Laughing with him, brushing up against him when he signalled he had something to say? Perhaps I really was to blame for this. Perhaps this was my own fault. But I had felt so safe with him. He was my friend – the very definition of the word implies comfort, safety, shelter.

I watched Gary's Adam's apple bob up and down against his shirt collar as he readied himself to speak. "Let me be very clear,

Anita. Nothing happened. And if you take this accusation, this patently false accusation, any further, if any of this nonsense ever leaves this room, I will consider it an act of aggression, a gross slander against my name. And I will act accordingly. Do you understand? Now get out of my office!"

I left in tears.

The following year, when Gary was promoted to Head of Department, I sent him a congratulatory note, knowing the danger I faced in advancing through the university. He would now be the one to approve every request for funding, every research proposal, every promotion I applied for. He would have the final say in assigning postgraduate students and prized doctoral students; he would be the one who recommended me for fellowships, prizes and residencies.

I silently thanked God that I had already passed my probation period, even as I steeped in the knowledge that with Gary at the helm, my career was now at a dead end. I would not advance any further beyond Senior Lecturer; not here, nor at any other university in South Africa. His networks at other institutions were strong – if I applied for a job anywhere else, they would inevitably call him for a reference, whether or not I'd listed him.

He responded to my congratulatory email in his usual collegial way, offering to meet me for lunch – a "peace offering", he wrote back to me. A peace offering made complete sense for both of us. We would have to work together now that he would oversee me, regardless of our history. I accepted his invitation with the hope that we'd restart our relationship, forgetting "the incident" ever happened.

But even as I hoped for the repair of our relationship, I wondered how this would work when one party in the relationship, the one who committed an act of violence against the other, would not even admit wrongdoing? It felt like the story of our nation, forgiveness and reconciliation, writ large again, on my skin. I did not want to, but I had to forgive Gary for my own survival.

Funny: once he was appointed, my hope for redress shifted to hoping that he would be the one to forgive me for ever making the accusation. But this is how power works. Until I could get a job elsewhere, it was best to accept that I had been made the aggressor, that I was the one with much, much more to lose than Gary.

Lunch invitation accepted, Gary suggested we drive out to the winelands to get away from the humdrum of the university. A fresh slate, perhaps? I knew that I was taking a huge risk, but to slight him would have been career suicide. So I made a mental checklist of ways to avoid physical contact: go in separate cars, not accept drinks I did not see opened and poured by a waiter, sit across the table from him, wear pants, boots, a buttoned-up shirt, and my scarf.

And so I found myself, two years after "the incident", at a beautiful wine estate at the foot of the Simonsberg, on one of those days when the winelands were a riot of competing greens and blues, beauty spread out before us like a feast. Gary chose well: the vine-covered veranda on which we sat overlooked a beautiful lake, framed by the not-too-distant berg. We kept the conversation cordial, if a little stilted, but a bottle of chenin blanc soon mellowed us. I took generous helpings of water between each sip of my wine. Gary would never find me drunk again.

An hour into lunch, it was like old times – we gossiped, laughed, caught up on episodes of each other's lives we'd missed during our estrangement. He outlined his vision for the department, and how I'd fit within that vision. He wanted me to apply for the rank of Associate Professor within the next year. Even though he'd just taken up the position, he had a long-term plan for the department and a succession plan. It was a shame, an indictment on the university really, that more than two decades into our democracy, our department had never been headed by a black person.

He delivered his manifesto with the usual aplomb: "You would be perfect. The first black woman department head. A double victory for transformation. We need to show that we have truly embraced transformation. And this would be great boost to your career, of course. It's a win-win, Anita. I want you to start thinking seriously about this, and get comfortable with the idea. Let's prepare you – get that publication count up. In five years you should be ready for the headship, if we start working now to get you to the rank of Associate Professor."

It felt like old times: Gary strategising and plotting around department politics; me enthusing about his brilliant insights. I was flattered that he regarded me as a potential leader, gratified that I'd once again have the protective mantle of his friendship.

He ordered a second bottle of wine after we finished our meal, and despite my protestations that I'd had enough to drink, forced me to toast to our plan. We drank some more, laughed some more. By the time we were ready to depart, it was after five. We were both a bit tipsy, about to drive straight back into rush-hour traffic, and his next proposition unfolded seamlessly from these circumstances.

"Have you seen the artwork in the main house of this estate? No? Let's give the traffic a miss and meander our way through the exhibition."

I agreed.

We left our table and headed towards the main farmhouse, which housed the exhibition.

As he ushered me through the door, his hand hit the small of my back. He leaned down and made his next move.

"Have you seen their magnificent suites? Perhaps we could book one and overnight here?"

It took a few seconds for his words and their implication to sink in; a few more for the weight of what saying "no" would mean.

The vision of the bright future he had just conjured before me was wiped away in the space of thirty seconds, which was the time it took for the "no" to fall quietly from my lips. As I turned my back and left him still standing at the threshold, the weight of this knowledge lodged in my stomach: that I was done for at this university, done in academia.

That was five years ago. Since then, we've made an art form of avoiding each other, except in meetings where we both have to be present. I stopped attending staff gatherings outside of work hours, becoming more and more isolated. Everyone left me alone, which suited me. I was labelled the problem child of the department, but they couldn't get rid of me, because, thank God, I had tenure. But Gary made sure that not a scrap of anything good came my way. No grants, no participation in projects, no advancement workshops.

This same Gary Simmons who stuck his fingers in my panties now stands over me at the side of his grey Oxford couch, my proposal in hand. The same Gary whose signature I desperately need if my research project, the first academic endeavour I've been enthusiastic about in years, is to get out of the starting block.

"Right, let's get down to business." He sits down next to me.

A million worms scuttle under my skin as I catch a whiff of his cologne. I feel sweat moistening the shirt under my arms.

I glance at the proposal, all marked up in red ink, as if it is a student assignment.

"I've had a thorough look-through. Now let me preface my remarks by saying that I am obviously not an expert in this field of participatory research. Nor have I read much around race, except the usual suspects – Fanon, Biko, Cesaire. My understanding is cursory. But I think you have a solid concept here. Very ambitious, but that is not unusual for you."

So far, so good. He continues: "I worry that the participatory aspect of the research puts you on an extended timeline between inception and publication. You know what it's like – I feel like a blessed bean counter half the time. You have to make sure you can publish almost immediately out of this, at the rate of at least two peer-reviewed articles per year. Your timeline does not reflect that. Can you rethink it?"

I am ready with a well-rehearsed reply: "Yes, I thought you'd make this critique. But I can't do what you suggest. My research is either participatory, or it isn't. It's essential for me to do it this way, not to have it be another mining project, extractive of people's knowledge. I simply don't know how to get around the time factor, which frankly, is an artificial constraint placed on me."

Now I have to ask: "Is it possible for you to advocate upwards on my behalf, make a case as to why my research will take longer to yield the results the university requires?"

Gary sighs. "Ah, idealistic Anita! The creeping neoliberalism we've warned about is no longer creeping, it is our reality! It has arrived, and not only that, has been embraced. We are in bed with it now, and as much as I've tried, as you know, to resist the onslaught, it has overtaken us. Austerity measures, more and more contract staff. I can hardly get a new post to replace our two retirees next year. Everything has to make fiscal sense before all else. You have to add value – God, how I hate that term! And the value we are having to add is money."

I wrap my scarf a little more tightly around my neck. Look down at my hands. I know what's coming next; just want it to be swift at this point.

He continues: "This isn't personal, you know? I want you to know that. I'm just a cog in the machine now, trying to churn out my own work as best I can. I know the mindset higher up. I'm sorry, I don't think this will fly with our research office."

"What do you suggest I do next, Gary? Give up? Sit and become dead wood, teaching but not producing research? It may not seem that way, but I have hopes and ambitions, a viable project to complete, and I don't see why a difference in ideological approach to research should get in the way of that."

Gary strokes his chin, looks past me. "I'm having a research retreat next month for a weekend with some doctoral students and postdocs. We're staying at a really nice conference centre. Why don't you come along? We're working on relevance in research, and framing that in proposal writing. Come and spend a few days or even a few hours with us. It might lead you in new directions."

I bristle at this suggestion. "My God, Gary, surely you're not suggesting I tag along with your postdocs to learn a thing or two? I am a Senior Lecturer in this department, with much more experience than your protégés. You people really do see us as forever emerging. Emerging researcher, emerging scholar. I am forty-seven years old, for God's sake!"

"Goodness, Anita! Having any kind of interaction with you is like negotiating a minefield! One never knows what will set you off. God, you're so easily offended. I am trying to help you, really, I am. Do you think your non-productivity makes me look good as a department head? Fuck, no!"

His face is red, eyes bulging. "I am tired, frankly, of explaining to the Dean once a year why there is so very little output from you, when we've invested so much. Training courses, research workshops. But you stubbornly resist all attempts to talk some common sense into you. Your research ideas, in a perfect world: Yes! Brilliant! But not here, not now. With subsidies shrinking every year, time-to-graduation lagging for most of our postgrad students. We simply do not have the luxury of taking forever with our research. And God knows, we have pressing social problems in this country. HIV! GBV! Pick any one of those and you won't be able to stop the grant money flowing. But no! Grounded participatory research on some obscure topic about how bloody teenagers perceive themselves.

Newsflash, Anita, nobody fucking cares!"

We are both surprised by this outburst, and when it is over, we are silent.

"Okay, Gary," is all I can muster in the end.

What else is there for me to say? Where else to turn? I have hit a wall in his office, in this university, a rat in a maze with no exit.

We sit in silence while the clock on his wall counts the seconds.

"I'm sorry, Anita. That came out wrong. But maybe you needed to hear that. And you're so quiet these days, taciturn. One wants to help. But you're like a wall. Won't take direction, nor advice. Ungrateful. You never are sociable with us anymore, refuse my mentorship. It borders on uncollegiality. There's just no helping you."

He places my proposal into a manila envelope. "For what it's worth, here are my notes. I've outlined a few suggestions for converting it from a participatory project to a more conventional study. At least consider it."

I take the envelope and stand up from the couch. On my way to the door, some wayward spirit comes over me, and before I can even reason it out in my head, I drop the envelope in the wastepaper basket next to his door. I leave without looking back. Lot's wife has finally found her feet.

Chapter Seven

Neill is home for once, sprawled across the beige couch in the TV room when I walk in. He is riveted to the Commission on State Capture's live broadcast on TV, his mouth turned down with disapproval. The personal assistant of a former minister is testifying about procurement procedures, and the chain-of-command in signing off on large payments, some of which have been found to be irregular. I sit down beside him, am drawn mometarily into the drama unfolding as she dabs her eyes with a tissue. Her evidence will be the bedrock for the National Prosecuting Authority to lay charges of corruption against her minister. She does not want to be there; he is a good man, she sobs. The allegations of irregular procurements and payments are part of a conspiracy to unseat him by his enemies within the party.

"You would not believe the day I had!" I sigh as I kick off my shoes and sidle up to Neill.

Without moving his eyes from the screen, he lifts his hand to shush me. I wait, resigned, for the personal assistant's testimony to finish. His sweatpants and t-shirt and the light sheen of his skin tell me that he's been to the gym. Still transfixed by the TV, he pulls me towards him, kissing my cheek absentmindedly.

"This is a disgrace, honestly. Going after these politicians who have been trying to build something. Yes, maybe they did some wrong. Yes, when the party was forced to transform from a liberation movement to a majority party, there were bound to be those who had deficits when it came to overseeing money, or other projects. And yes, of course they need to be held accountable. But this witch-hunt is ludicrous," he cries, eyes wide with rage. "What about the likes of PW Botha, who retired with a golden handshake to a luxury lifestyle in Knysna? What about De Klerk and his Third Force? What about Koornhof, Adriaan Vlok? Not for one minute did the evil minds behind apartheid see the inside of a prison. Free to the end, despite their destruction. Rewarded for it, even!"

He waves his free hand: "And they had plundered all the local government structures anyway in the run-up to 1994. Moved fat funds out of municipal coffers, setting us up for failure. Where is the commission on state capture for that, those greedy Nats? And don't get me started on white monopoly capital. Where is the accountability? Is the NPA going after all of those multinational corporations who continued to milk the country after apartheid ended? Where is the TRC for that? Will this damn commission subpoena them as well?"

I commiserate. Throw away a comment that it is in the nature of power to keep bolstering itself, to protect its own interests even as it seemingly gives up privilege. But I'm in no mood for a drawn-out political discussion about the ethics of post-transitional governance.

He turns to me. "Have you been crying? What have I done now? Thought you'd be happy I'm home, waiting for you like a good husband."

"It's not you, for once," I joke half-heartedly.

"What happened?"

I let out a huge sigh. "We're gonna need drinks for this."

Neill walks over to the bar in the corner of the room, where he pours us each a Macallan over ice.

He returns to the couch. I nestle into his arm. We sip our drinks while I relive my meeting with Gary. I end by recalling my power move of binning Gary's comments on my work.

Neil frowns. "Well, that might not have been the smartest thing to do, my dear."

"Please don't pile on. I've had the shittiest day. And I know it wasn't smart, but just being in Gary's presence still makes my insides boil, after all these years."

"Still? What do you mean?"

"Well, there's history there," I answer, glumly.

The lawyer in him is piqued. He sits up a bit straighter, angling his body slightly away from me. Reluctantly I share the story of Gary's assault on me.

"Fucking bastard! I'll kill him!" Neill shouts when I've finished.

The rage I couldn't unleash at Gary comes out at my husband. "Oh for fuck's sake! Come on now, Neill. That is not at all helpful!"

"What do you mean, not helpful? You're my wife. Any man whose wife has been violated will want to kill the bastard who did it!"

I have never seen this Neill before, this angry coil of energy: an element whose current has just been switched on, glowing red. He leaps to his feet, drains his glass and pours himself another, downing it like a shot. "Why didn't you report him?"

"I did!" I protest, and tell him what happened at ODI with Grace.

"You should have taken it further! The bastard!"

I sigh, say nothing. Not the victim-blaming again. How do I explain the subsequent years of advocacy and working with students in the aftermath of sexual violence? How the system fails them again and again, with the idea that mediation can dispense justice? How I have seen the brightest, sharpest, most beautiful young women with the most promising futures drop out, year after year in the wake of a life-changing assault or rape? After they are expected to stay on campus, attend tuts, lectures, even continue to live in residences with men who have raped, assaulted or stalked them? How do I explain to someone who has never had to think about it, that I am one of many survivors daily bracing themselves in the fish-pond of our university against catching a glimpse of, running into a man who has assaulted us? Or worse, being assaulted or harassed by him repeatedly? I could offer a lengthy exposition of the sexual politics of space on campus, but right now I don't have the energy.

Neill continues his tirade: "And to think he sees you at work every day, probably congratulating himself about what he did to you, what he got away with. Do you want me to go to the Minister of Education, have a word about this? That bloody bastard will never receive another cent from the National Research Foundation. Hell, I could get him fired – fucking pig!"

"Will you stop!" I scream.

The last thing I need tonight is a fight with Neill on top of Gary's rejection of my proposal.

He comes to a halt, focuses on me. He looks as if he is actually about to listen.

"Just stop this, stop making it about you! It happened a long time ago. I am over it. I don't need you go fight my battles for me. I'm a survivor, and I have held my own against him for years. Why can't you ask, just for once, what I need?"

He stands wordless for a few seconds, his drink splashing violently against the rim of the tumbler in his hand.

Then he surprises me by remaining calm. "Alright, alright," he says, his voice soothing.

The even-keeled, equanimous Neill returns to the body of the man in front of me. He walks back to the couch, sits next to me, and starts rubbing my back. "Alright, my precious Anita. I hear you. What do you need from me? Tell me."

I'm not even sure. But I take a deep breath and try to tell him. "I need you to listen. To hear my full story without wanting to fix it. To bear the weight of it with me. Without taking it as a slight against your masculinity that some other man has dared to touch your wife. To put yourself in my shoes and imagine how I must have felt without making it about you, without becoming territorial. Because I am not territory for you to protect. I am me. I don't belong to you. I belong to myself."

"Of course. Of course. You're right, Anita. I'm sorry. But this is a thing that hits you in the gut. To hear what that pig did to you." He quickly corrects himself. "But I'm here for you. Listening. Tell me what you need."

"I need you to help me figure out how to get my work done. I need for a sexual assault not to ruin my entire career. Because that is what happens so often to women like me. We disappear."

I pause, take another sip of my drink, and continue.

"My research is important. No one else in the country is doing it. You're a master strategist – help me to strategise so that I can do my work! That's all I have ever wanted at that damned university, to be able do my work. To be given the space and time to finish my research. To be able to focus on it without having to be on guard constantly against the next racist comment, or the next man trying to put his hands on me."

He pulls me against him. I feel the steady thump of his heart as I lay my head against his chest, feel the warmth of his palm protectively cupping my head. To have someone like Neill next to me in this moment, to catch me, to hold me, to sit with me as I process the pain of this day, of that night many years ago and its fall-out: this is everything.

As I melt into him, grateful for his presence, his calming words, his ability to hear what I need, the tears come. Tears of relief that I don't have to face this alone. That someone, after so many lonely years, has my back.

We sit like this for a long time while dusk settles into the corners of the living room.

When he speaks, I know Neill has thought this over carefully.

"Quit your job," he says, in a low, steady voice.

"What? I could never. I know I'm a bit stuck right now, but there's the teaching. I love that. And I know that I make a difference. I know how important it is for black students to see me, someone who looks like them, who knows what it's like to come from a shack and make it there. They need to encounter my way of teaching, of seeing the world."

"Yes, yes, of course. That is important, but really, Anita? What future does that university hold for you? Gary will be HoD for years. You'll never get promoted. And there are other ways to get your knowledge, your way of seeing the world, out there."

He continues: "You don't have to be at a university to teach. You don't have to be affiliated to a university to publish a book, or many books, for that matter. In fact, the university publishing system may be a liability."

His arm tightens around me: "Imagine this – just bear with me for a bit, my dear. Quit. Start a small consultancy. Given your expertise in race, psychology and education, you could offer diversity training, sensitivity training to corporate clients. Upskill your knowledge on employment equity laws, and you'll be golden, I promise you. You'll have to turn clients away. You could do workshops about race, employment and inclusivity in different spaces. You'll make a killing! You can still write, still publish in journals. You could teach at private colleges or even high schools. Guest lectures and such…"

"I don't know, Neill..."

He's in top form as he continues to outline his vision for me. "No, you don't want to know. Think this through as a real possibility. You've got connections nationally at schools – you could take on independent schools as clients too. I can introduce you to my business contacts. You could even tender for government contracts. You're a black woman with a PhD. Experienced at a top university. You could make a fantastic career out of this, make loads of money!"

His eyes are alive with excitement.

"Neill, it's not about the money. This has been my dream since I finished high school. I am actually living my dream – it's just this thing with Gary ruined everything. It's put me in a rut. It's really not about money."

He scoffs. "That is the problem with you liberals! You never want to think about money, never want to make it about money. Anita, come and live in the real world. Everything is about money! Do the consultancy and take the huge raise in your income that will inevitably flow from it, and use it to write all of the books I know are inside of you. Imagine an intelligent, sensitive, well-considered book for the lay person about race and how it functions. Race in post-apartheid South Africa. How to work with race in the workplace, schools, sport organisations. It would be a best-seller! And there's no one more qualified than you to do it! And it would have a wider impact than any journal article read by a grand total of five other academics. Think about it!"

I digest Neill's pep talk in silence. Yes, I could make money. But this has never been a driver in my career or life. I want to teach, want the privilege of being present to younger scholars and students.

"But I want to teach, Neill."

"You will still be teaching. Think of it as transferring your brilliant skills to the corporate sector. You will be reaching a far more powerful audience, one that really has the ability to change the world. Think about it, Anita. Perhaps it's time to let go of this fantasy of the utopian university and its importance in a developing economy like ours. Ninety-five per cent of South Africans will never see the inside of a university. You are working with an extremely elite, privileged minority. Business is where it's at, my dear! You need to think about your impact from a different set of imperatives."

I have seen him do this many times at political rallies – rousing crowds, inspiring them, sketching a vision of what the future could be. He works that same magic on me, his personal audience of one, who adores him with the same almost religious fervour as the masses. I can almost taste the beautiful future he conjures, see myself in a shiny office consulting with a business client.

"But I'm not a businessperson, not like you."

"Well, I am here for you, Anita. I can mentor you. Hell, you don't even have to work. You know that, don't you? I can take care of you, financially. You're my wife now. Our lives have come together and I am here for you. Resign, take a few months off … I'll take care of you, my precious."

I promise that I'll think about it. It makes sense – have I not reached a dead-end in academia? There seems to be no space anymore for a scholar like me, who needs time to build proper relationships with research subjects, time to think, time to write.

Leaving academia will be a huge loss. I have defined myself for years now by my position, the prestige it carries, the looks of surprise when introduced as Dr Fredericks to strangers. And my story, my origins in a backyard shack, make my achievement an almost superhuman feat! Once I'd accepted that I would never be a mother, at least I could placate myself that I was this. How I have dreamed of the title Professor in front of my name. How it's the first thing I write down at every strategic planning session. How would it feel to give this up? Who would I be?

Chapter Eight

I am at work a week after my meeting with Gary when an email from the Human Resources office pings into my inbox. Gary has filed a charge of insubordination against me for disregarding his direction on how to improve my research and for tossing his recommendations into the bin. The charge lays out how he spent hours reading and responding to my proposal – hours which have now been wasted by my insolence and unprofessional behaviour. I am to face a disciplinary hearing a month from now, consisting of the Dean, three academics from our faculty, one representative from an outside faculty, a representative from the HR Department, and a university lawyer. I am welcome to bring my own lawyer, or a member of my union to the hearing for support.

I stare at the email for a few moments of disbelief as panic rises from the pit of my stomach. I pick up my cell phone and dial Neill's number. No reply.

Closing my eyes, I remember my deep breathing to stop fear from spreading throughout my body. I sit quietly for the next ten minutes, focusing on my breath, summoning an inner voice for guidance. When I open my eyes, I know exactly what to do.

By the time I leave the office two hours later, I have emailed Gary and the Dean my resignation, effective immediately. My phone rings almost immediately after I hit the send button of my resignation email.

"This is unthinkable! You know we need at least three month's notice! Who will take over your classes, your postgraduate supervision? We need some time to find your replacement, time for you to do a proper handover."

"I'm sorry Gary, that won't be possible."

The drive from campus takes twenty minutes on autopilot. As I open the front door, the emptiness of the house rushes to meet me. I'm not even sure whether Neill is still in Cape Town, although I woke up next to him this morning. I try his cell phone again; this time it does not even ring, but goes straight to voicemail.

I look around the darkening living room, throw my bag down. The euphoria of sticking it to Gary has worn off, and a hollow feeling spreads through my ribcage. The emptiness inside me rivals the coldness of the house. Where is my husband when I need him? I pour myself a glass of whisky as I contemplate the changes of the last year.

Everything I have worked for since the age of sixteen, gone. My career, my home. The man that I love and now desperately need, nowhere to be found, with the earth beneath me crumbling, crumbling to dust.

By the time he comes home the next evening, I have stitched myself back together again, after hours on the phone with Thandiswa and Claire. I am calm when he walks through the door, but can see the defensive set of his jaw. He must by now have seen all my missed calls and text messages, but has not responded.

He walks in, overnight bag in hand, and heads straight to the shower without greeting me. Rage churns inside of me. I wait, try to get a handle on myself – it has taken me most of the twenty-four hours since I quit my job to calm down. But Neill ignoring me triggers another wave of violent anger within me. Despite willing myself to calm down, and deploying all my strategies for staying serene, I lose the battle to tame my roiling emotions and follow him into the bathroom. He is naked in the shower, soaping his body with a large sponge.

"Where the hell have you been? I've been trying to reach you for the past day!"

He turns his back on me, slowly, deliberately; lifts his head into the stream of steaming water while rinsing the suds from his body.

With slow, calculated movements he stretches out his arm to

switch off the flow of water. He turns back towards me, his face like thunder. Stepping out of the shower, he grabs a fresh towel from a stack and winds it around his waist.

"For God's sake, not this again. I was working. What part of my work do you fail, deliberately, over and over again, to understand?"

I am astonished at his attack on me, when he has been the one missing, unreachable, for more than a full day: "For fuck's sake. I needed you! My world has fallen apart. It was urgent!"

"Well, why didn't you leave a message saying so? Or a text, a WhatsApp? All you had to do was say: Neill, I need to speak to you urgently."

I scream at him: "You wouldn't have gotten that message anyway; your phone was off virtually the whole day! What the fuck were you doing?"

He doesn't miss a beat: "Fifteen missed calls, ten 'where are you' texts. What do you think that does to me when I am working my arse off, negotiating a very tricky situation? I switch on my phone and find this barrage from you. One message spelling out exactly what the emergency was, would have been enough for me to know exactly what was wrong."

"And one message telling me where the fuck you were going to be, why you would be completely unavailable to me for almost twenty-four hours, would also have done the trick! It's called communication, Neill. Why can't you just be open and transparent? Where the hell where you?"

Rage flaring, he paces around the bathroom. I see him warming up to this fight and know that I am in no way an equally matched adversary to him. A lawyer, he is able to destroy me verbally within minutes. Fully in thrall to his argument, he volleys his next shot.

"Transparent! Not this again. The same old argument. You don't trust me! Can never believe that I am out there and still taking care of you, of us. I have to be tied to you by some invisible umbilical cord so that you must always know my movements, where I am, who I'm with. For what? To appease your insecurities. I have never met a woman like you, wearing your insecurities like a new outfit! Every day it's something different with you! Work on yourself, woman! Work on why you're such a co-dependent ball of neediness. Pathetic!"

The ferocity of his attack guts me. All I can think of is the weak response: "I am your wife! Surely I have the right to know where you are, how to reach you?"

"Yes, you are my wife, and that right you have. But if you think I am hiding things from you, which is insinuated by your attack on me, then I don't know where we go from here. It is not the question itself, but the way you are asking! I am very well versed, my dear Anita, in strategic ways of questioning. Leading someone up the garden path to catch them out. It's like you are laying a trap for me to walk into."

"Laying a trap? What utter rubbish. Where were you last night? A simple, straightforward question, which should be easily answered by someone who has nothing to hide."

The argument spins us both out of control. My rage, too large for my body, stalks the room, heaping on itself. The main issue is never addressed. Here we are, fighting about his absence, as usual – but he has not even asked what was so urgent. He has still not responded to the very simple question of his whereabouts. I think about the hours I have spent strategising with him about the party, its politics, and getting ahead there. None of this time or attention has been reciprocated to me, or my career. Yes, I have certainly been a helpmeet, as his mother implored, but have I had one in return?

He towels himself off while staring at me, eyes glinting. I wait for another volley of shouting, but as he looks at me, taking me in fully, it's like a switch flips. The words that come are quiet, collected.

"Where did I sleep last night? I don't appreciate your insinuation. Ask questions if you must, but I must tell you, the way you've come at me disturbs me. I don't mind the question – it's the way you have framed it."

He continues, as if delivering a speech: "I've told you before, without the underpinning of trust, there is no foundation for a healthy relationship. If you think I am lying to you, deceiving you, or worse, unfaithful, it throws the entire relationship into question. And once that happens, it is almost impossible for things to go on. So, Anita. You must decide: do you trust me? And if not, what do you propose we do about it?"

The rage pulsing through my body evaporates, and an icy dread crystallises in its place. Nausea swirls inside of me. He still hasn't answered the simple question about where he slept last night. Tears trickle down my face as I struggle for breath. The sight emboldens him.

"Oh so now you want to cry? One minute so bold as to make the most disgusting of insinuations. How would you feel if I thought that of you, that you were whoring yourself around? I am your husband. I made a commitment to you, and you should know me well enough to know that I will honour that."

He walks out of the bathroom.

I follow. "I'm sorry, so sorry."

His eyes, unblinking, assess me while he dresses. Disgust is written all over his face.

I start to beg. "Please, Neill, I'm sorry, forgive me. I need to talk to you. Need to tell you what happened."

The disdain in his voice is clear: "You need a man who you just accused of cheating on you? What could you possibly need from such a man? Why are you still here?"

He steps into his Italian loafers, splashes on cologne.

"I've been working myself half to death for you, and this is what I get when I come into my own home. No peace. No understanding. No empathy. A man just wants peace in his home. Surely a woman as clever as you can understand this basic idea!"

With that he turns, walks down the corridor from the bedroom to the living room, and out the door.

I want to run after him and beg him not to leave, tell him a million more times how sorry I am for the accusation. Why had I said that? Did I truly believe he was betraying me in the basest of ways? But I still do not understand why I cannot know the simple fact of where he has been. I know that he must be tired and busy, but how many seconds does it take to text, or explain your whereabouts?

Once it is clear that he will not return, I sit down with a cup of tea, avoiding the temptation to pop yet another benzo. I scan my body the way Thandiswa has taught me. The ice in my stomach is gone, but there remains that fuzzy scramble of static interrupting a message. I still haven't told him that I have quit my job, still haven't had the comfort of my partner embracing me and assuring me that all will be well. I close my eyes and focus on the feelings. "Listen to your body," I hear Thandiswa's voice floating above me. What I have been dulling with the tranquillisers is my body's innate way of knowing. I sit long enough in silence, without distraction, without a pill or glass of something to take off the edge, until I hear my gut screaming. Despite Neill's increasingly acidic assurances, despite his protestations that he is guarding my best interests, what my body knows for sure and is telling me loudly, clearly, is that something sick has infected my marriage.

Chapter Nine

We make up. We always do. He comes back to the marital bed in the early hours of the morning and wakes me with his lips, his tongue, his hot breath. Relief thaws my body – I receive him gratefully. We sleep with me pressed up against him, his arm around my waist – the familiar locking together of our bodies lulling me into dreamless sleep. In the early morning, in the first light filtering through half-slanted blinds, he kisses me awake.

"My precious Anita. Let's never have a repeat of last night, okay?"

I am back in his arms, back to being precious, wanted, desired. I am only too happy to acquiesce to his request not to restart last night's fight. I resolve to ask no further questions.

But he's ahead of me. "When you question me like that it makes me feel so weak. You know things are difficult right now, with the national electoral conference just two months away. You know that I am being considered for the position of Speaker in Parliament, but to get there, I have to get elected to the executive. And I have to play my part to get my comrades elected into the positions that will hand us a decisive victory over the other side. But those bastards who want to see me trip and fall are trying to pull me down as they know I'm being considered. Things are getting dirty. And how do I stay strong in this battle if even my own wife does not believe in me? Please, my precious. I need you to be strong for me. For us."

I apologise for doubting him, for even the hint of a thought that his character is anything but unimpeachable. We kiss. I find sanctuary again within the laager of his arms, against his warm chest.

We make love again in an unaccustomed, gentle way. He is slow and deliberate in touching me, kissing me – his tongue teasing my skin with unhurried precision. It is only when we are done, with him drifting off to sleep, that I share the news of my resignation. I tell him everything about how it happened: the email charging me with insubordination, my reaction, the charred ashes of that fire now turned to regret.

He listens with his eyes closed while stroking my arm. "Don't worry, my precious. You've done the right thing. I told you, I'll take care of you. No need to suffer the indignities of that bloody university anymore. The microagressions. Gary keeping you in your place. It will all be okay. It will all work out. Sleep, my darling. We'll work it all out later."

I fall into a deep sleep. Later, he brims with delight as he brings me a cup of coffee. I try to keep up with the stream of ideas pouring out of him. He will help me register a consultancy. He has already scheduled an appointment with the interior decorator so that we can turn the study into a more formal office. Or do I want a separate studio built on the grounds? I must just say what I want, and not think too much about money. He has just the architect who could turn my wildest vision into a stylish reality. I need an accountant and a good marketer – he has good contacts there, too. And once I've registered my business, we will hire a PA who will focus on the everyday nuts and bolts, so that my time can be freed to craft a vision – and to write, of course. I listen in awe. Neill has a mind always figuring moves several steps ahead of everyone else, while I struggle with decisiveness and seeing what next tentative move to make. He has a full vision of what my new life will look like, whereas I have only vague inclinations about what to do next.

Have I always been like this – timid, unsure? I don't remember myself before Neill anymore. I try to cast my mind back to a time when I moved assuredly through the world, but conjure nothing. I know myself to be a fighter, someone who shakes things up, but there's no denying the glass ceiling that I have crashed up against at the university. And who am I without that venerable institution, a place which, through the years, seeped into my pores and has become part of my identity?

But my identity has also changed with Neill in my life. I am his wife; a partner. My life has increasingly taken shape around the contours of his, and with my job gone, I fear he will completely absorb me, mould me to his image.

I smile, feign excitement from behind my coffee cup over his plans for my professional life, but in the pit of my churning stomach, the static continues to hiss.

The next day, he is home early to greet the interior decorater as she arrives. Gwyn, with her short blonde pixie crop, face all sharp angles, has been primed and briefed – she arrives with several concept boards, visualising different styles the office might take: chrome and glass; warm cherry wood, cool white marble – none of them reflective of me.

I say this, and am met with the question: how, then, would you describe your style? Not a question I have ever thought of, or know how to answer. I think back to my old home, my study with the worn corduroy reading chair, the poster of Audre Lorde, arms outstretched, her well-cited words emblazoned across her body: "When I dare to be powerful, to use my strength in the service of my vision, then it becomes less and less important whether I am afraid."

I see again the hodgepodge of images stuck against my wall: pictures of feminist writers I've admired, postcards from friends, a photo of me, Thandiswa and Claire at a sisterhood brunch, affirmations written in my own hand, stuck to the wall with Prestick to form a mercurial collage of dreams, wishes, imaginings. I had taken them down when I moved, feeling the echo of the precious moment or aspiration each one held. I could not envision them anywhere in the house I shared with Neill. Imagining his horror at the fatty stains the Prestick would leave against the expensive wallpaper in the study, I put my colourful, inspirational confetti in a folder and away in the bottom drawer of my desk. Away from my house, my Audre Lorde poster looked tatty and faded, and I threw it in the bin. I pictured them now in the shiny new office being conjured by this maven.

"I have no style at all!" I joke.

"Well, this is what Gwyn is here to do, get you some style," snaps Neill.

I had meant to be humorously self-deprecating, and his comment stings.

I chose a light-blonde wood setup with comfortable chairs, upholstered in blue batik, and matching armoires. Gwyn says she can have my dream office up and running within a few days. I do nothing after choosing the particular "look"; I just watch as Gwyn and her crew march in at eight every morning to work their miracle in converting a spare bedroom into my office.

A week that feels like a fever dream later, it is done. Gwyn, Neill, Thandiswa and Claire surprise me with fresh flowers and the ever-present bottle of chilled Moët, which Neill decants expertly into flutes before he makes a short speech congratulating me on having the audacity to strike out on my own.

"You are exemplary of what this country needs: a smart, hardworking, savvy black woman with so much expertise, so much passion, so much love for what you do. In taking charge of your own destiny, you are also changing the shape of things to come in this country. Anita, I am absolutely in awe of you, and your vision, and what you are about to become! To my wonderful wife!"

We clink and drink. He hands me a gorgeously wrapped box, in which I find a beautifully engraved glass nameplate: Dr Anita Fredericks, Director. Thandiswa and Claire clap and cheer, ululating as I place it at the centre of my desk. Neill reminds me that this is a soft launch; he will have his PA organise a bigger, glitzy event at one of the hotels at the Waterfront so that we can invite key stakeholders who could benefit from the services of my new consultancy.

"My God, you are so lucky to have him," whispers Thandiswa as she kisses me goodbye after our party. "He has vision, great ideas, and the means to help you make it all a reality. And not forgetting the connections. Don't be weird now about it, Anita. This is how you must play the game. Tap into it, all the connections he has, everying he wants to give. Receive it! Don't overthink this, please. Accept your good fortune with grace!"

When they've left, Neill pours the last drops from the fourth bottle of Moët. I feel light, tipsy, floating at the excitement of starting this new venture. No more marking, no more cringing at student evaluations. No journal editors sending anonymous venom, no more Gary Simmonses and their ilk.

I look around at my beautiful home, my beautiful man. It is all mine. For a moment, I smell again the damp cold shack in which I grew up. Who could imagine that life could exceed all expectations, that I could live like this, drive my BMW, go to sleep next to someone like Neill? He is standing with his back to me, looking out over the garden. I sidle up behind him, wrap my arms around his waist, and rest my head against his back.

"Thank you, my love. For everything. This life with you is a dream."

He squeezes my hand. "No, I must thank you. You have made everything worthwhile again. I have felt so lost, so numb, for years."

Later that night, as we're nodding off to sleep, he whispers: "I think you should see less of Thandiswa. She is just too ... I don't know, raucous. So loud. Raw. You need to think more strategically about your image now. You're a businesswoman, and your image, your brand, is everything. See less of her, please."

The words, like a splash of cold water to the face, wake me. "What? We've been friends forever!"

"Don't make it a big deal now, Anita. Stop overreacting. I've been in business for years. I know what I'm talking about. For once, just listen."

He turns his back to me.

The grey spot on my stomach announces itself yet again. "She's my oldest friend. I'm not just dropping her for appearance's sake, now that I've changed my job."

He turns again sharply, faces me. "You should have done that long ago. Got rid of her. Not only is she loud, she's always spouting that backward crap. About cleansing your space, burning imphepho, covering your chakras. A new-age fraud using superstitious nonsense. And the way you eat it up ... I can't stand it! Gullible! That's what you are."

There it is again: the unmistakable taint of contempt in his tone.

"But..." I try to protest.

He cuts me off: "You never know when to stop, do you? Always must have the last word. This conversation is finished. I've said what I have to say about her, and I won't discuss or debate it anymore. We've had a wonderful evening. And now you've gone and spoiled it. It's becoming a habit with you!"

He gets out of the bed and makes his way to the spare bedroom.

I lie in the dark, the wake of his words churning confusion and terror through my body. What the hell just happened? He's never had a problem with Thandiswa before. Yes, she has been coming round more often to the house since I quit my job, but only to be of support. He is hardly here when she's around, and when he is, they get on well.

Must be something going on with work, with the party. The national conference is looming, and the jostling for power is heating up. What I know about the various factions in the party is dangerous, but I do know that my husband is firmly aligned with one camp, the camp seeking to unseat the current power block. He has forged tight alliances with the men who will challenge the current incumbents for the position of president and Secretary-General of the party. If their bids fail, Neill will lose the power and influence he has silently, meticulously accrued behind the scenes. His dream is to be awarded the position of Speaker of the National Assembly. If the growing power bloc within the party's bid for power succeeds, he will be rewarded with that position. Ever the tactician, he has spent hours on the phone in his study strategising with the would-be president and Secretary General. The tussle for power has been merciless, and Neill's future rides on the fates of the players he backs.

Still, this is no excuse for the way he has spoken to me, like a disobedient child needing to be put in her place. But that's the thing, isn't it? It is beginning to dawn on me that a man like Neill, for all his progressive talk – his holding forth on women's rights as human rights, the feminisation of poverty, his passionate defence of the quota for women within the party's candidates list – is still a man who needs the women closest to him to know their place. For all his well-articulated, gender-progressive stances, I am starting to see that the political is not the personal for Neill. He requires the woman by his side, especially, to know her place. She will be secure as long as she doesn't challenge, doesn't question; as long as she accepts, believes his version of reality, of truth; while closing her eyes and her mind to the things that do not add up.

How can that woman be me? How does a woman like me get squashed into the box that Neill requires for any woman who is to remain in his life? It is impossible. Surely he must have known that as he got to know me? That I am not obedient, compliant; that I have never known my place? That I do not take direction from any man, on when to stop talking, when to stop thinking. A woman like me, born into poverty, rejected by all, does not get to the places I've been, get to hold the positions I have, by knowing my place. It is precisely because I refuse to know my place that I have achieved, albeit modestly, what I have set out to do. It is because of not knowing my place that I have been able to enter a place that gatekeeps so ferociously that it has taken almost superhuman determination to get through its doors in the first place. Both times. First as a student, and later as an academic.

An icy river courses through my body as I consider this new turn in our relationship – the contempt, the reprimand, the put-down, him removing himself from our bed, the one place where everything is guaranteed to work out. I am here with this man, in his house, my fate now irrevocably tied to his. I have quit my job, sold my house, and I have nowhere to return to, should this not work out. And now he wants me to stop seeing my friends. Panic rises in me. What have I done?

Chapter Ten

The weeks running up to the national elective conference are fraught. Neill sits me down and explains the importance of his going back to the Free State to campaign for himself and the comrades he supports. Whoever controls the branches, controls the province, and he will have to do grinding legwork to secure the province, and ultimately the outcome at the national convention.

"I am telling you this so you will understand, so that there will be no drama, no unnecessary tears, no looking for me. I will be gone for most of the next six weeks. I will not be sleeping, will not have time to eat some days, will be exhausted. Days will run into nights. Please, for the love of God, don't look for me, don't bother me. Don't make this a question of my love for you, or what you mean. You mean the world to me, but I will be busy. I will get in touch as often as I can. I cannot tolerate drama or baseless accusations from you. Do you understand?"

I nod, feeling numb.

"You have a new consultancy to build – I suggest you focus on that."

I ask if I can join him in the Free State some of the time.

Absolutely not, he replies. He cannot be worried about me, my comfort, my safety while he does the important work of securing victory. There's a lot at stake; this is a battle for the very soul of the party. Have I not read the papers? Political assassinations are the order of the day, especially in the Free State and KwaZulu-

Natal provinces. He cannot have my safety on the campaign trail as another burden to bear. When he puts it that way, I must agree.

"More than ever, I need your support, Anita. And what that means, in this instance, is for you to trust me and not question my whereabouts or motives."

I nod some more.

He holds both my hands in his, then plants a kiss on each one.

"Things won't always be this way. Once we've secured the presidency of the party, things will change. I promise I will make this up to you. We have the rest of our lives, our forever, ahead. Please be patient, my precious."

When he speaks like this, I believe him with my entire heart. I know he is right. I chose him, a politician. I knew the life I was getting into. I need to be strong, stronger than I've been, unflinching in my faith in him.

He is about to leave.

"I almost forgot something," he smiles, standing up from the sofa. He pulls a box from the inside pocket of his Hugo Boss suit jacket. It contains a sparkling diamond bracelet.

"Now promise me, you won't take it off," he says as he clasps it around my wrist. "Any time you miss me, just look at this bracelet. Let it be a reminder of how much I adore you, Anita."

The gift gives me the freedom to weep openly. He believes these to be tears of joy, and holds me tightly while stroking my back, comforting me.

"See my darling? This is just the start. There are so many more good things to come. You'll see. This house, this bracelet, it is only the start. Once we secure the party again from the forces that have taken it over, there will be many more such rewards for you – for us."

I allow myself the luxury of sobbing against his chest. He has become increasingly impatient with my tears, which these days gush at the merest hint of discord. That he allows them is a blessed relief.

I want to pull away from him, look him in the eye and tell my truth: that I don't want any rewards, can do without the fancy house, the car, the jewellery. That all I really need is him, with me, consistently. That more than anything, I want to start my days beside him, and end them in the same way, curled up in bed next to him, going over the mundanities of everyday life, kissing each other good night. That I would live back in the two-roomed house in Athlone if it meant that he'd be present; that I don't know how to be happy in a marriage where my husband is away for half of our lives together. Yes, I should have known; but I did not know exactly how desolate this life would feel until I had been dropped into it.

I say nothing, swallow the words. They would only lead to another fight, and I don't want him to leave me like that. Things have been bad enough. I need to hang in there for the next two months, until the elective conference is over. Maybe then he will be less busy, less distracted.

He sits with me until the sobbing subsides. He wipes my face with a handkerchief he keeps, always neatly pressed, in his trouser pocket. He kisses my face tenderly, while telling me how much he loves me. Soon, soon, he'll be back, and and then I'll have my hands full with him.

And then he is gone. I sit quietly in the spot where he's left me, watching the sun's rays dim through the floor-to-ceiling windows. I sleep fitfully, but wake with calm and clarity. This is how I will structure my days: work, networking, writing proposals, exercise, cooking, reading the latest journals in my field. In the evenings: exhibition openings, dinners out. Weekly trips to the spa, the hair salon. Training at the gym. Volunteering. My life is full. And when his absence aches, I will fill it with even more.

Over drinks with the coven, Thandiswa jokes that this would be the perfect time to take a lover. "Nothing serious, you know, just a little diversion. A nice hot Ben 10, perhaps?"

I fake a laugh, finding the joke distasteful. Maybe Neill is right about her?

I spend long days in my new office, studying the contours of the landscape I'm about to enter as a consultant, sending out introductory emails to potential clients and working with an event planner to organise the formal launch. Leads start to trickle in, but I am yet to secure a substantive contract. This is fine – I knew this phase would take time. I am fortunate not to have to worry about money – Neill takes care of everything. I get an allowance for running the household and for buying food, generous beyond any kind of discretionary money I've ever had. I pour money from my house sale and my meagre pension into the consultancy – Neill has told me many times that to earn big, you have to spend big!

I live for that one five-minute phone call per day from Neill. It is usually around six in the evening, when he is having a break to eat, or resting in a hotel room before the night's work. Perfunctory conversations: How are you, how is everything going; an exhausted performance of how are things at home. I miss you. I love you. We repeat the same words in the same sequence every evening. But I would rather have this than him not calling at all.

I think back to the heady days of falling in love, when we'd talk for hours, with depth and vulnerability. How that which was a great pleasure has now become a stilted duty, like so many other things in the marriage.

Against my better judgement, I reminisce about my first years of marriage to Keith. We were giddy with love, could not get enough of each other. Weekends meticulously planned to maximise our time together. We cooked together, prayed together, shaped our dreams for the future together. There was not a question in my mind about whether he loved me, or the state of our relationship. I took all of that for granted. Until it slowly started crumbling away under the weight of the empty cradle in the nursery we'd started to furnish.

I brush these thoughts aside. I shouldn't compare marriages – Neill is a different man altogether, a grootman, an important man, with the weight of the world on his shoulders. So much responsibility, so much of the country's trajectory riding on his actions, his decisions. He does not belong to me only, but also to the party and the nation. I need to accept that, once and for all, make peace with it, carve my own path alongside his.

A new anxious worm burrows in my gut. Our first wedding anniversary is coming up, and of course I want to spend it with him, celebrate with him. But I am too afraid to even mention it, lest an argument ensues. I want to keep the fragile peace, not ruin the five minutes a day I have of him. I cry about it to my mother, who advises me to stay silent. This too shall pass, my child. The first year of marriage is always the hardest. Next year will be better.

Next year will be better. And we have the rest of our lives together. We have our forever. I cling to that.

But what about this year, the now? This, right now, is my life too, and for how long will I defer my own happiness on the promise of a better tomorrow? Almost like the slogan they came to power with more than twenty years ago: a better life for all. When does the better life start?

I needn't have worried about the anniversary. Two days before, he arrives, unexpectedly, his arms full of two dozen red roses. I cannot believe he is actually there, within touching distance. We hug, kiss, fall into bed.

"You didn't seriously think that I'd forget our anniversary, Anita!" he jokes.

He is there for one night. I must pack my bags because we're escaping for a weekend to celebrate. Just us. No meetings with anyone from the party. No strategy sessions. No constituency work, no drinks with comrades. No calls from his ex-wife about some emergency with the children. He has told everyone he is not available this weekend. And he is spending it with me. I am elated.

On a plane next to him is the best place to be. He settles in a way I hardly ever see him do, into a bubble of tranquillity, unpierced by the trill of his phone ringing or the pings of text messages and emails landing in his inbox. We both read, holding hands while we do. Bodies in synch, breath in sway – our own private oasis.

A driver scoops us up from King Shaka Airport and deposits us at the Dolphin Coast's most exclusive hotel, where men in colonial garb silently open doors for us. The concierge greets Neill with a deferential bow – he is known here, and we are escorted to a luxury sea-facing cabana, all chinoiserie upholstered, and filled with four dozen roses. On the private balcony overlooking the Indian ocean, Neill raises a glass of Moët to his beautiful wife on our first anniversary. He promises to make each remaining year of our lifetime together better than the preceding one. I melt into him, wondering how this blissful moment could possibly be topped. He is resplendent in a Mandarin-collared linen shirt, chinos and leather sandals. I hardly ever see him like this anymore: relaxed, radiant, glowing with love, laser-focused on me. It's like we're back in the first heady days of our love affair.

I match him in a white Dolce & Gabbana sundress, bodice tight with a flared skirt, and spaghetti straps showing off my toned shoulders. My wardrobe has changed so much since our wedding

– sometimes I hardly recognise the elegant woman I've morphed into. I have transformed my appearance subtly, embodying a type of feminity I know Neill finds attractive. My hair, once mildly untamable, swishes below my shoulders with the high gloss of regular blow-dries, treatments and colouring. My nails are always manicured – never gaudy, always subtly painted. I've abandonded my glasses for contacts, and my eyebrows are shaped every second week, the furrows between them ironed out with a touch of Botox. My trainer at the gym, until now an unaffordable luxury, ensures my waist-to-hip ratio never strays outside the bounds of curvy-but-petite. Neill's love, and his money, have honed me from dull to sparkling diamond, each facet of my exterior reflecting him in the very best light. As it should be. Neill is a man who is beautiful to look at in every way – well put together, bespoke suits, well groomed, hours of gym evident in the shape of his body. In this, too, we must be equally yoked.

As we sip our champagne overlooking the ocean, I marvel at the perfection of him, the perfection of this moment. As the sun sets, I feel like I've been dipped in gold; not only me, but my entire life. I wish I could post these beautiful moments, this gilded life, on Instagram, but he forbids that, finds it tacky. To be showing off these kinds of indulgences would not sit well with the party – and most of all constituents. He has a public persona that he crafts meticulously. He is adamant that the personal – me, his children, his homes – are off limits and should remain out of public view.

I settle into a giant overstuffed wicker chair while Neill pours more champagne. The combination of alcohol and sun loosens the grip of my anxiety, and I feel, for the first time in months, relaxed. A weekend with Neill all to myself.

We are laughing about how the year has flown by, when his cell phone chirps.

"One moment, my precious. It's the Secretary-General," he says as he walks back into the suite and shuts the door behind him.

I suppose it was too good to be true, to expect that he'd be able to turn off his phone for the entire weekend. Hopefully the conversation will be over soon, and I'll have him back all to myself.

The minutes slip away and dusk falls as I drain my glass of Moët. I help myself to another. Neill emerges from the suite, and the look on his face tells me I'm about to be unhappy.

"I am so sorry, Anita…"

I refuse to be understanding; launch straight into a confrontation. "What now, Neill! What are you sorry about this time?"

"There's an emergency, an urgent lekgotla's been called. They need me. I am sorry, but I have to get to Bloemfontein."

I can hardly believe it.

"But it's our anniversary! You left me on our honeymoon and now you're leaving me again, a year later, in exactly the same way? Fuck this, Neill. Fuck the party and fuck you!"

He stares at me wordlessly as the cogs whirl in his mind. Will he attack or placate? What is the best way for him to deal with me? Everything is a game of strategy for him. He decides not to rage.

"Look, I am sorry. Obviously, I didn't plan for this to happen. Why would I waste money, time, in this way, if I hadn't really wanted to be with you? Please, come on now, be reasonable."

And then, the words: "I'll make it up to you, I promise" – the constant thread that runs through our relationship, stitching together all the rough patches.

The will to argue leaves my body; tears start streaming despite my attempts at stoicism. This is really how it is going to be – promises broken; time together stolen, being stolen back from me; our life together constantly off-kilter, fractured. Nothing that he says or commits to can ever be relied upon.

I retreat to the bathroom to fix my face. I see that he has already started packing to leave – his toothpaste and cologne, which he had unpacked an hour earlier, have already disappeared back into the Louis Vuitton toiletry bag perched on the edge of the bathroom sink.

I splash cold water on my face and wipe it down with a soft white towel. I look at the bag – strange how it is the first thing he's repacked for an emergency lekgotla – and on a whim, unzip it to see what it contains. Nothing out of the ordinary: there is his special toothpaste and toothbrush, the cologne, antacid, paracetamol and dental floss.

And then there is an inner pouch – in it, a blister pack of four blue diamond-shaped pills, and three condoms.

My blood runs cold. We've never bothered with contraception –

it hasn't been necessary. Irresponsible in the beginning, I know, but he had assured me that he checked his HIV status regularly, and that he hadn't had sex with anyone in at least a year before he'd met me.

I am frozen again, like Lot's wife. Perhaps the condoms are from the time before he met me? Then I remember that the Vuitton bag is a recent acquisition, brought home from a work trip away a few months after we married. The condoms had thus been bought within the course of our marriage.

A cloak of detachment falls over me. I take out the blister pack containing the blue diamonds. That he uses these comes as a surprise, although I suppose, at his age, things might not be as reliably functional as one might like. But I would have expected him to tell me, his wife, about any sexual difficulties he was having.

A knock on the bathroom door jolts me. "You okay, Anita? I need to leave soon, need to finish packing."

I stuff the pills and condoms back into the inner pouch and zip up the bag, careful to place it exactly where I found it. I flush the toilet and open the door, allowing him to enter the bathroom as I exit it to go back to the balcony.

I pour another glass of the Moët. It tastes like vinegar in my mouth. I must admit to myself that I have known this all along, in some small way – that my husband was having sex with another woman. The knowledge was there, in my body, even as I tried to shut it down with my mind, rationalise that he was busy, had a gruelling job, needed to travel frequently. My mind was playing games with me, an accomplice to Neill's deceit. But my body was never fooled; it clearly signalled Neill's betrayal and the presence of an interloper to me with nausea, stomach aches. My body spoke loudly; in fact, it screamed at me to wake up! Wake up! But I wouldn't listen, didn't trust the knowledge that comes from the visceral; had needed this evidence, this hard, shattering thing. Like my husband, the lawyer, I had started believing that only facts counted, only the tangible, measurable ways of knowing. That which you can touch, can see, which can be verified over and over again, is the only measure of truth that counts for anything.

And here now was a truth I could no longer smile away, drink away, fuck away – Neill has betrayed me.

The calm that settles over me is a blessing. Later I will fall apart, assess the damage, pick up the pieces. For now I am in survival mode – flight, fight or freeze? None of the above, just a deathly, serene calm that tells me to proceed with extreme caution as I plot my next steps. My enemy has been revealed, and he is cunning, sly. Rich and powerful. A man like this – there is no telling what he will do when confronted with the knowledge that I have seen behind the façade of care and honour he has so carefully cultivated.

Neill reappears on the balcony – his Hugo Boss blazer tells me he is on his way.

"Bye now, Anita. I'm sorry, my precious. I'll be back as soon as humanly possible."

He walks over, bends down and kisses my cheek.

I look at him dispassionately, trying to discern the real man who resides behind the loving look he casts upon me. I see nothing.

"Travel safely, my love."

He offers a sad smile, then turns and leaves.

Night falls on the balcony. I sit in silence, watching the sea turn to black ink. The moon rises, trailing a giant shaft of light across the smooth surface of the ocean. It is only a good half-an-hour after he leaves, once I am sure he will not return in a hurry for some forgotten thing, that I allow myself to let go; allow myself to let the full weight of his betrayal crush me. My heart struggles to pump against the clamp of an invisible vice tightening around it. When I can no longer stand the pain in my chest, it courses down my arm into my hand, crushing the empty champagne flute I've absentmindedly held on to. It shatters, breaking the spell and cutting into the flesh of my palm, allowing me, at last, to release a guttural howl. I fall to the floor, on my knees, sobbing. Neill – beautiful, brilliant, honourable Neill – my love, my life. A fucking fraud.

Chapter Eleven

I wake up on the floor as the sun pierces the horizon, my head in the grip of a hangover that is the Moët-benzo lovechild from hell. Shards of glass lie scattered around me. Fortunately, the cuts in my hand are superficial; blood has clotted in my palm. I read somewhere that the heart is the same size as the palm of one's hand. My bloodied palm, ripped to shreds, could well be my heart. My perfect blow-dry has patches of blood sticking to it where I touched my hair. My white dress, the pristine outfit in the scene of enchantment I savoured in the moments before my life shattered, is stained with blood.

I struggle onto my knees, trying to avoid further cuts from the glass strewn around me. I make it to the bathroom, dislodge a small shard of glass still stuck in my hand. The bleeding starts afresh – I hold my hand under cold running water to wash both the clotted and newly flowing blood off me. I find cotton wool and bandage in a first-aid kit under the basin, and press the cotton wool down on the re-opened gash.

I check my watch – it is 8am. God knows when Neill will be back. And when he does get back? Then what? Confrontation? Accusations? Never that simple with a man like Neill. I know now that he will resort to the gaslighting he has used on me all along, will simply flip the argument on me. How dare I go through his stuff? What's in his overnight bag is private, I have no business there. I was snooping, invading his privacy. The tongue-lashing he's bound to unleash on me will be so calculated, so precise, I know I'll end up being the one apologising for ruining our anniversary celebration. As certain as I am in this moment that Neill is cheating, so certain will I be, when he is done arguing his case, that I was wrong, misguided, a paranoid wreck for even thinking this way.

I turn the shower on to almost scalding heat, lathering my body with fragrant shower gel, careful to keep my cut hand out of the stream of water. My emotions vacillate between grief and rage. I need to stay clear-headed with Neill. He might even throw me out on the grounds that I invaded his privacy, betrayed his trust. And where would I go? I no longer have a house of my own, and my savings are dangerously low after the office make-over.

As I inhale the geranium-scented steam of the shower, I will myself to be strong, stay focused. By the time I am dried and dressed, a dim outline of what I need to do next starts to form.

I need more evidence. The condoms, the Viagra – these are not enough. I need to know who the other woman is, where they meet, how often. I have to find solid, irrefutable evidence with which to confront Neill, so that there will be no room for him to twist this, to turn the tables, making me the wrongdoer.

No, there will be no confrontation today. I will wait, bide my time. Out-strategise the strategist. Waves of panic drive bile into my mouth. Neill is the smartest man I know. Someone like me, so unsavvy, gullible – oh, how right he was about that – how will I outwit him? He has hidden his affair from me for this long. He knows what he is doing. I have gone into this relationship blindly trusting, naïve, and despite knowing that something was off, gaslit myself even more than Neill did to convince myself that everything was okay.

Clad in a comfortable, loose dress, I take in my image in the mirror – the dark circles under the eyes, my wet hair still matted, and make a decision right there: Neill will never see my distress, will never see me cry over this betrayal. I am far too proud a woman for that.

I apply a serum to my hair and leave it to air-dry. My hand is too sore to manoeuvre the hairdryer.

Next, I do my make-up, expertly camouflaging the undereye circles and contouring my face with highlighter. Whatever comes next, I will look good.

Will my marriage survive? Do I want it to survive? Do I still want Neill? Yes. Yes, I do. I check my gut and it screams at me to fight for him with every ounce of strength my body and soul can muster. I will not cede him. I love him, still love him despite this. But first I must know the extent of the damage.

I call housekeeping and ask them to clean up the broken glass from the balcony and bathroom, then depart the room for breakfast. My stomach churns as I enter the dining hall and the smell of bacon assaults me. With no appetite, I gulp down two cups of coffee and force myself to eat a small bowl of yoghurt.

I find a spot by the pool, an Olympic-sized monstrosity flanked by sculptures of young women, next to a patio bedecked with red and white umbrellas. My eyes hurt, my hand, wrapped in a bandage, hurts, my heart hurts. My career is gone, my home is gone. And I have to remain the faithful, loving wife I've been until I can figure out what to do. How to live with this betrayal. How to move forward loving Neill when I know that this love has not been reciprocated.

The listless day drags on, with me lounging next to the pool. Neill returns at four in the afternoon. I welcome him back to our suite with a cool demeanour – pleasant, happy to see him, but not too happy.

He folds me against his body, lifts me up and swings me around, puts me down again and grabs my face with both hands, planting a big, soppy kiss on my lips.

He notices the bandage on my hand.

"What happened?"

"Nothing much, just clumsy me."

"Now where were we…" he smirks while starting to unzip my dress. I let him. He slips the dress off my shoulders; I watch it billow around my ankles as it falls on the cream carpet. He plants a myriad of tiny kisses along the contours of my neck, then plunges his tongue between my breasts, licking up and down while undoing my bra. I sigh, wondering if he's been with her. His clothes, immaculate as always, betray nothing. I inhale him – not a trace of another woman's scent lingers on his body. I take off his shirt. Not a scratch, not a bite mark, not a hint of skin discolouration left by an overzealous lover. He discards my bra on the floor, and grazes my nipples with his teeth. I want to push him away, shove him against a wall and ask him just what the fuck he has been up to, but I stand, rod-straight and still, allowing him the liberty of my body.

My body betrays me. I feel the dampness spread between my legs as his tongue and lips lick, suck, probe the dips and rises of my body. He kneels in front of me, tugging my panties down around my hips with one practised move. I shudder. He plants his face between my thighs. I look down at him and resist the urge to plunge my freshly manicured nails, filed into sharp points, into the flesh of his exposed neck. I want to draw blood. Instead, I close my eyes and allow him to do what he wants with me. We end up writhing on the bed, then collapse into each other as he orgasms. We lie together for a few minutes, limbs entwined, heavy breaths punctuating the silence.

"Happy first anniversary, my precious," he says, kissing my face, my shoulders, my hands. "Here's to many more years together. I promise they will get easier from here on."

I say nothing, keep my eyes shut, and float on the feeling of release still coursing through my body. He gets up from the bed, wraps a towel around his waist, and gets a flat box out of his bag.

"Here's your anniversary gift."

I open it. It is a A4-sized lithograph by Sophie Peters, his second gift to me by the artist I most love. A thoughtful gift for a paper anniversary. In spite of everything, I am touched.

My own gift now feels inadequate, but I produce it anyway, from a folio in my bag. An embossed piece of paper, inscribed with the words of a poem I wrote for him. What else could I possibly give to a man who has everything, but my words of love? He reads it and smiles, bends down to kiss me again.

"You are certainly a gifted wordsmith. I didn't know your many talents included writing poetry. Thank you. I will treasure this."

He gets up from the bed and runs me a bath.

"Come, get ready. I've booked a special table for us for dinner tonight. You go get cleaned up first, and I'll hop into the shower when you're done. I need to make a few quick calls anyway, so we can dine in peace. Tonight, I promise you my undivided attention."

I lie stretched out on the bed, listening to his movements around the bathroom as he prepares my bath. I run my hand down the centre of my naked body, from my neck, over my stomach, and down between my legs. I wonder: how does a man make love to his wife so passionately when he has just returned from being with another woman?

Yet the love I feel from him is real. It is there, in the way he touches me, the way he cannot tear his eyes away from me, the way he kisses me. What kind of man is he if he has been with someone else last night, perhaps even this morning?

Perhaps he wasn't. Perhaps there really was a lekgotla, and also a perfectly reasonable explanation for why he was carrying condoms in his overnight bag. Perhaps they belong to another comrade, or are left over from his single life. We haven't been together for that long. Heaven knows, I have lipsticks older than our relationship in my make-up bag. I should just talk to him, ask him – gently, of course – and he will straighten out this whole mess. Tell me, show me, how foolish I've been to doubt him for one second.

The tap stops running and seconds later, Neill reappears in the bedroom.

"Your bath awaits, my precious. It's the perfect temperature."

I ask: "How was the lekgotla?"

"My precious, I won't bore you with the details. Come, come don't let your bath get too cold."

He pulls me up by my wrists and slaps my bottom as I pass him, naked. The large oval bathtub brims with bubbles. The air is perfumed, sweet. I open the cabinet under the bathroom sink and see Neill's toiletry bag tucked way back, unpacked from his suitcase, and I know what I have to do. I lock the bathroom door and, with my heart pounding in my throat, I pick up the Louis Vuitton bag and unzip it. I go straight to the inner pocket, where I find the condoms. The three condoms that were there have returned, intact. I sigh with relief. At least he hasn't used them! I pull out the blister pack of blue diamonds. Two of the four are gone.

My heart shatters again. He has used two Viagra pills in the last twenty-four hours away from me, and what is more, whoever he's been with, he's had sex with them without a condom.

I pack everything away neatly, and step into the bath, wishing the water would dissolve me. I wish I could leave this gilded lie of a life immediately and run, run as far away from Neill as possible. But I can't. This is my life now. I have traded my old life for this one with him, putting all my faith in a man. This man who, it is clear, has betrayed me. I cannot wish that fact away, live in denial for a second longer. My body knew. It knew all along, was screaming for me to wake up, but I wouldn't listen. I sink further and further into the bath water, completely numb.

Our evening together in the restaurant passes in a blur. Neill is animated, happy, telling the waitstaff what a special occasion the night marks. I pick at my food, then excuse myself to go and vomit in the bathroom. I return to tell Neill that I am ill, and we leave our dinner early. He makes me chamomile tea in the suite, watches with concern while I drink. Soon he is softly snoring next to me, sleeping peacefully while I toss and turn for half the night, before reaching for my trusted benzos.

We get up early to catch a flight back to Cape Town. Before we leave our suite, Neill pauses at the door and cups my chin in his hand, tilting my face up towards his.

"Well, we've made it, Anita. One year. Thank you for sticking with me. I know I haven't been the easiest. There were times I didn't think we'd get here. But I love you more and more with every passing day."

I say nothing, but smile and reward him with a kiss on the cheek, hoping that will be enough of a response.

In the back of the car taking us to King Shaka Airport, I snuggle against him, thread my arm through his, and lay my head on his shoulder.

"Still feeling ill, my precious?" His voice is full of concern.

I nod and close my eyes, relaxing into his body as the car exits the driveway.

He pulls his phone out of his pocket. It has been switched off all night, and as he starts it up, he bends his head to look at me. I keep my eyes shut, feigning sleep, but open my eyelids just a crack as he punches in the six-digit code to unlock his phone. I see the numbers he inputs and commit the PIN code to memory before closing my eyes again. The coming weeks will bring enough time and space to figure out how I will use it going forward.

Once we are back home, Neill makes it clear to me, yet again, that the final few days running up to the national conference will be extremely busy: "I will not be around, will most likely not be able to take calls or reply to your text messages. Please my love, know that I will do my best to stay in touch. But, I am asking you now already, forgive me for the neglect you are going to suffer over the next two weeks."

I nod. Always so thoughtful.

Since my discovery, I have been obsessed with the identity of his mistress. I wonder if she will also be "on the ground" campaigning in the run-up to the national conference. On her back, more likely. I wonder what she does for a living: president of a branch in the party, or perhaps a young, hotshot lawyer in Bloemfontein? Heaven forbid she is still a student and my darling husband a pathetic sugar daddy, the likes of whom we see all too many at the gates of the university on Friday afternoons. Transactional sex, they call it in Gender Studies, as if all sex is not transactional. And the old men lining up, waiting for their young girlfriends – they look like utter fools. Surely Neill would not be this foolish. Perhaps she is married too; maybe he longs to be with her and has settled for me because she is already taken.

I picture her: tall, young (if one is going to take a mistress, it makes sense that she would be younger than the wife), pretty (obviously), with long jet-black hair and doe eyes. Definitely a professional, a beautiful go-getter; Neill, wanting only the best of everything in life, would not deign to mess with anything less than a stellar woman.

I need to know who she is, so that I can properly focus this jealousy rending my heart. I want to know who to hate, despise with my entire being, and then start plotting to destroy her. Because that's how I feel. I do not merely want to remove her from Neill's life, from our life together; I want to destroy her; beat her up like I did the girls in primary school who waited for me outside the school gate before they knew what I had in me. The girls who came off much worse than I ever did, and never tried shit with me again.

Part of me is ashamed that I feel like hurting another woman. Before this happened, I was one of those people who judged betrayed women who took their rage out on the "other woman". You know the argument – the other woman is not the one who betrayed you: your husband is. Your anger and vengeance should be reserved for him. The other woman broke no vow. But here, in the thick of it, it's not Neill whose eyes I'd like to gouge out – it is hers, this mythical, beautiful, thin and whip-smart young creature who has usurped my place in my husband's heart and bed. I promise myself that I will find her. And she will be sorry.

Neill visits the pharmacy and returns with a cornucopia of drugs for my upset stomach. He is sorry to be leaving me while I'm ill, he says, eyes full of concern. He will keep his phone on and closer than usual, and if my condition worsens, he'll be on the first flight home. I assure him that I'll be fine, but enjoy the fuss nonetheless, even though I know the performance to be a pretence.

His leave-taking is filled with much less anxiety than usual. It is a blessed relief when he pulls the front door closed behind him. Finally alone, I have time to think, to plot, to figure out what I need to do. I resolve not to tell anyone about this. I still want to be with Neill; I want to have him without the humiliation of my friends' and my mother's pity. I will deal with the emotional fallout of his affair by myself – I just need to find out who and how long – and then I'll make him stop.

Chapter Twelve

My nausea and stomach cramps clear as soon as Neill leaves. I wait an hour, knowing that after this amount of time, he would have checked in for his flight, making it impossible to dash back home to pick up something forgotten. The plan has been brewing in my head since we left Durban, and further refined on the plane while I pretended to doze.

I send the domestic worker home, lock all the doors to the house, and make my way to Neill's study. With its panelled walls, book-lined on one side with all his law journals, its leather couches and heavy imbuia desk, it is the one place in the house I never go. Something about it feels stuffy; its style an articulation of a world in which I don't belong. Neill always shuts the doors when he works here, especially when taking phone calls. Since he is not home, the heavy, dark-green curtains remain unopened; the study, dusk-like, retains the faint aroma of the cigars he smokes in here from time to time. I turn on the desk lamp and make myself comfortable in his chair.

The desk is clear – no notepads, no scraps of paper. So like Neill, not a thing out of place on the surface, but who knows what lurks underneath the pristine veneer of his life? I open each drawer. In the top one, I immediately find what I was hoping to – the old iPhone he upgraded from two months ago, neatly stashed in the box in which the new one came. I place the phone, still in its box, on top of the desk, and continue to rifle through the drawers. Nothing untoward.

A few scraps of papers with odd cell phone numbers, with no names attached to them. An old, weather-beaten leather wallet with a stack of business cards, and two blue diamond-shaped pills tucked inside. A birthday card, undated, from a woman called Kelley, addressed to "my love". Not hard evidence – this could be from a time before he knew me. Two receipts: one for a dinner at a restaurant I don't recognise, a second for an Apple watch. I've never seen him wear one.

In the bottom drawer I find a leather satchel containing his old laptop – the one he replaced about a year ago, just after we were married. I try to switch it on – it prompts me for a password, which I don't have. I leave the laptop open on the desk, then return to the obsolete iPhone I found earlier. I am counting on the fact that, like me, Neill keeps the same PIN when he changes phones – it is always such a drag to think up and commit to memory a new one.

I punch in the six-digit code I memorised in the back of the car. It is the magic "open sesame" I need. The iPhone home screen wakens, its apps springing to life and glistening like jewels. My stomach lurches, not knowing where to look first, but also for fear of what I might find. And I am not only snooping, but breaking the law. It is a criminal offence to read someone's personal data – emails, texts, SMSes – without their permission, punishable by up to twelve months in prison or a fine.

I'll take my chances. Any judge would sympathise with my predicament at this moment.

My hands shake; I rationalise the invasion that I instinctively know will change my life by telling myself that anyone in my situation would do this; if not to catch out her husband, to get the peace of mind that comes with knowing he is not doing anything wrong.

I take my time looking at the twinkling screen. First, I need to disable the wifi, in case opening one or other app pings to his more recent phone, alerting him to snooping or an attempted hacking. I go into settings and switch the phone to airplane mode, then take a deep breath, knowing that what I'm about to do will change my life. What I am about to find out, I will not be able to unsee, unknow. For a moment I consider turning the phone off and putting it back into its box, back into the drawer; continuing with the life I have, making the best of it, knowing that my husband is cheating. Not knowing the details will allow me to retain this knowledge as an abstraction.

If I focus on the good things – the house, the cars, the gifts, the expensive holidays – I can forge a good life for myself here; a great life, even. Be grateful when he is present, choosing my bed over hers. It is not as if he neglects me sexually. Be content to be happy when the sun of his affection shines on me; lap it up, and get the most out of it – money, things. He is generous. He tries to make me happy, materially at least. He is discreet. I have found out what I did because I went looking. If I could just know my place in this arrangement, I could make it work for me.

I laugh at myself. What have I become? Avoiding a truth I finally have access to, to stay in the good graces of my benevolent patriarch, to keep wearing the rose-tinted glasses through which I have viewed him thus far. My liar, my gaslighter. My wonderful Neill. What have I become? A woman more loyal to the image of a man than to herself. No, there is no turning back now – I must confront the truth.

The first app I choose is WhatsApp. The messages are between all the regulars I would expect: me, his mom, his sisters, some comrades whose names I recognise, his PA. I scroll down. Nothing untoward. I close the app and go to the direct messages. Not as many messages here as on WhatsApp, which is clearly his preferred mode of text communication.

I close the app and go to the one for booking hotels. A range of hotels have been booked in the past year, many of them I don't know. Not untoward, necessarily – he does travel a lot and needs to sleep somewhere. But some of these hotels are not in the Free State or KZN, ostensibly his main destinations when he leaves me. I click on one, a game reserve in Mpumalanga. A weekend booking for two. The date stands out as significant – my mother's birthday. We'd had plans with her which he had to pull out of at the last moment because of a constituency crisis in Mangaung. Which is nowhere near this game reserve.

I shudder. He even rated the experience with five stars. The bastard! This was one of the weekends I remember not being able to make contact with him at all. Several other bookings at five-star hotels reveal themselves, all for two people, all within the period we were engaged and married; none of the people he was with, me. He has been at the hotel we've just arrived from several times – is a regular there.

My stomach lurches violently. Who is the bitch? I want to know. I have more than enough evidence here already that my husband has been cheating on me for the entire duration of our relationship. Should I really try to find out more? Yes. Yes! I want to know. I will drive to her house right now and see her straight!

I dip into his emails, but my swirling head doesn't allow me to see anything clearly. My hands shake. Back into the WhatsApp messages I go, and this time I open the archived texts.

What I find makes me dizzy. Message upon message from multiple women. Scrolling through them is like a ride on a high-speed rollercoaster, tossing me against invisible walls and turning my stomach.

From:

Lynette: "I miss you and wish I was entangled with you right now."

Tumi: "Good morning to the reason for my smile ☺"

Shireen: "So good seeing you last night!"

Kelley: "I can't stop thinking about last night."

Gilda: "I love you, Neill, always!"

Carla: "Oh my God, please answer Neill, don't do this to me!"

Sharda: "At the airport, see you soon, sexy!"

Nontobeko: "Don't forget about our date."

Antoinette: "Too busy for a quick drink? I'm around this weekend!"

And on and on it goes, a seemingly endless list of women sending the most intimate messages, the most intimate pictures. Young, middle-aged, older than me; skinny, sculpted, big, curvy. Blonde, brunette, black, coloured, Indian. Every race, age, body type is represented in his gallery. He has no discernable type.

Salty saliva rises from the back of my throat. I run down the passage to the guest bathroom, which I reach just in time to vomit. I retch up undigested food and the pills he administered just before he left. I vomit some more, until there is nothing but silvery liquid exiting my mouth. And even when there is nothing else left to vomit out of my system, I dry-heave. I hunch over the toilet for what feels like hours. There can be nothing left in my stomach, and yet the painful spasms continue, my body's attempt to expel the horror of what I have just seen. Grief lodges in my throat.

I thought I was a cherished wife. Precious. Instead, I've discovered that I'm merely the whore-in-chief of a skilfully-tended harem. Yes, that is what he has made of me, without my knowledge or consent – an interchangeable body on a endless conveyor belt of women, ready to be picked up and sampled at his desire, his pleasure.

I wash my face and go back into the study. I just do not have the stomach for further investigation right now. I pack everything away as I found it, shut the drawers. The air in the study starts to suffocate me; I need to get out, as far away from here as possible.

My red BMW purrs along the winding streets of the city, and for the first time since owning it, I floor it on the highway. No idea where I'm going, I go faster and faster, swerving in and out of traffic to get beyond any car in front of me, just to get the hell away. Maybe if I'm lucky I will lose control, go off the road, and this whole nightmare will end. I drive up the N1 highway into the winelands and back again, turning off towards the west coast. I keep driving, eventually finding myself on the beach at Melkbosstrand. It is a cold day, with not many people about. As the sun readies itself to dip behind the ocean, I get out of the car and wade into the frigid water, so icy it jolts me out of the haze I've wrapped around myself since Durban. The rage that has welled up in my body over the days, months and years dislodges, coming out in great heaving sobs. I sit on the beach for God knows how long and weep; not only for the man whom I loved, or for the betrayal, the sick games and lies, but also for the future I thought we'd have together. The idea of growing old with him, of having him beside me to weather whatever this fickle life might throw at me – not for one moment thinking he would be life's chief agent in dumping the most unimaginable despair on me.

It's completely dark when I get back into my car and steer it back towards the city. I cannot go back home. But where is there left to go? I've sold my house, used a large chunk of the proceeds to fund this foolish venture of a consultancy. The house is his, my fledgling business is tied to it, and would be impossible to access if I left.

I could take the furniture with me, but where to? Even my old car I sold for a song, flush with the excitement of zipping around town in a new BMW.

As if by autopilot, said BMW finds its way to Athlone and pulls up in front of the modest two-bedroomed home in Bokmakierie. My mother is probably already in bed, but I need her. She opens the door after I've knocked for quite a while, and only once she determines it is really me.

"Anita, what…?"

She takes one look at my face, and asks if something has happened to Neill. I start crying. She soon joins me, knowing that whatever has happened must be catastrophic.

"What is it, my girl, what happened?"

I cannot speak, but my mother's arms allow the sobs to wrack my body. It is a relief to be here, with someone who truly loves me, who will tend to me. She comforts, soothes, clucks around me sympathetically, her task just to be there while my emotions wash through me.

When I am done crying, she gets up from the couch on which we've huddled, and puts on the kettle. In a minute she returns from the kitchen with a cup of strong, milky tea. I know it will burn my throat with the amount of sugar she will have ladled in for the shock.

We sip on our tea as I voice the obscene tale of what I've seen today, what I've been living through, unknowingly, for the past two years.

She starts crying again, softly: "Oh my girl, oh my girl! Are you sure? Are you sure?"

"Yes Mum, I am absolutely certain of what I saw."

"But how could he do this? How could he do this to you my child? It makes no sense. He loves you, it is plain for anyone with eyes in their head to see, how much he loves you. Look at everything he's done for you, given you. The car, the jewellery, all these beautiful things? Why?"

"I don't know, Mum. I wish I knew what to tell you."

We sit in silence for a while, staring into the distance, each with her own thoughts.

My mother breaks the silence with a heavy sigh. "Have you eaten today?"

I haven't, but feel no hunger. Nor can I swallow down my favourite chicken soup that she warms from an ice-cream container pulled out of the freezer. All I manage to get inside of me is a slice of toast.

Her phone rings. It is Neill. She looks at me, her face a big question-mark.

"Tell him I am here, but sleeping. I wasn't feeling well and came to your house to rest."

I listen to her answer Neill's questions, as they become more and more insistent. "No, Neill, she doesn't need to go to hospital. No, she's exhausted, just needs to sleep off this bug. My neighbour, Junie, also had this stomach bug last week, the only cure is rest." I hear his voice on the other end, but can't make out the words. She answers again.

"No, no Neill, please don't come home. She wouldn't want you to come now. We know how close it is to the national conference. You are needed there, my child."

My child. The words are a dagger in my heart. The son she has always wanted, now doing this to the child she never wanted. The irony. I know she loves Neill fully, has accepted him as her own. How could she not, with all of his charm and the gifts he has showered on her? A kitchen renovation, a new Samsung phone, a smart TV.

I open my own phone and find several WhatsApp messages and missed calls from Neill. Where was I? Was I feeling better? Did I need a doctor? Should he arrange a car to take me to the doctor?

I will reply to him tomorrow.

For tonight, I take another benzo – I am popping them these days at the same rate my husband pops Viagra – and go to sleep on the couch in the spare room, which my mother has made up with bedding. I drift off into a meagre sleep, punctuated with dreams of me following Neill around the house, trying to catch up with him, but never reaching him.

I wake at 3am, unable to sleep any longer. My mother is awake, and comes into the room after hearing me return from the bathroom.

"My girl, what are you going to do?"

"I don't know, Mum. I don't know."

"Surely you are not going to leave him? My child, tell me you are not going to leave that man. Another divorce. A second failed marriage. What will people say? That there's something wrong with you. That you can't keep a man. Sometimes I wonder if all that education was a good thing."

I look at her in disbelief. Not this, not now. Not this pushing me towards perpetual ordentlikheid, when he is the one who has fouled up my life.

"Mum, I told you, I don't know. I can't think straight."

"You can go back there, Anita. Make it work. Look at you, you have everything your heart desires with that man. He gives you everything! You can say what you want of him, but he's a good provider. And it's not like he hit you. Pray on it. Don't let your pride be your downfall, my girl!"

I have nothing more to say to her. "Leave me, Mum, I need to sleep."

I suppress the urge to shove her through the spare-room door.

After she leaves, I crawl back onto the couch, where I'm lulled back to sleep with the aid of another benzo. At least these tiny white pills never let me down.

Chapter Thirteen

I don't know what to do, I tell my mother. But I do, I do. My first duty is towards *my* safety, *my* survival. A lever switches within me. My body knows; it knows what I need and what to do. The instinct to survive this takes over.

I am at my gynaecologist's office, to test for a variety of sexually transmitted infections. She is kind, obviously trained in counselling, because she listens quietly, attentively as I tell her my story.

The test for HIV yields immediate results: negative.

I break down and cry as she shares this news. She walks around her desk, hands me tissues, pats me on my shoulder. "You have dodged a bullet."

The other test results will take longer to get back from the lab, but most other STIs are not chronic conditions, so should I have one, she'll decide on a course of treatment. She orders an HPV test from my previous pap smear with her, just months earlier. HPV, she explains, can be a silent killer. Transmitted during sex, the virus can lie dormant for years before it triggers cervical cancer. Anyone who is sexually active can be infected with HPV – the worst part, she tells me, is finding the virus in women who have had sex with only one man their entire life.

"We've had huge HIV campaigns in this country warning people about safe sex when they have a series of partners, but women are most susceptible when they believe themselves to be in a monogamous relationship with a man who is not."

She treats many women whose husbands, whom they assume to be faithful, infect them. When you believe you are in a monogamous relationship, what need is there for barrier protection like condoms?

"Do you think you will remain in this marriage?" she asks.

I shrug. I've hardly started to process Neill's multiple affairs. My head feels stuffed with cotton wool, and this minute, I can't see beyond the fog.

"If you do, I'd strongly advise you to go onto PrEP."

"What is that?"

"PrEP stands for pre-exposure prophylaxis. Many people in high-risk sexual situations use it. It is medication that prevents you being infected with HIV. You take it once a day."

I nod. Good God, I am in a high-risk sexual relationship, with a man who has vowed fidelity to me. What kind of man claims to love you while exposing you to HIV and HPV, life-altering viruses that might kill you in the end? I already know Neill doesn't use condoms with whomever else he's having sex. The untouched condoms in his overnight bag proves this. How could he be so thoughtless, show such utter disregard for my safety, if not his own?

A painful silence hangs between me and the doctor. In the end, she breaks it. "Would you like me to refer you to a counsellor, Anita, to help you think through these decisions?"

I shake my head.

"Alright. You're a very tough woman. I know you will get through this and make the right choice for you. Remember, there is no good or bad, wrong or right decision here. It's complicated. You've merged your life with his. I know it's not easy to disentangle yourself. But whatever you decide, please be aware of the risks. Take precautions. Take care of yourself. Because your husband surely isn't doing that."

I thank her as I take the script for PrEP.

My next consultation is with Claire, not at a bar or fancy restaurant, but at her office.

Once the shock of hearing my story subsides, she gets down to business. We revisit the prenup – how different this time, a short year after I signed it!

"Well, it's fairly standard. In the case of dissolution, each walks away with what they brought into the marriage. What assets do you own?"

Nothing really, since I've sold my house. The furniture in the consultancy rooms Neill bought me as a gift, and I wouldn't know where to take that anyway, as my office is in his house.

Claire goes on. "You are not entitled to any of Neill's earnings or investment income for the year you've been married. And there are obviously no children for him to support."

Not that old wound again, on top of everything else. I sigh. Flush with love for my future husband, I had also signed away any entitlement to spousal maintenance in the event of a divorce.

"I think you could still ask him for some support, seeing as you no longer have a home to return to. He's not at all obligated to do that, but he might be generous, given that he's the one who messed up here. If you decide to end the marriage. You are going to leave, though, aren't you, Anita?"

I don't answer.

Yes, the old Anita of two years ago would have baulked at the idea of a weak woman standing by her man – a man without an iota of loyalty. But what has happened to that Anita? I hardly know the woman I've become, the one who has contorted herself, become a shapeshifter to please a man, to keep the peace, keep him happy.

"What about the car he gave you, Anita? Do you own it?"

"I don't know."

"For the love of God, my friend, how do you not know this? We talked about this before you got married. You have built in so very little protection for yourself in this relationship. I hope to God he will be kind to you if you decide to separate, but men like this usually aren't. A man who could do this to you will have no qualms about your financial security post this relationship. You need to think very carefully about your next steps, play your cards right – or you will walk away with less than nothing. That is, if you choose to walk away at all."

"What are my options, Claire, legally?"

"You don't have many. My most cynical advice would be to tough it out, stay another year or two, get what you can out of him during that time. But you'd have to fake it, the whole thing, the marriage, the love. He'll feel it. Anyone with emotional intelligence would know you were faking it."

"But that's what he did!" I start crying again. "He faked it, everything – the texts I saw between him and these women go back to before we were even married. And did I feel it? No! I thought he loved me! How could I not have felt this … this gross betrayal? What was wrong with me? My instincts, my intuition?"

My friend looks at me, sadness pulling down the corners of her eyes. "Please don't do this to yourself, Anita. Don't beat yourself up. He has abused your trust, your love. He may not have physically abused you, but what he has done is a profound act of psychological aggression. Don't add to that. Please don't."

She looks down at her hands, then back at me: "I deal with divorces all the time. There's a class of men who do this, who prey on women. It may not be physical abuse, but emotional abuse hurts just as much. A woman like you is on the back foot, because you want to trust, want to see the best, think the best of the man you love so much. Men like Neill count on that – abuse that love."

I nod. Yes, I have wanted to see the best in him, always: "But now that I think of it, I don't think I ever trusted him. But he would guilt me for that – imply that there was something deficient, damaged in me for not trusting him. He did that so well, so skillfully."

"Yes, that is what manipulators do. Turn the tables and project blame onto you when they know very well what they are doing is wrong. I am sorry that he did this to you, Anita. But please do not take this on as your fault simply because you had the courage to love someone, because you wanted so badly to believe in him."

Silent tears trickle down my cheeks, pooling below my neck.

"You're gonna be okay, Anita. I know this hurts like hell, but you'll get through it. I promise. For now, you need to figure out how to get out of the relationship, if that's what you are sure you want to do. Without Neill harming you even more. Because I fully believe he is capable of that, once you let on what you've found out."

She frowns. "Does Thandiswa know?"

I shake my head. Claire calls Thandiswa, who appears within half an hour. Our consultation morphs into a proper coven circle once she arrives with a bottle of Johnnie Walker – no more 18-year-old Macallan for me – and a bag of ice. We spread out on the couches off to the side of Claire's office. Thandiswa lights some incense while pouring all three of us doubles, on the rocks.

She is much less restrained than Claire as I tell her the whole sordid story. "What the fuck, my friend?"

She is incredulous. "Die vark!" she interjects at key points of the story.

The whisky, chased by Thandiswa's fiery outrage, is just what I need to melt the icy shell of detachment around my heart. Whereas Claire's cool demeanour was what I needed to help me see the practical steps I should take, what could go wrong, what I should consider – Thandiswa's rage on my behalf is the fire I need.

Drunk and empty-stomached, I cry, scream, reel in the retelling of the story. The tears that come in the company of my friends release me from a spell, bringing relief. Something visceral leaves my body with these sobs, so unlike the ones I shed yesterday, at the beach – tears of sorrow. Today's tears, shed while surrounded by a circle of loving women, are cleansing, healing.

Claire and Thandiswa take turns to hold me, hug me, soothe me through the telling, never once reminding me that they told me to be careful, never once uttering the words, how could you have been so gullible? How could you not have known? Not have seen, smelled, felt another woman on him? Because those of us who have honed that sixth sense, who don't disavow it as mere superstition or a woman's hysteria: we do know. But I had dulled that sense, blunted it into submission – and all to keep a man happy. I toed the line, and took it all as he construed it: a fault in me, damaged as I was, unable to trust a man.

When I'm done, Thandiswa announces: "You can come and stay with me. We will go and pack your bags right now, both of us, and bring you over to my place."

"Thandiswa, I don't know."

"Don't know what? If you're going to leave him?"

Claire tries to shush her, but Thandiswa won't be silenced. "Nee, fok daai man, Anita. You are a queen, now pick up your crown and put it back on, and leave that bastard and all his little blue pills in the gutter where he belongs. Please!"

We screech with laughter. Trust Thandiswa to turn tragedy into comedy.

"Seriously, though," I say. "I am going back home. I have nowhere else to go. Thank you for your offer to have me stay, but that house is my home, after all; the only one I've got, for now, and I have just as much of a right to it as he has. He deceived me out of the home I made for myself; the least I should have now is space to figure it out. And he's never home, anyway."

If Thandiswa or Claire have anything to say about this declaration, they keep it to themselves. We hug again and part ways. I call my mother to let her know that I will not be back with her tonight.

As I walk back through the front door, my bravado evaporates. Entering the hallway with its familiar scents brings more tears. Though I have never quite settled in here, it is the closest thing I have to a home. Desolation settles over the grand entry way as soon as I shut the front door behind me. Alone again. I should be used to this by now.

I walk into the kitchen, rifle through the refrigerator. The nausea is back, and I have no appetite. I sit down at the kitchen counter, pull out my phone.

One WhatsApp message from Neill. "You okay, my precious? Just checking how you're doing. Better, I hope?"

My world has shattered around me, and it strikes me he will not know, will not be here to read it on my face, might never know – if I decide to become as deceptive as he is.

I type back, thumbs dancing across the keypad. "Much better, thanks."

And then for good measure: "I miss you 😘!"

I watch the two ticks fall into line, see his status blink "online" for a second, before the word disappears. Two blue ticks. No reply. Why would he bother? I've let him get away with this for so long.

Rage rises again in my chest. I wonder who he's with tonight. I toy with the idea of actually calling him, but he has trained me so well, I never do so anymore without texting for permission to call first. What a fool I've been, what a docile, compliant idiot.

I walk over to the liquor cabinet and pour myself another whisky. I swallow a quick benzo with the drink, waiting for that comfortably numb feeling to spread through my body. I don't have to wait very long.

On the mantlepiece stands a large, framed photo of me and Neill on our wedding day. He looks bright, shiny, his gaze confidently level with the camera. I am smiling, tucked under his arm, gazing up at him adoringly, my ringed hand resting possessively on his chest. Typical – Neill outward-looking, meeting the gaze of those looking at him head-on, while I see only him.

This is the only photo of the two of us together – he despises selfies or couple photos. He forbade me from posting our wedding pictures on social media, citing privacy reasons, not wanting to expose me to unnecessary risk from his political enemies. I can still hear his voice: "There is no need for us to parade our marriage in public. I have always kept myself out of the public eye. I prefer doing my work quietly, without fanfare. No reason for that to change…"

For that same reason, he did not bring me along to SONA, when Parliament opens and political couples walk the red carpet in designer gear. He despised those comrades who dressed up and hammed it up on the red carpet: "Such tacky behaviour, when so many in our country live in poverty!" It had made sense at the time.

But now I know why – I was to be kept out of sight, out of the public eye, an open secret of a wife. I had thought that the other women must have known about me, must have known that they were sleeping with someone's husband. But reflecting on it, I realise that there is no public knowledge of our marriage. Since our wedding, we have spent little time in Bloemfontein, his home town. His inner circle knows about me, but that's it. Even his comrades who came to the wedding: we have not seen them again, or socialised with them, the way normal couples do. I have been neatly compartmentalised, set up in this house while he spreads his wings all over the country.

My drink and drug kick in, and woozy, I stumble to the guest bedroom, where I crawl into bed in my underwear.

In the morning, I cut through the fog in my head with two strong cups of coffee. I text the domestic worker to take the day off and brace myself for a task that I must do, even though I would rather walk barefoot over a bed of broken glass.

I arm myself with my phone, my own laptop and a writing pad. It is time to truly face reality. I am a trained social scientist – have made my living collecting and analysing data, looking at patterns, drawing conclusions through observing human behaviour. And in Neill I have found my most heartbreaking case study, which I now will mine for every iota of data I can find. I brace myself for what I will find over the next few hours, as I take a scalpel to Neill's old phone.

I make myself comfortable at his desk, open my laptop and place my pen above the writing pad. Next, I turn Neill's phone back on, and return to his archived WhatsApp messages. On the pad, I write down the names of all the women. With my own cell phone, I snap pictures of all of the conversations – I am not leaving this desk without receipts.

My next step is to open three social media tabs on my own laptop – Twitter, Facebook and Instagram, and search for the women there. Almost all of them have some social media presence. From Facebook I get their approximate ages, birthdays, and where they live. It's astonishing what people will put on the internet for the whole world to see!

Twitter shows me who they follow, and their views on politics, TV shows, their griping about men who don't love them back, and stupid memes about how they have learned to get up from the table when love is no longer being served. On Instagram I see their homes, their cars, their children; where they have recently gone for short romantic breakaways – all the places where Neill, creature of habit has taken me. Their profiles are adorned with the same bouquets of red roses he regularly brings home to me. I download all their relevant pictures to my laptop. It's easy; with one click of the mouse I capture the visible markers of the good lives they've put on show for all the world to see.

Next, I open an Excel spreadsheet on my laptop and create a table, with the following headings: Name. Age. City. Children. Profession. Marital status. Dates together. Role.

I create a row for myself – it's the first one I fill out.

Anita. 47. Cape Town. None. Academic. Married. 2016–2018. Wife.

And so I continue, slowly piecing together the puzzle of Neill's multiple dalliances and affairs.

Next I go to Neill's Facebook profile on his phone, the one I didn't know he had, given that he blocked me without my knowledge, apparently at the start of our relationship. I photograph the relevant direct messages there, jotting down the dates he made contact, the times they met for drinks, the "oh so lovely to see you last night" messages.

I work methodically, chronologically, scouring all the apps on his old phone. His Gmail account opens without a password, and here I find one or two more women of the harem, along with further clues of the when and how he managed to conduct his sordid affairs. I find icons for Tinder and the much more upmarket dating site on which we met, open them, and note the dates when he was active. His "last seen" on the dating site is the previous night.

By mid-afternoon a picture emerges. In the two years that I've known him, as boyfriend, as fiancé, as husband, Neill has had ten other relationships. I use the term "relationship" loosely – they range from a marriage (to me), through a long-term, kept mistress, to short flings lasting weeks only, and one-night-stands arranged on Tinder.

He has no discernable type, no preferred age, body type or race. When I had first suspected him of cheating, I had imagined my rival to be a beautiful, younger woman – accomplished, well-educated, well-spoken. Someone like Neill; a younger, female version of him. But his tastes span the gamut: some of the women are older than me, some younger; there is a more-or-less permanent mistress, just below me, the wife, in status, installed in a flat at the Waterfront. There are a range of other women, cycling in and out of his life – a municipal manager in KZN, a TV presenter in Johannesburg, a PA at a law firm. Younger women who clerked at his law firm before he got into politics, eager for an opportunity to scramble up the career ladder. Women whose deceased husbands' estates he wrapped up, whom he continued to advise pro bono in return for sex. He keeps some of them in reserve, with just enough money and attention to make them stick around. Others, he discards once the thrill of the chase, the novel sex, has worn off.

He has had longstanding relationships with the two chief "other women", Carol and Shireen, who both know about me, and both have been promised that he will leave me as soon as he is able; that I have psychological disorders that cost me my job, that he can't leave me now, while I'm down and out. That I drink too much – increasingly true, thanks to him – that I am unstable, insecure, volatile and jealous. That he should never have married me in the first place. He blames Shireen, the previous Queen Bee, for our marriage – she had broken up with him in a fit of pique because of his constant unavailability – their texts reveals that he was devastated, or claimed to be. He proposed to me the next day – with the ring she had thrown back at him.

She forgave him, of course, after three months, and they resumed their relationship, ignoring the small detail of Neill now having a wife. She just had to wait until a seemly amount of time had passed, and he'd divorce me, and go back to her. She lives here, in Cape Town, in the Waterfront flat, from which she regularly dispatches selfies. Most of his long nights at the office, when he is in town, are spent with her.

Then there is Carol in Rosebank. A short two-hour flight away, and a quick hop on the Gautrain. No one recognises him as the Speaker-in-waiting; there are benefits to being a behind-the-scenes type of guy; a power broker who makes deals in backrooms.

He spends at least one weekend per month with her, lavishing her with gifts while he's away to keep her pliant. I cannot help but compare gifts – Shireen has a Mercedes Benz sports car to go with her Waterfront lifestyle, while I have a mere BMW. Carol has one-carat solitaire diamond earrings, received as a belated birthday gift when he could not be with her on the day; they look more expensive than the bracelet he gave me before he left.

Shireen's Instagram shows off her gorgeous body, always exquisitely clad. It is a window into her Loubouton-wearing, One-and-Only lifestyle – the envy of her twenty thousand followers. There are spa treatments, horse-riding lessons, the cringeworthy selfies in business class, sipping Moët: "about to take off!" No doubt Neill is next to her, but cropped out of all the pictures. All three of us get the same flower bouquets from Netflorist, on the same days. Must have been a three-for-the-price-of-one special.

Then there are the not-so-serious liaisons – the little snacks he nibbles on to fill the gaps between the three mains. He meets them at a flat he owns at a residential hotel in the CBD, barely ten minutes from our home. This is where he entertains women seeking mentorships, women he finds on dating sites, women he befriends on Facebook and tries his luck with. They bite – who wouldn't? He is smart, educated, good-looking, wealthy, in good shape, well-spoken. Any woman's dream. The perfect man.

These women are wined, dined, sexed and discarded within

dizzying cycles of a few weeks. Some of them are kept on as more permanent fixtures, but that usually means he has to phase out a longer-standing dalliance. This he does with devastating callousness. Several of the breakup texts show the same formula:

"If you weren't so self-centred and selfish, you would see that I am struggling a great deal with work…"

"I cannot stand this self-righteousness. I don't like feeling like I'm walking on eggshells all the time. Not for me…"

Followed by an unceremonious: "This is not working. I would rather be single than tolerate your suspicion, listen to this constant nagging…"

The woman apologises. He refuses to accept it. "You have ruined this for me." Followed by a block.

I compare all the break-up notes on WhatsApps; it's as if he cuts and pastes them from a master document. They are blamed for their insecurity, their trust issues, for wanting more, and then cut off.

By the end of the afternoon, I have a devastating idea of the type of man I have been sharing my life and bed with for the past two years. I sit, stunned, as I survey the spreadsheet and multiple open social media tabs, piecing together the multiple lives Neill has successfully hidden. While I had made him my whole universe, he has cultivated an array of other worlds, galaxies of intimacies between which he flitted as if from one room to another.

How did he do it? I try to wrap my head around the extent and levels of his deception. How do you keep multiple stories straight, how do you memorise the most tender intimacies whispered at night before falling asleep, keep them in order, which story for which woman? How do you remember which one had a good day, which one's mother was in hospital, which one had a spat with her best friend? How do you keep your stories straight?

And me? I am Bluebeard's wife, who disobeyed his instructions to be docile, obedient; I opened up the one room in my husband's kingdom he forbade me to enter, and found the rotting corpses of his affairs littered all over my life. How had I not smelled their stench?

The self-flagellation starts: how could I not have known? How did I not see this, feel the other women on his skin, feel them in the way he moved inside me? I dull the ache around my heart with a benzo. Tomorrow I will stop with these pills. I need just one more, to get me through this day.

I end the day by packing up all evidence of my presence in his office – put his used phone back into its case and into the top drawer, fold up my notepad, power down my laptop after saving my spreadsheet of horrors in multiple places, including the Cloud. This man who always wants hard evidence in every argument, who dismisses my feelings as paranoia and hysteria: he is about to get hit with all the evidence he needs.

Chapter Fourteen

I return to Neill's study the next day to pore over more of his apps. Like a dedicated researcher, hooked on my topic, determined to answer the research question – just how many women did my husband fuck? – I will leave no stone unturned in this quest. On his obsolete phone, I find a file with all his passwords – giving me futher access to the laptop in his bottom drawer, and all the information stored on it.

At last having full access to both of Neill's devices, I start my unholy work. The trick with combing through emails to find evidence of wrongdoing is to go not only through the inbox, but also the sent messages. People will delete the latest inbox message, forgetting that the "sent" folder holds a different kind of breadcrumb in the trail of infidelity.

I find a different category of evidence there. Plane ticket bookings forwarded on to his women; reservations to five-star hotels and restaurants; proof of payment of bank transfers to some of them. Shireen gets a monthly allowance of R50 000, in addition to having her prime property paid for. Carol has received three payments during the past year of R25 000 each, the reference line in the proof of payment email stating simply "reimbursement". For what, I wonder. Services rendered?

I have never received a cent from Neill. Yes, there have been the expensive gifts, the holidays away; yes, I live in a mansion for which I do not pay a cent. Yes, there is the household fund to which I have access via a credit card that I use to get my hair and nails done, and to buy clothes. But money is a different kind of currency, for which I now wish I'd had the foresight to ask. How stupid of me to not want any money from him, to think I would never need any. And how do you even start a conversation with a man you are supposed to love, asking him for money? I did not have the words the others so patently had. What a naïve, trusting fool.

I call Claire, sharing what I have found.

"Oh my God!" is all she can say, over and over.

"What else should I be looking for?"

I start a Zoom call from Neill's laptop to Claire and share the screen. Her first concern, knowing the terms of the prenup and the ownership details of the house, is the BMW Neill gave me after I returned from my wretched solo honeymoon.

"Try to find whose name the BMW is registered in."

I search the emails. Nothing. Desperate to see whether I am the legal owner, I find the registration details in a dropbox folder called "Cars". My wedding-gift BMW is registered to his family trust.

My heart sinks.

"You won't be able to take it out of the marriage, then," Claire sighs.

"Let's look for information on the family trust that's got everything registered to it."

This bit of sleuthing brings another clue. I search the laptop for details of the trust. Sure enough, Dropbox reveals yet another secret: all the documents of the family trust.

The trustees: his oldest sister, his brother-in-law and a lawyer friend I have never met. The trust owns the house we live in, his mother's home, his house in Bloemfontein, the flat at the Waterfront, the hotel apartment in Bree Street where he entertains women. It owns his Porsche and my BMW, as well as three other cars: the Mercedes sports car Shireen drives, a Polo and a Volvo.

The trust owns several properties around the country.

"Do you know who lives there, Anita, or are they being rented out for profit?"

"God alone knows, Claire."

I do another search of the laptop, using the keyword "passwords". I find a document containing login details to all cell phone apps, his banking apps, as well as PIN numbers for his bank accounts. And boy, does he have bank accounts! Of course I had not expected to know about all of them. In the Neill-Anita universe, there is only one joint bank account, set up by him, which I access for household expenditure. Money for fixing things, cleaning things, car servicing, buying groceries and homeware, that sort of thing. He often encouraged me to use this account to buy clothes, have my hair and nails done, or buy nice things I wanted. I had done so reluctantly at first, but quickly became accustomed to this. Well, that was the Neill-Anita universe, but Neill's pluriverse reveals a level of expenditure which makes me gasp.

Once I find the logins and PINs for his bank accounts, Claire cautions.

"What you're doing is illegal. Everything you have been doing so far is illegal, by the way, but the banking stuff … this is dangerous, Anita. As your lawyer, I want to caution you that this is a serious transgression. And this is where I'm out. Take care."

Having printed out the password document from his phone, I have a manual to Neill's financial world.

His bank statements give me a completely different picture of the all planets to which I've been an unwitting satellite. Shireen has retirement annuities and an Allan Gray portfolio to which Neill has contributed to for five years. She has a standing account with the spa at the One-and-Only, which he funds. Carol gets a standing R5 000 monthly payment to her veterinarian. Her dogs' vet, for Gods sake! From her Instagram photos, I know them to be two schnauzers, Gigi and Georgy, who regularly appear in her feed with fresh haircuts and bows – blue and pink for her "boy" and "girl". I seethe as I scroll through yet more transactions.

There are various random payments to various other women. University fees of R60 000 last February for a Carla. I consult my spreadsheet. Carla. 46. Johannesburg. One son (19 yrs old).

Monthly school-fee payments of R20 000 to one of the most exclusive girls' schools in Cape Town. Back to my trusty spreadsheet I go, where I filled in from Facebook the following: Sharda. 42. Crawford. 2 daughters, 12 and 17. Neill is supporting an entire ecosystem of women and children! Not to mention dogs, and even their worms and fleas, as a detailed bill from Carol's documents reveals!

I look at the two bands on my ring finger. It's more profitable being a side chick to Neill than his wife. I've traded the monetary perks Shireen and Carol enjoy for these rings, not even bought with me in mind. As the wife, Neill is my prize. Living in his house and sleeping in his bed alone is supposed to be the ultimate status symbol aspired to by all of these women. Cooking his meals, making his doctor's appointments, calling DSTV when the TV stops working. How royally I have played myself for the empty prize of the title "Mrs". I would have been better off as one of his concubines!

Bile rises in my throat; I swallow it down with scalding tea. The burn in my throat feels satisfying, matching the rage swirling in my stomach.

The ring. My frazzled mind races back to the proposal, how he produced the engagement ring out of his suit pocket, not a box. It all makes sense now, how he pulled it out like a magician pulling a rabbit out of a hat because that day, when I opened the door, he saw that I was done with him. He read me like a book, and panicked – and in an act of desperation to keep me hooked, produced the ring.

I go through his WhatsApp exchange with Shireen one more time.

Neill: "I'm sorry. Yes, I did ask her to marry me. What was I supposed to do, after you broke it off with me like that?"

Shireen: "You told me Anita was just a fling! But it was serious enough for you to propose to her! You did not even try to fix things between us!"

Neill: "What did you expect me to do? I told you I needed a wife, stability, to rise in the party. And my mother. She's ageing. Health failing. She wanted to see me settled."

Neill: "Anita loves me. She'll make a better wife than you ever could."

There it was. If I did not know it before, here was the evidence that confirmed what I was in Neill's life: a pawn, an object to be shifted across the giant chessboard of his life, manipulated to create a certain impression, to bolster the image he needed to uphold for his family, the community, the goddamned party. "Devoted husband" – the façade he polished, in addition to savvy businessman, political kingmaker – to humanise himself, to be seen as dependable, loyal, stable. I had just happened to be there – the right woman, stupid enough, at the right time. It could just as easily have been Shireen, had she not wounded his ego by breaking off their engagement.

I thought he had loved me for all I was. But none of that mattered in the end. I was a useful object in a woman's body he happened to come across at a time he needed a wife. Neill was correct about me. Despite my heaps of book-learning, my smarts, my detached exterior, I was gullible. Utterly and naively, charmed by the most calculating, Machiavellian of men.

The ping of my cell phone interrupts my sliding thoughts.

"You okay, precious?"

"Fine, and you?"

"Okay, just missing my woman."

On autopilot, I reply. "I miss you too."

"Still so beautiful?"

😄.

"I should be home in a few days. Wednesday, Thursday by the latest."

☺.

"Will fly out again for the weekend for last round of campaigning within the branches. It's a tight race."

"Yes of course."

"Got to run. Chat more later. I love you."

The power of habit prevails: "I love you too."

Chapter Fifteen

He is away, and I don't have anywhere to be. Poring over his life's most intimate details becomes my habit, a macabre wake for the death of our marriage, a necessary excavation so that I can set things straight in my head once and for all. No, I was not insane. No, I did not overreact. No, I was not overly clingy, paranoid, suspicious. The reason my head and stomach swirled continuously was because he was lying; because he was consistently warping my reality, weakening my ability to think; deactivating my personal, internal defence system, meant to keep me safe. For these two years that he has lied to me, he has not only betrayed me; worse, he made me turn on myself.

My mother calls, Thandiswa calls, Claire calls – I do not reply.

My entire world has collapsed around me – I need to sit in silence, be with myself to at least try to put it back together again. To know where he really was on that night he had to leave suddenly from our anniversary (with a new conquest he'd been courting for months, who eventually texted something that made him realise she would let him into her bed); to know whom he was with when one of the twins had an accident and needed to go to hospital (with Carol); to know where he was on the many, many nights he worked so late and crept into bed at 2 or 3am (Sharda or Shireen). To note where the many fights, coming out of nowhere, provoked by the most insignificant things, causing him to storm out, led him. To have this knowledge is like piecing small, lost parts of myself back together again, to restore the me I once was. I want to know everything: every name, every time. I imagine him with them – I know what they look like, where they live, even what beauty products they use – every groan and shudder as he made love to them; every pet name he called them as he lay against them in postcoital bliss (the same names he called me: gorgeous, precious, darling, love).

Going over the emails, the text messages, the DMs becomes a ritual, a practice of finding out exactly with whom I've been entangled, and how craftily his life was hidden from me. I know I should stop but I can't. I commit to memory snatches of their text conversations, the tease in Shireen's voice when she voicenotes him, the little endearments he exchanged with them, so familiar; what I had taken to be the sacred, inviolable expressions of love between us. How cheaply I came to him. How much he further cheapened everything I was, everything I held dear, all of the love I poured into him. How he would sometimes use the very words I had used to express my love to him on the other women. The long conversations we had about politics, race, gender, précised and parroted to another woman in their courting stage, to impress her with his progressive politics. I could almost see the one he was hunting thinking, what a man!

I live on tea and benzos, haven't showered in three days. I keep my vigil at his desk until I am certain I have squeezed out every particle of information about his affairs. What I'll do with this, I don't know, but I need all of it. I scrape the sordid details together as if my life depends on it.

I lay off the whisky. I cannot afford to be drunk at this stage. Casting off the benzos must wait for another day – without them I would completely lose my mind. I summon every ounce of brainpower, intuition, discredited knowledge to the task of unravelling the web in which I am caught. I need to get out, even if it means amputating a part of myself to get free. Because of one indisputable fact, the knowledge of which screams through my veins with every beat of my heart, louder and louder until the blood rushes and rings in my ears: to stay here will be to die.

Not by his hand; no, Neill is far too sophisticated, far too much of a tactician to get that kind of dirt on his hands. A different kind of death: a suicide perhaps, but more likely the slow strangulation of my energy, my spark, the force that animates me, until I, too, will be a husk, like Neill, pretending, performing; putting on the appropriate mask for the appropriate audience and occasion. And becoming so accomplished in it, like Neill, that putting on the mask will become *the thing*, the substance of my life, so that the real me is sublimated beneath the dizzying ritual of changing acts, scenes, plots, co-actors. If I were to stay, I would have to learn to perfect that act, like my husband; and in that process, I would lose myself, my mind. To stay here will mean the loss of me, a soul death.

I have trawled through every conceivable text, email, Facebook message and WhatsApp note on his phone and laptop. And yet again I sit, one morning, with my first cup of tea at my post, his laptop. My eye catches a folder I've noticed before, but have passed over as some run-of-the-mill policy file. Something tells me to click on it. It is password-protected, so I consult again the list of passwords I have printed from his phone, which gives me instant access.

I find a list of documents – not policy briefs or research, as I had suspected, but arrangements for travel. Flights, accommodations, an itinerary for a trip to China. It is from a time before I knew him, before Parliament, while he still practised as a lawyer. I find it odd that he has never mentioned this trip to me. His flight booking was in Business Class, of course, nothing less would do for my Neill; but clearly not a romantic tryst as the electronic ticket shows only one traveller. The itinerary, once opened, sheds light on what was a business trip, sponsored by the province, to facilitate economic and commercial links with China. Where have I heard this before? An internet search leads me down a rabbit hole: yes, this was in the news a while back. One of the activities flagged as irregular: a delegation of local politicians and businesspeople, paid for by taxpayers, when the lines of what the delegation was actually doing in China were more than a little blurred.

Clearly, Neill has been living a double life, but this surprises me. I'm not sure why. I know he is close to power, is hungry to enter its upper echelons, but I have always assumed him to be above this. I cannot imagine him capable of this: stealing from the very people for whom he purports to have gone into politics. I think back to the countless conversations we've had about poverty, the indignity of it, how it is gendered, how its worst dividends accrue disproportionately to black women; women like his mother, whose suffering he witnessed first-hand. That experience has been the driving force behind most of his life's work. These things were never said to grandstand, as performance; they were spoken in our intimate moments when there was no need to impress, win me over. In my heart, I believe that he believed this; that his purpose was tied to alleviating the indignities of poverty, racism, sexism. His work in the portfolio committee on gender attests to this too – the painstakingly researched policy briefs commissioned, his fight for a Basic Income Grant stymied at every turn by many opposition parties, and from within the ranks of his own party. He has nevertheless carried on with it, pushing slowly at intractable boundaries, with a determination bordering on obsession. This Neill, this part of him intimately wrought with why I love him; this Neill could not possibly steal from the poor, from the working-class black women and children from whose ranks he rose.

But if you can act immorally, despicably, in one sphere of your life, how ethical can you be in the other parts? It is a well-known defence of politicians, when they are caught in sex scandals, that the personal does not, and should not impinge on the political, the public. That who a man sleeps with has nothing to do with how well or how ethically he conducts his job. He may be flawed, yes; he may have certain weaknesses; yet those personal flaws and predilections do not necessarily have a bearing on the professional. But can a man who is deceptive and duplicitous in private be counted on not to act in the same way in his public life? Character is character, and surely the lack thereof permeates the entire sweep of a life? Or are there people who can compartmentalise so fully, so neatly, that they are able to switch on the morality button when they step into the public view? That is even more sick.

I flatten the heels of my palms against my eyelids. This is all too much. A week ago, I was living a beautiful life with this beautiful man. Yes, we had problems, but I thought they were circumstantial: a politician in election season, gone a lot. Neglectful, yes. But at his core, a good man, good to me, faithful. Having my best interests at heart. Loving me, wanting the best for me. Not this – the very foundation of the relationship built on lie upon lie; the most egregious multiple betrayals, the warping of my reality, my sanity, to the extent that I no longer know up from down in my own life. Not this.

I step out into the garden – pristine, manicured, with late spring blooms promising a lush, fecund summer. The scent of jasmine perfumes the morning air, so sweet, I feel as if I could float away on it. On the nights he has been here, we've spent hours talking, or sitting in silence in this garden, hands intertwined.

Back inside, I sit at the desk and start a new spreadsheet. This time, I do not fill it with lovers' names, or dates of trysts.

I start with the name of the person who invited him to China, the secretary in the Premier's office, and move on to the Premier himself. I search for those names in the emails, texts and WhatsApps that I've haunted these last few days. Their names come up a great deal, of course. Nothing out of the ordinary – they are comrades, they came up in the party together, work together. Neill was one of a few lawyers kept on retainer by the Premier's office, so of course there would be correspondence between them. And most of the correspondence between them is brief, matter-of-fact, above board. Before taking up formal politics, while still in practice, he also did a lot of work for the Mangaung municipality, representing them in numerous cases. There's substantial email correspondence between him and the Chief Financial Officer of the municipality – perfunctory briefings or follow-ups from meetings.

But then I spot an anomaly. A search using the Premier's last name brings up a number of different results in the email inbox; same surname but different first name, a name I have not ever heard Neill use during our relationship. Google comes to the rescue, and I learn that the second bearer of the Premier's surname is his younger brother, a man not widely known in political circles, or at least not to me. I enter his name into my latest spreadsheet, saved as "Neill's political network". I sift through these emails, most of which I fish out of the "Deleted emails" folder, dating all the way back to 2008 until fairly recently. These are emails purged from Neill's sent folder, but forgotten in the trash can, which he neglected to clean out. A few of these emails are less detailed than the ones between Neill and the Premier, consisting of one word, or a few phases: "Done". "Company set up". "Complete". When I scour the trash folder for the Premier's brother's name, my heart lurches as I see the contents of the emails sent to him: calls for tenders from the province and the Mangaung municipality. I count a dozen emails with details of tenders sent by Neill to the Premier's brother.

What marks Neill's emails of tenders as not-quite-right is the fact that they are not sent directly from the regularly published government Tender Bulletins. They are Word documents, some containing typographical errors, others incomplete in their wording or formatting. I copy the messages into a separate document, along with dates sent, collating a new archive of all the tender announcements Neill sent to his contact.

My next step is to find the official tender announcements, as published by government. I search these tender bulletins to find the announcements that correspond with Neill's emails. Noting the dates, my worst suspicions are confirmed. In every case, Neill's emails predate each official call for applications by six to three months. I record these official tender publication dates, too.

I read, write, record with an anaesthetising efficiency. What becomes clear to me is that Neill had prior knowledge of tenders before they came out, that he was passing this information on to his comrade before the official announcements were made; and I can guess why: in order to form companies to bid for them. My suspicions are confirmed when I search the South African Companies Registration database: between 2008 and 2012, Neill has registered twelve different companies. For six of these companies, the Premier's brother is listed as co-director. I track the dates on which these six companies were registered: all two to three months before the tender bulletins came out. They formed these companies specifically for the purpose of bidding for these tenders.

I Google some more, find the website of a governance accountability organisation, which holds the records of all tenders awarded during the last fifteen years. Soon I am piecing together the grotesque puzzle of procurement, of which my husband is the chief architect. Before me, on my various spreadsheets, notes and jottings, his rapacious design comes into view with devastating clarity: a motley assortment of companies that have raked in millions through tenders ranging from auditing municipalities, through construction of hospitals, to road maintenance.

Neill had knowledge that these procurements would be coming

up, formed companies just in time to bid for these lucrative awards, won every single tender for which he competed. It is impossible for a layperson like me to calculate, but he has profited, during the decade before he became an MP, by hundreds of millions of rand as a tenderpreneur. For Neill, born and raised in the squalor of an apartheid location, without a father, having suffered the most humiliating indignities of poverty and dispossession, going to bed hungry more nights than he cared to remember, the mid-2000s had been a time in which the tables turned fully, definitively, in a life-altering way. It had been his time to eat.

And eat he did, a gluttonous, voracious stuffing of the belly, which groaned, distorted out of all proportion, under the onslaught of all he had stolen. The houses, the cars, the insatiable appetite for women: all symptoms, all growlings of the distendend, ravenous stomach which, having once been so cruelly deprived, could now never have enough. And so stuffed itself with the desire for more, more, more and even more, even as it clogged itself, sickening the rest of the body politic – taking food out of the very mouths of those he purported to serve.

I breathe deeply, shaking at the scope of the betrayal spread in front of me. The hard crust of ice that has been crystallising around my heart all afternoon as I worked, starts to thaw. The study walls close in on me, a fog displaces the oxygen in the room. I flee back into the garden, bathed in the light of the setting sun as it plays between the branches of the stately oak trees surrounding the property. The scent of jasmine, so intoxicating this morning, hangs sickly sweet, cloying in the air. A wave of nausea rises, and once again I retch, doubling over to vomit, expelling a trickle of saliva. I haven't eaten in days.

Once the retching subsides, the sobs overtake me. I cry like a baby, heaving for breath between guttural cries. Neill, my beautiful Neill. The wise one, the earnest fighter for freedom, for social justice. The man who declared so many times that he would not rest in his lifetime until the plight of the downtrodden improved. And I had believed him, had the utmost faith in his goodness, his integrity. Not only has he betrayed me, but he has betrayed himself: his calling, his intellect, his gifts. He has betrayed the people who vote for the party, year after year, with the stale hope, barely intact, of a better life. Because what he, and others like him have done, has been to steal their futures.

With every pothole, with every hospital that does not have the necessary medicine because of these frauds, with every tap that runs dry, with every pit latrine that remains in every schoolyard, with every dysfunctional state system that cannot pay student bursaries or electricity on time – a little bit of the future once promised us is eroded, stolen. The futures of our children, our collective futures. And all we are left with is this dazed despair, incredulity that what has started with such beauty, such promise, has degenerated into this. This putrid mess of a country in which the one per cent drive around in their Porsches and their red BMWs, while the underclass barely survives on paltry state handouts. A better life for all, indeed.

I look around, from the garden to the house in which I have been happy to live this past year; see it now afresh for what it really is, from whence it came – and I vomit some more.

Chapter Sixteen

My red BMW cleaves the air. I feel like I'm flying. Yes, I am flying through this city, early in the morning, my mission clear and purposeful. The buildings whizz past me. I see them as if for the first time. The last few days in my husband's study has remade this place, causing it to appear foreign. In a way it is. I have never been here before, never been in the city that I love with the new knowledge that has sunk into my skin and bones, the knowledge that I have married one of *them*, the despicable ones; have lain beside him, offered my flesh willingly for him to eat and eat, as he has eaten away at the musculature of our country. Eaten the things that are supposed to make a democracy work.

A vampire, you might call him, and you would be correct. Has he not sucked the lifeblood out of me, and every other woman who is part of the charade that is his life? Has he not built that life with the spoils of what was meant to fuel a functioning state? Has he not constructed the very edifice of the false, empty self from the expensive and beautiful things that make him who he is, the adoration reflected back from the eyes of the women he has conned and deceived?

It is a basic tenet of the gender theory I teach that gender is socially constructed. And Neill exemplifies this construction of masculinity: this manliness shored up by the numbers of homes and cars, the number of bodies of women he can bend into supplication. This is the self that Neill has constructed, and as he has crumbled before my eyes, so has everything else – our home, the city, my sense of self. Because who am I now, having been the wife of Neill, having been complicit in his fraud? Who am I without him?

He has destroyed the person I was before we met. I have given up everything that gave my life meaning at his behest, trying desperately to be the perfect wife for the perfect man. Who am I?

It is relationships that anchor me, contain vestiges of the me I was before I met Neill. And these are the people to whom I now cling: my mother, Thandiswa, Claire. I am on my way to Claire's office. Next to me, in the passenger seat, sit three stuffed manila envelopes, each containing identical information. The first one I deliver to my bank safety deposit box as soon as their doors open, before continuing on to Claire's office.

She hugs me as I arrive, offers freshly brewed coffee and the oat biscuits I love. My stomach is too tight to eat them. I open the Pandora's box of Neill's tendepreneurships on her desk, spilling the entrails of his hidden life. She looks through everything: the tender notices, the company details, the bank statements of the companies I downloaded from the Cloud I hacked, a skill I have acquired through ferreting out his mistresses.

After hours of sifting through the papers I've provided, she is ready to give a verdict: "You seem to be in the clear. He did all of this stuff, the companies, most of them shells and shelves, before he became an MP – and most importantly, before he met and married you. You aren't implicated in this, thank God. But there's the consultancy he encouraged you to start. Could it be…?"

Claire struggles to complete her sentence. "I'm not implying anything about your integrity or honesty, Anita. But, did he discuss any intention *he* might have had for your company?"

I'm left speechless. I comb through my recollections of the countless conversations we had about my consultancy. How reluctant I had been to start it, how he had encouraged me, arguing that my talents were wasted in the untransformed university. How he had "mentored" me every step of the way, savvy businessman that he was. The start-up capital he had offered me, which I could not bring myself to accept. How I had berated myself afterwards for being a fool, too full of pride to accept money from a man who loved me and wanted to see me succeed.

"I honestly don't know, Claire. I don't know anything anymore. I don't know who he is. I can't reconcile the man I fell in love with, that soft, gentle soul, with the man I have come to know him to be over the last week. I have no idea what is going on in my own life. No idea who I even am anymore."

I allow the tears to course freely down my cheeks in the company of my friend.

She reaches across the table to hold my hand for a few seconds. "You will get through this, Anita. I promise you, we will get through it, okay? Your life is about to get extremely difficult, but when you are on the other side of this, it will be better, my friend. Now, let me speak as your lawyer. This is what I advise you to do next."

I listen without interrupting and take copious notes. I know what I must do. I don't know what will happen after I have done it, where I will end up, but there is no question in my mind about how to move forward.

I can stay, pretend to unsee what I have seen, turn the proverbial blind eye, enjoy the house, the holidays and the gifts, and delude myself that he is only mine. I can carry on, play the game, squirrel away enough money to leave in five years' time, and continue to live the lifestyle to which I have so quickly become accustomed. Or I could leave right now.

I know what I have to do.

After another long hug, I leave Claire's office, flooring my little red car as I head back into the city. Stop at the couriers at the Gardens Centre on my way home, and send off the third envelope, containing all I have just discussed with Claire, to an address she has supplied.

I am just in time for my appointment at the swanky spa a few blocks away, where I have booked a full body exfoliation treatment, a massage and a facial. My husband is, after all, coming home tomorrow, and I want to look beautiful for him.

Chapter Seventeen

It is the morning of the day my husband will return home, after the week that changed everything. It must have been the sheer exhaustion of going through all the skeletons in his closet, hauling out the bones, dusting them off and piecing them back together, that has made me sleep through the night for the first time in two weeks. I am sipping a cup of tea at the kitchen counter when my cell phone vibrates. The caller name popping up on the screen surprises me: Neill's mother hardly calls me.

I answer, immediately worried that something has happened to him.

"Is Neill okay?" I blurt before even asking how she is.

"Oh, no no, he's fine, my child. How are you?"

"Well enough," I lie.

"I wanted to talk to you, as one woman to another. Do you have a few minutes, Anita?"

My heart starts to race. Do they know that I've been digging? Or is something else wrong? Perhaps Neill is preparing to discard me?

"Yes, sure, Aunty Sophie. I have time. What do you want to talk about?"

She gets straight to the point. "It's about Neill. I just said goodbye to my son last night. I'm sure you must be happy that he's on his way back to you."

"Yes, of course, Aunty."

"I want to speak to you about a topic that might be delicate.

Neill confided in me last night. He said you were going through a difficult period, that you are not coping well with his workload and him being away so often. He thought you would have adjusted by now."

She pauses, waiting for a confirmation or rebuttal.

"Yes, Aunty, it has not been easy, but I am trying my best."

Fear rises in me. What is Neill planning? His mother almost never speaks to me – I wonder if he's asked her to do this, as a precursor to something more sinister?

"Well, good. I'm glad you're trying. Marriage isn't always easy. And you knew who Neill was when you married him, what your life with him would be. Surely you know you cannot expect a big man like Neill to be home all the time, following you around."

"No, not at all. I don't expect that. I know his work comes first."

"Good. Now the reason for my call. My son is stressed. He is fighting the biggest fight of his political life right now. The conference is weeks away, and he needs to be elected to the executive for his plans to work out. His survival in the party, in government, depends on this. I'm not sure if you understand how important the next elective conference is. You know his dream is to be Speaker of the National Assembly. That can only be achieved if he wins this battle."

"Yes, Aunty, of course I know this. It's all he talks about."

"Well, now more than ever, you need to stand by your husband. Look after him. Support him. He may be grumpy, he may be short with you. Don't take it personally. Be there for him."

I laugh to myself as she says this. I wonder what advice she would give me if she knew all I've discovered about her adored son this week. Perhaps the advice she gives here applies there too – don't take it personally that he has kept a menagerie of other women on the side. Yes, I should definitely not take that personally.

"Of course, I will be there for him. Of course I will support him, Aunty. It goes without saying."

"Good, my child. You married Neill for better or worse. Now is the time for you to really live that vow. He is on his way back to you. Give him a good, home-cooked meal. Welcome him with open arms, without any nagging about him being away so long. Tell him how much you've missed him. Tell him you love him."

I smile as I reply, as if she is standing in front of me. "Yes, Aunty."

"Thank you, my child. Thank you for loving my son, for taking care of him."

"My pleasure, Aunty."

It is the politeness of the call that lingers with me throughout the rest of the day, the coaching in being a respectable, good wife. Has she thought to do the same to her son, schooling him on how to be a good husband, on how to treat his wife with respect, care and dignity? But this is what it comes down to – as a woman, you are responsible for the success or failure of the marriage. He went outside the marriage? You must have done something wrong: let yourself go, become boring, forcing him to look elsewhere for the very spark that he slowly, insidiously extinguished within you. Yes, it is you, woman; it is always your fault.

I have cooked Neill's favourite meal – roast rack of lamb with a chimichurri sauce, and roast vegetables – in anticipation of his arrival. Garlicky aromas float around the kitchen, giving the house a warmth it has been devoid of this last week. In the dressing room adjacent to our bedroom, I cast an appraising glance at my reflection in the mirror. I am wearing a red sheath dress, one of Neill's favourites, usually skin-tight, but now hanging slack against my curves, after the weight has melted off my body over the past few days. I've washed my hair and styled it in loose waves that tumble down to my shoulders; my concealer is doing double duty underneath my eyes, disguising the dark hollows blooming there. My make-up is muted, as always, except for the deep ruby shade on my lips. This is new for me; the colour makes my mouth look like a gash against the pale skin of my face. Ruby Woo – Shireen's favourite lipstick shade. I look drained, but I will smile when I meet him, fake it till I make it, or whatever the hell that saying is. I finish my outfit with a spritz of Chanel, a gift from my husband, a perfume he liked and thought would suit me. I know from his texts, emails and shopping receipts that he has gifted us all the same perfume, so that none of us will detect the others' scents upon him. He has really mastered betrayal as a fine art, evil fucking genius that he is.

I pull my roiling mind away from the database of debauchery; tonight I must be chipper, delighted even. A good wife – the perfect wife. I am not giving anything away, not at this stage. I need time to think, plot, figure out my next move. Unlike him, I am neither a strategist, nor a street fighter. I wear the tides of my emotions plainly on my face. Anyone can see through me. But not today, not tonight. Tonight I will tear my focus away from the sordid underbelly of my marriage. Tonight I will shine for him, and make him feel shiny.

I hear the click of the automated gate, and see his car flash in the driveway. Before he enters through the front door, I am there, waiting for him in my red dress and red lipstick. I breathe in, summon the courage and fortitude of my mother, and her mother, and the many mothers before them; the strength they've had to draw on in the face of a million humiliations and degradations by the state, the law, unholy bosses, their husbands. I draw this energy to my very core, willing myself to stay proud, stay standing. Serenity falls around me like a cloak. The door opens and Neill walks through it. My smile is unforced, sincere. He stops when he sees me, stands still for a second, drops his bags by his sides and exclaims: "Wow! You look amazing!"

I laugh; despite everything that I know about him, I am still as grateful as a lapdog for his approval.

"So aren't you going to give your husband a kiss?" he teases.

I rush into his arms, my body trembling as I'm pulled back into his orbit. I want to hate him, slap him, have it out with him, but the familiar scent of sandalwood has a narcotic effect on me – warming me, soothing me. He scoops me into his arms, lifts me up and puts me down again, covering my face with kisses.

"God, how I've missed you, my precious."

His words break whatever it was in me that shored me up and tears start to fall down my cheeks.

"Oh no, no no, my precious, don't cry. I'm here, right here," he coos, as if I am a child.

I don't say a word. I leave him under the misapprehension that these are tears of joy at being reunited with him, not the despair of a betrayed woman who cannot do a thing to hold her husband accountable. I wipe my tears and smile.

He kisses my mouth greedily, as if he means to swallow me. He lifts me up and carries me into one of the guest bedrooms, where we are soon naked, him writhing on top of me while I bury my face in his chest. If he is exhausted from campaigning or whatever else he has been doing, his body does not betray it. He is as energetic as ever, driving my body to the edge of explosive desire.

There is nothing quite like a good fuck, even when you know that your partner is getting it on elsewhere. The inevitable climax releases my pent-up fury and settles my frayed nerves. For the first time in almost two weeks, I exhale, my body relaxes, and the knot in my stomach disappears. In the aftermath we lie with limbs entangled, my head on his chest. I listen to his racing heartbeat as it steadies, matching his breath as it becomes more even.

"Wow! That was amazing! I should go away more often," he teases, kissing the top of my head.

I tuck my arm around his waist, close my eyes, and exalt in this closeness with him. He starts telling me about the trip, how campaigning is going, how close he feels his election to the NEC of the party. His dream of being Speaker is within reach – he can taste it. Less than two weeks to go now to the elective conference.

"I'm afraid I'll have to leave again, quite soon, my love. We've got to canvas with even more intensity at the level of the branches. I'm trying to hit every major branch in the province one more time before the conference. We've built such good momentum – we've got to keep it going."

The "we" he refers to is the faction of his party that is just a hair's breadth away from clinching political power internally. Not supported by centrists or liberals within the party or the country, but a populist faction championing the cause of the poorest of the poor. Radical transformation is what they stand for. Ideologically leftist, Pan-Africanist; unflinching in their unwillingness to kowtow to global capital, white monopoly capital, and its nefarious agenda. Unequivocally opposed to the Washington Consensus and its neo-liberal tentacles.

They are so close to tipping the scales of power within the party – something they have strategised and organised and coalesced around for years. And it is here, the moment: almost within grasp, and Neill is set to be a prime beneficiary of it – a reward for his loyalty towards this faction, even when the going got decidedly tough. The fruits of his fealty are about to be harvested. His voice, animated, rises as he explains the micropolitical shifts over the last few weeks, the standoffs, the powerplays, the way he put some people in their place.

I laugh, smile, cluck over him, praise his brilliance as I run my fingers through the hair on his chest. My brilliant strategist, my Machiavellian prince. All for the good of the people, of course.

Naked like this, my skin still flushed, and with Neill spilling the intimate details of party warfare, I can almost forget what he has done to me. I am drawn back into his orbit; back to being his confidante, his lover and co-conspirator. I feel wanted and needed and desired as I trace the contours of his hips with my hands. I long to go back in time, back into the sweet and blissful ignorance of just a few weeks ago.

He chats, animated. I listen, focusing on his steady heartbeat, thumping against the chest beneath my head. When I focus on that, I am able to centre myself in the love I have for him – almost, almost forgetting about the other women with whom he shares beds, sweat and semen.

When he has caught me up on party politics and gossip, a silence falls between us.

"And what have you been up to, my pretty woman, while I've been away?"

"Oh, nothing much. My week was nowhere near as exciting as yours."

He runs his hand over my naked torso, down my hip and thigh. "Have you been working out a lot? You've lost so much weight. I must say, it suits you. You are stunning at this weight."

I stay quiet. Well of course – the smaller I am, the more attractive I am to him. Not only in the flesh, but also in the way I have been quietly shrinking my life to contort around his.

"What else has been going on while I was away?" he asks.

"Well, I did get a surprise call from your mother. Very concerned about the state of our marriage, she was."

He groans. "Oh God, she didn't! Sorry, my precious. I spoke to her, and told her we were having some growing pains. She must have blown it out of proportion. I'm sorry, Anita. Sorry I said anything to her at all. Because that's really all it is, growing pains, my love. Two people, set in their ways. And both of us strong-willed too. There's bound to be some fireworks as we settle into married life."

I look into his eyes and smile.

"But I tell you this much, my precious. I love you. And I believe in you. I believe in us. So you're not getting rid of me, ever."

There are so many ways to respond to this, none of them wise, so I reply with a kiss. "Don't worry too much about what your mother said. Her main instruction to me was to cook you a good, solid meal. Speaking of which, you've made me quite hungry," I tease.

"Let's go eat, my love."

He jumps into the shower; I use the one in our bedroom, amazed at my ability to fake happiness and excitement at seeing him, when, until the minute he walked through the door, I was not at all sure how my body would respond to him. But I was genuinely happy to see him; craved him, even. And it felt good to be with him, to make love to him, to feel the weight of the body I had missed so much on top of mine. Even though I have hated him every second since I discovered his secret lives. But that hate turned to dust the minute I saw his face. God knows, I love this man.

He devours his dinner while I pick at mine.

"Can I come with you to the conference next week?" I ask impulsively, despite already knowing what his answer will be.

"Only if you are a paid-up, card-carrying member of a branch in the Free State Province, my love. That is the only condition on which you may accompany me! And then you must promise to vote for me!"

A flippant reply, meant to deflect. I know why he doesn't want me there. Who knows how much fresh meat will be up for the eating during the long nights of the conference? How scornfully I laughed at the media reports a few years ago that cited the party's annual national conference as providing the busiest weekend of the year for sex workers in the town that hosts it. But now the joke's on me: my husband most likely qualifies as a top customer for such industrious women.

"You stay at home, love. Hold the fort. Practise these magnificent cooking skills, and your even more impressive boudoir skills. I'll be in need of both once this conference is over. I'll want nothing more than to come home to you and make myself a glutton for you."

I blush. He laughs. Us, the happy couple, once more.

I sleep fitfully next to him that night, unaccustomed to his alien body beside me in bed. He heads to his study early in the morning. By lunchtime, he is packed and ready to depart for the airport.

He kisses me goodbye. "Not long now, my love," he says, and is gone.

As the door shuts behind him, I turn to survey the empty house, and exhale. All the emotions I've suppressed during the twenty-four hours he's been here come bubbling to the surface. I burst into laughter; loud and maniacal, a laugh that bounces from the walls of the house back into my face. So, this is how it feels to pretend, to put on a grand show of love. He's had many years of practice, but I'm astounded by the remarkable ease with which I have slipped into the role of devoted wife, basking in his attention, showering him with adoration. If I wanted, I could continue like this for years, for the rest of my life even. But at what cost? What would happen to the core of me, the essence I have taken years and years to accept, imperfections and all, and learned to love? How do I do this for the rest of my life and still love that core, still look that woman in the eye in the mirror without flinching?

I won't choose this. I will never choose this gilded lie of a life. I will choose myself.

The next week passes in a haze. Planning, strategy sessions with the coven, dinners with my mother, who forces me to eat, and whom I allow to lay prayerful hands on me. She prays that I may find strength and wisdom, but most of all, that I will be protected, delivered from evil. I accept her prayers as an invocation of the life I seek.

Thandiswa visits the big, lonely house, filling it with the jingle of her many brass bangles, the scent of neroli, the spells she weaves around me with her cleansing wand of imphepho. She strips me down to bare flesh, washes me in bath upon bath filled with salts and herbal concoctions. She submerges me in the water like a child being baptised, conjuring a freedom I cannot yet imagine.

Claire stops by, dropping off a pay-as-you go cell phone when I meet her at the gate. Her terse instructions: "Don't give this number to anyone, not even your mother. Only use it for calls, not texts; only speak on it when you are outside, as far away as you can get from the house."

The calls to this phone start coming soon after, and flowing from these conversations, the requisite meetings are set up in Claire's office. I drive to these meetings, sit through them like a zombie, listening to my own voice as it drones on, as if from some distant recording device.

That weekend, I watch the party's electoral conference as it is live-streamed on TV. The toyi-toying on stage, the speeches, the skirmishes; almost half the conference staging a walkout in protest of the faction opposing Neill's. Breathless journalists doing live crossings; analysts in the studio spinning meaning out of chaos. What is not being shown is the wrangling behind the scenes, the deals going down in hotel rooms, the compromises being hammered out in conference rooms.

Then there is the coming back together, the show of unity. The country – no, the world – is watching this party with its proud history tear itself apart. It cannot break so publicly, so violently. It is known by every cadre that the electoral process should not tear the movement apart. The centre must hold. And it does, it always does, eventually, because power must be consolidated to be maintained. To fracture too far, too publicly, is to loosen its grip on power, the continued grasping of which is the ultimate end game. The show goes on.

I watch listlessly as the candidates for the top six positions deliver their manifestoes. Then comes the next level of candidates up for election to the National Executive Committee. Neill is electrifying. He starts off slowly, deliberately, in the calm, measured manner for which he is known. He plays the room like an instrument, plucking at its strings, starting at *mezzo piano*, and rousing them through *forte* to *fortissimo*. By the time he reaches the crescendo of his speech, every person in the conference hall is on their feet, swaying to the mesmerising beat of his song, chanting his name. His comrades come onto the stage and embrace him. Not one to dance, he allows their energy to carry him so that he seems to be floating, floating above them all; beaming, a beatific sun shining down on those whom he will lead to a more glorious tomorrow; to that imagined community where poverty, violence, racism – the indignity of it all – will be voided, and we will live in the land of milk and honey, sated by the movement itself and its glorious thrust into the future.

After he is carried from the stage, I switch off the TV. I imagine my husband shaking hands backstage, hugging his comrades and thanking them, then breaking loose from the huddle to find his way to the bed of whichever woman he has chosen from his harem for the occasion. Or perhaps a new conquest has been lined up, and she, having stood in the crowd at his feet, still high on his speech, will give him the fuck of his life.

I pour myself a glass of whisky, go out into the garden, and gulp down the first sip. Its satisfying burn scalds my throat. I sit down and contemplate the blades of wayward grass poking through the usually immaculate lawn as the tree shadows lengthen. And I wait and wait.

Chapter Eighteen

Neill's return home is jubilant. He flies down his mother, the twins, his sisters and their husbands to celebrate with us. Not only has he been elected to the National Executive Committee, but from there, the NEC has appointed him to the National Working Committee, the much smaller, elite steering group, saturated with power. The year hurtles to a close, with Neill assured that the coveted position of Speaker will be his once Parliament reconvenes. His faction has won the electoral contest, and he was pivotal in making that win possible with his behind-the-scenes negotiations. A political influencer, a kingmaker: now his reward is all but assured. And he is still young enough for the positions of Secretary-General, even President, to be beckoning in the not-too-distant future.

We celebrate, eat, drink, dance, make endless toasts to Neill, who remains sanguine throughout. The house – for once, a home – throbs with laughter, speeches, recollections of childhood and music – to which we dance late into the night. A small affair, Neill had decreed, but the alcohol warms and loosens us, even the sisters, who are usually reverential in his presence. The food is catered, drawing reproachful glances from my mother-in-law. What is the use of a wife who cannot cook for parties? Neill is moving up rapidly in the world, and he needs a partner who can hold her own as a political wife.

"Now that you've made her a stay-at-home wife, the next step is catering school," his mother jokes.

I laugh along with everyone else. Yes, how fortuitous that I have left my job just as Neill's ascent begins. He will need someone strong to anchor him, not a woman who is preoccupied with her own low-stakes power struggles. Yes, yes. I chuckle along with the rest of the family, who toast my own good fortune, my having landed so undeniably with my bum in the butter.

Underneath it all, I am hollow. I laugh, dance and make merry; a performance plastered over a great big void, the nothingness that I have become.

They stay for the weekend, by the end of which I want to run away. When the last of his family has left for the airport, Neill thanks me for having them with a peck on my cheek, then retreats into his office.

I am almost asleep when he slides over to me in bed. "Hope you're not asleep yet, my gorgeous."

I turn to him, sighing. I inhale the warm, musky scent of his cologne, and feel like crying.

"Here's something for you. It's a small token, to say thank you, Anita. I couldn't have done this without you by my side."

This time, the gift comes in a tiny box. I open it to find two brilliant, diamond solitaire earrings, and gasp. The same ones he has gifted Carol.

"They're almost as beautiful as you," he says.

I kiss him as a thank-you, tears spilling from my eyes. He mistakes them for tears of gratitude.

"Now, now, my darling, don't cry," he soothes. He wipes each cheek with the back of his hand, then kisses my eyelids with infinite tenderness. "This is only the beginning of all the good things yet to come."

"Promise me one thing," I say after we've lain together motionless, locked in an embrace.

"Anything, Anita."

"I want you always to remember how much I love you."

His eyes widen. "What a funny thing to say. We have many years together still for you to show me just how much you do."

I turn over so that he will not see the fresh tears seeping from my eyes. He pulls me into him, his chest hard and warm against my back. He wraps a protective arm around my waist, cradles his knees into the crevices at the back of mine, and tucks his feet underneath mine – speaking the wordless intimacy of two bodies that have created their own skin language.

He kisses the nape of my neck and I doze off in his arms. Despite everything, the space against his chest remains the one place that drives off my insomnia. For the first time in weeks, I drown in slumber, falling into leaden sleep.

I wake at four, as if a beam has been shone into my eyes. He lies on the opposite side of the bed, in foetal position, gently snoring. I make my way through the dark bedroom and shower briskly, putting on an orange dress, with small, cornflower-blue blossoms, shirred at the waist, one of Neill's favourites. I apply a smattering of make-up, pull my hair back in a simple, loose pony tail. I daub the Chanel on the bathroom shelf on my wrists and neck, and adorn my neck with a simple gold chain, a long-ago gift from my mother. I tiptoe back into the bedroom to my side of the bed. On the nightstand, in a shell-shaped porcelain holder, my engagement and wedding rings rest. I slip these on, revelling for the last time in the sense of belonging these rings have given me. I remember the diamond bracelet and new earrings, slip the bracelet around my wrist, take the earrings out of their box and thread them through the lobes of my ears. I am grateful for these gifts. Because with Neill's taste and money, I am sure they are worth a great deal. I pause only once to catch my reflection in the mirror to see how well they suit me. No need to get attached to things that aren't really mine. Just like my husband, I suppose.

I slip my feet into my favourite tan pumps, left next to my nightstand, and walk over to his side of the bed. He sleeps peacefully on his side, his chest rising rhythmically with each breath he takes. It is too dark in the bedroom for me to really see him, but I don't need to: I know so very well the features I have loved above all else. I bend over and kiss him on the cheek, the way a mother kisses her baby. He stirs, opens his eyes and smiles, then falls back into sleep.

In the kitchen, my hands flutter around the kettle, which I fill with water, but then decide to leave unboiled. I wouldn't be able to get anything, not even coffee, down my throat. I am perched at the kitchen counter when the cars, lights flashing, start to arrive. I clasp my wedding rings sitting snugly on my ring finger, to anchor myself, to make sure the they are still there. Claire has drummed it into me. Put on your most expensive jewellery before they come; remember, you'll be walking out of that house with only the clothes on your back.

No sirens blare. The knock on the door is restrained, polite almost; not at all how I imagined a police raid would begin. I open it before the knocking becomes too loud. I am expecting them, after all. Once the door is open, they swarm in. The commander explains to me politely that they are the Hawks, they have been alerted by the Special Investigative Unit, and that they have a warrant for Neill's arrest. I tell them that he is asleep in our bedroom, please not to startle him. He has PTSD from being in hiding and being hunted by Special Branch during the 1980s. And then it hits me: I start crying, begging – please please please, can you just turn around, can you just go? I have changed my mind.

But it is too late. The manila envelope that I couriered to the SIU weeks ago has sealed Neill's fate, providing a more than solid case against him. He has illegally procured state money meant for roads, meant for buildings, through nefarious means – and I have provided them with all the evidence. It is too late now, far too late.

An army of men swarms through the study, already starting to disconnect Neill's desktop computer.

And then I hear it, his voice from the bedroom, filled with confusion. "Anita? Anita!"

Confusion soon turns to fear. "Anita!!"

Hearing his voice, two officers closest to the passage that leads to the bedroom place their hands on their holsters.

I scream: "No! No! No! He doesn't have a gun! Please God, no!"

Neill's voice rises with panic, echoing down the corridor from the bedroom: "Anita! What the fuck is going on?"

The cops surge forward, intercept him as he comes out of the bedroom, completely naked. He folds his hands protectively in front of him.

"What the hell, where's my wife? Anitaaaaa!"

I have never seen or heard my husband this out of control. The fear, palpable in his voice, infects me.

"Please, please. Just leave him alone. Don't hurt him!" I scream.

"You are only supposed to arrest him!"

Neill is now in the kitchen, confused and dazed, while a phalanx of cops surrounds him.

The commander speaks: "You are under arrest."

"For what, bloody bastards?" His fear mutates to anger. "What the fuck is going on? Anita!"

They shove him back down the passage towards the bedroom, giving him five minutes to put on trousers, a shirt and shoes so that he is clothed, at least, when they take him in. The next time I see him, he is dressed and hand-cuffed, and they are dragging him down the passage, into the atrium that forms the heart of our home.

The commander shows him a warrant, explains that he is being arrested for corruption, and that details of the charges will be made clear to him once they get to the police station. Not only that – his bank accounts have been frozen, pending the outcome of the case being brought against him. And all assets belonging to his family trust – the houses, cars, and all the contents of his homes, are untouchable, as the court has granted a restraint order against all assets, with a view to forfeiture, should the charges against him result in convictions.

"This is ridiculous! Do you know who I am?" he cries. "You will pay for this. Once this misunderstanding is cleared up, I promise, you will pay."

He looks at the men carrying computer equipment out of his study. His rage flares to even greater heights.

"I swear, I will have your job for this," he spits at the commander.

"We have enough evidence to charge you. So please co-operate, Sir, and let's make this as painless as possible."

"Evidence – what the hell?"

He turns to me, still anchored to the kitchen counter, twisting the bands on my ring finger. The light of realisation dawns in his eyes.

"You?" What starts as a question becomes an accusation. "You! You did this? Why, Anita? Why?"

Tears stream down his face. I have never seen him cry before.

I stand silent, unmoving, my eyes never leaving his; neither denying that I did this, nor defending myself.

The officers start to lead him away through the front door, into the waiting police car. At the door, Neill turns around to take one last look at me. Face contorted with rage, he spits: "You fucking cunt!"

The words pierce the air, landing on me like a glob of phlegm.

How foreign these words sound, coming from my Neill, who never swears.

But what a strange relief, I think to myself, to hear it said out loud at last.

Cunt.

Yes, cunt; how appropriate, because this, after all is what I was to him: a cunt, a thing, a body part, interchangeable with the cunts of at least half a dozen other women – the other cunts in his life. The thing he used as a receptacle to expel his semen and his rage into. Yes, a cunt. That is exactly what I was to him, and having his words finally align with his actions – the actions that made me into a cunt, an object – is a blessed relief. No more smarmy "I love yous", no more "precious", no more "we have the rest of our lives together". No, thank God, no more lies. For once he has said it exactly how it is; exactly what he means. For once he has told the truth of our situation. And with that word spoken out loud, spat at me, the spell is broken.

"Cunt" is the freedom that I need to let Neill go.

I follow him out the front door, watch as they bundle him into the waiting black car. At least it is not the back of a police van – what an indignity that would be. I stand on the steps of my home, the house I will never go back into, and watch as the car taking Neill to the police station recedes down the driveway. Before it moves completely out of sight, Neill's head turns back. I see the hurt and confusion of betrayal in his eyes. And in that moment, I do not give a single fuck.

Unlike Neill, and unlike Lot's wife, I don't look back. The house is being sealed off anyway, and I will not be allowed to re-enter. With my handbag at my side, my rings on my fingers, my diamond bracelet around my wrist, and earrings adorning my earlobes, I step into the taxi I've ordered, and into my new life. Claire's words echo in my ears: remember, you will have to leave with only the clothes on your back. This I do, and it feels like freedom.

At the shopping mall where the taxi drops me off, I return to the jewellery store I visited a few weeks earlier. The manager recognises me and after we greet, escorts me to the lift and up to the jewellers' business offices. I have already been offered R450 000 for my engagement ring. Shireen had wonderful taste – I silently thank her as I hand over the ring and start filling out the paperwork to make the sale. Then there is the bracelet, and now I have the unexpected boon of these earrings, too. I remove them from my ears and hand them over to the valuator, who disappears with them into a small back room. Two carat diamond weight, set in platinum, is what the assessor comes back with. The store can offer me R250 000 for the earrings, an offer I accept. The bracelet is worth a further R200 000.

I leave the jewellery store with R900 000 in my bank account. A small amount, relative to the life from which I've just walked away – too small even to buy a house or a luxury car – but enough to start over. I call another taxi, and take it back to Athlone, back to the matchbox house I fled from all those years ago, the minute I had the piece of paper that signalled the start of my better life.

I walk through the door to find my mother sitting on the couch of her three-piece lounge suit, hands folded in prayer.

"What happened, my child?" she asks, her eyes brimming with tears.

"They took him in. Like I told you, Mum."

She now openly weeps. "Oh my girl, oh my girl! Why did you do that? You didn't have to do that!" she keens, as if she has just heard of Neill's death.

I say nothing.

"I wish you had listened to me! You didn't have to do that! You could have left him, yes, if you were so hell-bent on destroying another marriage, but why did you have to involve the law? You know what they say. Revenge is like drinking poison and expecting the other person to die. You should have worked through it, worked on forgiving him. That is what Jesus would have wanted you to do. Neill was wrong, yes, but vengeance is the Lord's. You should have left it in the Lord's hands."

I disagree fundamentally. Why shouldn't vengeance be mine? But still I say nothing; I just sit down next to her and watch her weep for both of us.

Chapter Nineteen

I buy a modest second-hand car, and pick up short-term teaching gigs at two different universities. My jobs mean that I race between one campus and another for the best part of each day. I apply for permanent jobs, but I'm an academic who never broke into the field, with few publications, no book authored, and no references from my previous job. I am pushing fifty – an altogether unattractive proposition for anyone. But I find a strange freedom in the lack of any structures to weigh me down. The things that I've always wanted – a marriage, job security, a home of my own – will now always elude me, but once that dreaded knowledge settles into me, I feel lighter than I ever have before.

Neill is, of course, released on bail the very same day he is arrested. His lengthy and much publicised trial ends in a conviction – fifteen years, suspended for five. It is strange that I never, ever see him again after that morning, but not entirely unexpected, as our lifestyles depart in such radically different directions, that I would never even have the chance of running into him by accident. There is a moment when I turn on the TV, and hear him answer questions at a press briefing: "…a woman scorned … fabricated evidence … hell hath no fury." So predictable. Yes, I fully own that I am a woman scorned, but I do not allow the shame that should be his to settle on me. I disown it, rebuke it. I pin "woman scorned" on my chest like a war medal and wear it proudly. Yes, I am a woman scorned – this is what you have made of me, my darling Neill.

The city's landscape changes inexorably. Everywhere I go reminds me of him: the mountain under which we lived mocks me, the very highways hold memories of us driving around the city, hand-in-hand, in cars considerably more luxurious than my current one. I exile myself from the city, finding a flat deep in the South Peninsula, on the side of a mountain overlooking the Silvermine wetland. The space is more of a spare room, really, with a bathroom and kitchen; a flatlet attached to the side of a much larger house, home to a family of five. I reach the front door of my flat by climbing two flights of whitewashed wooden stairs. This nightly trek up winding stairs gives me the sense of living in the tower of a castle. A modest double bed, a bistro set on which I eat, and a wing-backed chair furnish the single room that is my home. It is enough for me.

I dub it my house of joy. In the mornings, when I have nowhere pressing to be, I watch the sunlight stream through the windows, brightening the day. From the top floor, I look across the wetland, where the reeds sway in the wind as sun-rays splay across them. I draw in an immense feeling of calm watching the swathes the wind cuts through the reeds and the sunlight playing on the bright green leaves. I start my day at the window with a cup of tea, a notepad and a pen. I breathe in the green of the valley below, and the blue of the sky, and with my body and pen, transmute these breaths into words.

Every day, I try to walk through the grass that makes up the swaying, heaving wetland, listening for the sound the wind makes as it breathes life into all things. Slowly, gently, it breathes something new into me, too.

I start again, to make peace with myself, and commit to loving myself the way I would have loved any children I might have had. I have learned to stop mourning them. Here, I learn, with time, to love every single inch of myself: my greying hair, the lines growing more pronounced around my eyes, my rounder, softer body, which expands as it relaxes away from Neill's penetrating gaze. I go about my days gently and reverently, feasting on this simple, glorious life.

These are the good mornings, the good days.

On other days, I wake up hating him, sobbing for the life I had and gave away to him – the life I will never get back.

Then there are mornings when I wake with an unbearable

longing for him, for his arm draped around my waist as he first stirs from sleep, pulling me towards him. I stretch my hand across the bed, eyes still closed, hoping to feel him there, but find nothing. On those mornings, my love for him is as strong and ever-present as the day it first announced itself. Unmistakable, undeniable. On those days, my longing for him becomes the blade of a knife, broken off and stuck in my flesh: whichever way I turn, I feel it; with every move I make, it hurts, reminding me of him.

These mornings, too, I pull the pad closer, grab the pen, and release the pent-up grief inside me onto the page. I start scribbling this story about him, about us, over and over again, one I cannot seem to finish.

These are the opening lines I have down pat: "If I had to describe my husband in one word, that word would be devoted." I write that first line over and over again, never knowing what next to write. The ink on the page is still wet when I rip it out from the notepad, ball it in my fist, and drop it, crumpled, to the floor.

In time, I hope to write a different story.

Acknowledgements

I am grateful to the women of my writing group, Kharnita, Pregs and Marion, for our many writing and swimming dates. Your gentle encouragement and reading of my work in various drafts enabled me to complete this manuscript. My beloved Malika Ndlovu, who supported and worked with me to help this book take shape – thank you! I am thankful to additional readers: Nina, Sandra Young, Nadia Davids and Hermione Cronje, for their insightful comments on the first draft of this work. I am thankful also to Sorayah Nair, Lynelle Kenneth, Nadine Dirks, Yazeed Kamaldien, Natasha Diedricks and my mother and son for their assistance and care.

My thanks extend to the Jakes Gerwel Institute, which offered me space for writing at the enchanting Paulet House in Somerset East – just what I needed to complete this manuscript – and my home institution, the University of Cape Town, for its generous support. Sarah Bullen's magical writing retreat gave me the final push I needed to complete this manuscript – thank you, Sarah!

I am exceedingly grateful to be in the safe hands of Jacana Media, and my publisher, Maggie Davey, editor Helen Moffett, and proofreader Lara Jacob, in bringing this work into the world. Thank you Helen, for being the best and most entertaining editor. I remember, with gratitude, the life and work of Nadia Goetham, a beautiful human being who encouraged me to take my dreams seriously. You are loved and missed.